A DISCOVERY JOURNEY TO FAITH

Islamic Insights into Theism, Atheism, Agnosticism, and Truth-Seeking

HAFIDH SAIF AL-RAWAHY

NYBP

NY BOOK PUBLISHERS

Printed in the Sultanate of Oman

Dedicated to those souls seeking the divine truth. May The Almighty God guide you with grace along your journey.

About the Book

"A DISCOVERY JOURNEY TO FAITH" is a thoughtful work that bridges the gap between faith and skepticism by delving into complex themes such as belief, denial, and doubt, focusing on Islamic theology, philosophy, and Qur'anic discourse. The book sheds new light on problems such as the rationality of faith, the compatibility of science and religion, and how dubious yet interested minds might delve into the profound levels of metaphysical reality. The book invites believers, non-believers, and skeptics alike to expand their knowledge of faith by embracing theological, philosophical, and scientific ideas.

Humble Advice to the Atheist and the Agnostic

"Do they not reflect upon themselves? Allah created the heavens and the Earth and everything between them in Truth and for an appointed term. Yet many people deny they will meet their Lord."
~ *(Qur'an 30:8)*

Every prudent adventurer crossing an unknown frontier must devise a backup plan to get them to safety. If you were climbing a mountain that you had never climbed before or that no one had ever climbed, you would plan your major route to the top and back down safely. You would also devise an alternative route or a backup plan in case of a miscalculation, unanticipated circumstances, or plain bad luck.

In Islam, "death" is a known frontier because it is explained in good detail in the Qur'an and Hadith, but it is unknown to most of humanity. They have never experienced it before, nor those who have experienced "death" have ever returned to explain to us what the situation beyond this life is. So, my question to atheists and agnostics is: What

is your backup plan when the truth is revealed the moment you die and exit this life? What will you do when you encounter the reality of the Afterlife?

The wise words of seventeenth-century philosopher Blaise Pascal (d. 1622) echo this sentiment in "Pascal's wager." Picture this: You're wagering your life on God's existence. Living aligned with God's will, might mean some constraints in this life. But if God exists, it promises boundless rewards—an eternity of bliss in Paradise, evading the infinite torment of Hellfire (Popkin, 1999).

Pascal's wager can be persuasive to atheists and agnostics. The Qur'an presents a similar argument dealing with the Pharaoh of Ancient Egypt, *"And a believing man from the House of Pharaoh who was concealing his belief said, Will you kill a man for saying My Lord is God, though he has brought you clear proofs from your Lord? If he is a liar, he is deceiving himself, but if he is telling the truth, then the promises will be fulfilled: Truly, God does not guide the prodigal liar"* [Qur'an 40:28].

Of course, the Islamic faith does not endorse God's existence based on Pascal's wager. In Islam, faith in God has "rational foundations as well as the purpose, meaning, comfort, and guidance that it gives to our lives" (Parrott, 2022). On this note, we must also acknowledge that "the Qur'an inspires conviction by appealing to aspects of human inner life, specifically the heart and mind. To get at a condition of certainty in faith, intuition, and experience work in combination with logic and reason" (Parrott, 2022).

Foreword
By Jasser Auda

Praise be to Allah and peace be upon His final Messenger

The foundation of every knowledge of Islam is the Qur'an, the Book of Allah, which is also demonstrated in the most beautiful example of the tradition of His Messenger Muhammad, peace be upon him. These are the two fixed sources of true knowledge. Yet, the understanding (*Fiqh*) of these sources of knowledge is not fixed. Understanding Islam should be developing based on the original two sources but in different ways in every place and time, in order to achieve their higher objectives and goals.

The Call for Islam (Da'wah) is an area in which this dynamism is most evident. With every generation, humanity has new questions and faces new challenges that require new answers. That is when it becomes necessary to take a fresh look at the original sources before answering them.

And that is why I was immensely happy to see this monograph written by my brother Hafidh Saif Al-Rawahy. His approach merges between references to the original sources of Islam and the evolving wisdom of humanity, in order to tackle some of today's most challenging questions and obstacles in the way of the Call for Islam.

I am sure that the reader will find this book useful and seekers of truth everywhere will find it encouraging and affirming.

All praise is due to Allah, the Lord of the Worlds.

Jasser Auda

President, Maqasid Institute Global

Preface

"...will you you not reason?" ~ (Qur'an 21:10)

In the name of God, the Most Gracious, the Most Merciful.

As the dawn of contemplation breaks upon the horizon of human intellect, it reveals the shadows of life's most profound question: "What do I believe?" It is this basic inquiry that stirs within us a relentless pursuit of understanding, a journey that often treads the delicate line between conviction and curiosity. "A Discovery Journey to Faith" is an odyssey into the heart of this interrogation, where the realms of Islamic theology, philosophy, Qur'anic discourse, and science converge to illuminate the pathways towards belief.

This book does not merely present an exposition of faith as a static concept but rather as a dynamic, living dialogue between the soul and the signs of God that pervade our universe and in ourselves. It is an invitation extended to believers, non-believers, and skeptics alike—to embark upon a quest that traverses beyond the veil of tangible reality into the profound depths of metaphysical existence. Through the lens of Islamic intellectual tradition, "A Discovery Journey to Faith" grapples with the predicaments of the rationality of belief, unearthing the fertile ground where science and spirituality coalesce. It challenges the reader to confront the perplexities of denial and doubt, not as adversaries to faith but as instruments that carve the intricate designs of a more resilient conviction.

This work is an earnest attempt to transcend the superficial dichotomy between faith and skepticism. It endeavors to construct bridges with the sturdy stones of reason and the resilient ropes of revelation, offering a passage for those who stand on the banks of skepticism to cross over into the lands of belief without the forfeiture of critical thought. Each chapter is a tapestry woven with the threads of Qur'anic wisdom, the insights of Muslim philosophers, and the discoveries of modern science. It is a text that aspires to speak to the intellect as well as the heart, to resonate with the innermost yearnings for truth that lie within every human soul.

As the author of this humble venture, first and foremost, my eternal praise and gratitude be to Allah, The Almighty God, for enabling me to take on this journey and to support me in every step and turn. Second, my heartfelt appreciation is extended to a distinguished assembly of individuals whose support has been the anchor of this journey: To my cherished family, whose unwavering faith has been a constant source of inspiration and illumination for both my academic journey and personal growth. To the management of the Sultan Qaboos Higher Centre for Science and Culture of the Diwan of the Royal Court for giving me the opportunity to serve the Islamic Information Centre at the Sultan Qaboos Grand Mosque. To my esteemed colleagues at the Islamic Information Centre, whose rigorous religious and cultural discourse and interfaith activism have sharpened the edges of this work. Special thanks to Sister Saada Al-Ghafry and Dr. Aboud As-Sawafi, whose insightful contributions and exceptional editorial acumen were instrumental in elevating the quality of the initial manuscript, and to Sheikh Hafidh Al-Kindy and Dr. Yusuf Al-Oufy for their discerning evaluations and sustaining encouragement. Finally, to Jeremiah Hofsted and his editorial team at NY Book Publishers for their unwavering dedication and meticulous attention to detail, which were pivotal in the metamorphosis of the manuscript into a published work.

This book is also a tribute to the pioneering scholars of the past, whose shoulders we stand upon, and to the inquiring minds of the future, for whom this work may serve as an inspiration as they navigate their own journeys to faith. As you engage with the pages that follow, may you discover that the journey to faith is not a solitary trek but a shared voyage, buoyed by the companionship of those who have walked the path before us and those who walk alongside us. May this book be a worthy contribution to that timeless journey. As you turn these pages, may you find that what began as a search for answers transforms into the discovery of questions that elevate the soul. May your journey through this book be one of enlightenment, reflection, and, ultimately, a step closer to the ineffable essence of faith itself.

With heartfelt prayers for guidance and understanding.

Hafidh Saif Al-Rawahy
Islamic Information Center,
Sultan Qaboos Grand Mosque
Muscat, Sultanate of Oman
March 25, 2024

Table of Contents

CHAPTER 1

Introduction

"And those who strive for Us - We will surely guide them to Our ways. And indeed, Allah is with the doers of good."
~ *(Qur'an 29:69)*

The term "atheism" is complex and often challenging to define due to its intricate historical context. It typically contrasts between "lack of belief in God," termed "agnosticism," and "disbelief in the existence of God," known as true "atheism." An agnostic holds that the existence of God cannot be proven, allowing for skepticism toward the concept. Conversely, a committed atheist firmly denies God's existence, rejecting any possibility thereof.

This book adopts a straightforward approach, defining atheism as denial and agnosticism as harboring doubts about God's existence and the Afterlife.

Throughout history, atheists have existed within various civilizations, often existing on the fringes with a passive stance. However, in recent times, atheism has gained traction in the West. The emergence of "new atheists" has marked a shift towards more assertive expressions of disbelief. These individuals actively engage in anti-religious social activism, aligning with secularist and liberal movements.

Prominent figures like Richard Dawkins, Christopher Hitchens (d. 2011), Sam Harris, Daniel Dennett, Stephen Hawking (d. 2018), Lawrence Krauss, among others, have authored numerous books and articles on this subject. These self-proclaimed new atheists have risen as influential public intellectuals in the West, achieving celebrity status and landing their writings on bestseller lists.

Throughout previous centuries, a notable circle of atheist thinkers included Sigmund Freud (d. 1939), Bertrand Russell (d. 1970), Karl Marx (d. 1883), Friedrich Nietzsche (d. 1900), among others. These renowned Western philosophers held strong intellectual disbelief in religion. However, they didn't advocate anti-religious sentiments or aim to convert the public to their viewpoint. They recognized that removing religion from society could lead to a moral crisis.

These philosophers acknowledged the role of religion in instilling morality within individuals and societies. They perceived religion's primary purpose as the cultivation of ethical and compassionate individuals capable of finding happiness and success in this life, prior to considering the next. As Voltaire (d. 1778) famously said, "If God did not exist, we would have to invent Him" (Voltaire, 1773). In a similar note, Nietzsche (d. 1900) articulated a profound critique of modernity, highlighting that the decline of religious and metaphysical belief systems, symbolized by the metaphorical 'death of God,' precipitates a crisis of nihilism. This crisis is characterized by the absence of objective truth, moral values, and inherent meaning in life. This reflects the notion that without God, not only would precipitate a crisis of nihilism, but neither the universe nor life itself would exist—everything is contingent upon God's existence.

God stands as the sole "Necessary Being," existing without reliance on a cause, untouched by non-existence, the foundation upon which all existence rests, and the source of moral values and ethics.

Today, the forefront of the new atheist movement is led by the prominent figures known as the "four horsemen": Richard Dawkins, Christopher Hitchens (d. 2011), Sam Harris, and Daniel Dennett. These individuals not only challenge the existence of God and the Afterlife but also critique religious beliefs, advocating for a more secular worldview. They actively promote their atheistic and materialistic beliefs through various mediums like writings, public speeches, engagements, and social media, often criticizing religions and religious institutions.

Their vision imagines a world where religious spaces such as mosques, churches, synagogues, and temples cease to exist or transform into entertainment hubs, believing that such a world would be more peaceful and improved. However, this vision seems more like an elusive daydream rather than a plausible reality.

The teachings of various faiths, including Islam, highlight that the nature of life on Earth involves purposeful trials and tribulations. The Qur'an elucidates, *"He who created death and life to test you as to which of you is best in deeds ... "* [Qur'an 67:2]. It suggests that meaningful lives are lived with optimism for the eternal Afterlife.

Those yearning for a world devoid of suffering, pain, and injustices may struggle to reconcile such aspirations with the inherent realities of earthly existence. The Qur'an further states, *"So truly where there is hardship there is also ease; truly where is a hardship there is also ease"* [Qur'an 94:5-6], emphasizing the coexistence of good and evil, ease, and difficulty in this life.

Anger towards God due to the hardships of this world often stems from a lack of understanding of its nature and the simultaneous existence of challenges and blessings.

The new atheists' stance presents three remarkable characteristics in their attitude towards disbelief, dissemination of skepticism, and anti-religious fervor.

Firstly, in the search for truth about God's existence and the Hereafter, one might expect a comprehensive evaluation of theistic claims. However, many leading new atheist intellectuals in the West seem markedly uninformed about theology and religion. Their opinions on Islam and its teachings often emerge from limited understanding, creating a stark contrast with the theistic portrayal, especially in Islam. Interestingly, Muslims also reject the distorted view of God and God's nature endorsed by new atheists.

Secondly, new atheists tout intellectualism, aligning themselves with science and reason. They propose an irreconcilable conflict between science and religion, using science as the cornerstone of their argument against God and the Afterlife. Paradoxically, an objective approach to science and rationality actually supports belief in God's existence and the Afterlife. This paradox is exemplified by the case of Sir Antony Flew (d. 2010), a well-known atheist philosopher, who, in his later years, reversed his position and embraced belief in God. His book, "There is a God: How the World's Most Notorious Atheist Changed His Mind" (Flew, 2007), elaborates on arguments familiar to theists, supporting the existence of a Divine Creator. Flew's work serves as a comprehensive guide for Western audiences on the scientific aspects of religious belief (Oppenheimer, 2007).

The third significant aspect distinguishing atheism and agnosticism in the West often originates from a Judeo-Christian background. The conflict between their scriptures and modern science led many to perceive religion as irrelevant. They were taught that nature acts as a barrier between humanity and God, fostering a secular attitude towards religion. This backdrop explains the Western drift towards skepticism and disbelief.

Contrarily, Islam hasn't encountered a conflict between its scriptures and science. It also rejects the notion that nature separates people from God. Instead, Islam encourages deep contemplation, reasoning, reflection, and rationality as pillars of faith. It condemns blind belief and advocates for a harmonious relationship between faith and reason. The Qur'an commands the study of nature as a means to comprehend "God's work," akin to reciting the Qur'an, deemed "God's word." According to Islam, denying the Creator reflects a lack of wisdom.

Islam intricately interweaves religion, life, nature, reason, and science, establishing a coherent link. Therefore, it's unjust for new atheists to project inconsistencies from other faith traditions onto Islam.

This book aims to present Islam's insights on belief, disbelief, doubts, and truth-seeking. Specifically directed at open-minded atheists and agnostics genuinely seeking the truth about God and the Hereafter, it offers an Islamic perspective grounded in Qur'anic discourse and philosophy. It delves into how the Creator, evident in the natural world and within us, offers abundant evidence of His existence. The Qur'an states, *"We will show them Our signs in the universe and within themselves until it becomes clear to them that this 'Quran' is the truth..."* [Qur'an 41:53].

Additionally, the book addresses common questions about God and Islam, shedding light on fundamental theological and scriptural distinctions that differentiate Islam from Judeo-Christian teachings.

CHAPTER 2

Genesis of Western Atheism and Agnosticism

"Indeed, Allah does not forgive association with Him, but He forgives what is less than that for whom He wills. And he who associates others with Allah has certainly fabricated a tremendous sin." ~ (Qur'an 4:48)

Understanding the rise of atheism and agnosticism in the West requires delving into the deeply religious Middle Ages of Europe (Durant, 1993). The seeds of skepticism and irreligiosity in the West trace back through historical contexts, gradually growing over the past four centuries.

The Western notions of atheism and agnosticism emerged as Europeans began expressing doubts and skepticism towards their Christian faith. This skepticism arose during the aftermath of the sixteenth-century Reformation Movement and subsequent religious conflicts. The seventeenth-century Scientific Revolution and the subsequent eighteenth-century Enlightenment marked crucial phases in the birth of atheism and agnosticism in the West (Shapin, 2018).

During the Renaissance and Enlightenment eras, many religious beliefs were discarded due to being deemed irrational and superstitious. While some intellectuals retained the notion of God as the Creator, theological innovation emerged, such as Deism, which proposed a supreme but non-intervening Creator with no concern for individual moral conduct. This ideology allowed for absolute individualism and personal freedoms (Gay, 1969).

To restore confidence in religion, European Judeo-Christian scholars proposed desacralized theories of epistemology, ontology, and morality. However, inadvertently, these theories laid the groundwork for a new secular foundation that gradually weakened faith in God and religion.

Atheism and agnosticism in the West reached maturity during the nineteenth-century Industrial Revolution. Intellectuals critical of religion used past Church errors as ammunition against religious doctrines. They advocated individuality, personal liberty, and freedom of expression, openly criticizing and challenging religious beliefs.

A central tenet of this movement was the idea that religion and science were incompatible. The rise of Darwinian evolution and the Big Bang theory provided scientific explanations for natural phenomena without reference to God or religion. This shift gave rise to scientific naturalism or "scientism," an Enlightenment humanism that emphasized science and reason while rejecting the supernatural entirely (Haack, 2003).

Scientists began relying solely on natural explanations, excluding the need for invoking God or religion to explain natural events. For many new atheists and agnostics, science became a surrogate for God.

As empirical science uncovered more natural laws, the need to invoke a Deity to explain gaps in knowledge diminished, known as the "God of the Gaps" concept (McGrath, 2010). An act of God was something you could not explain based on available scientific data. Faith was assumed to begin where scientific knowledge ended and the other way around. Initially, the presence of diverse species and their adaptation were attributed to God's work. However, as more natural laws emerged, the necessity of invoking a Deity decreased, leading science to be viewed as a substitute for God. This misconception persists in modern scientific culture.

In the late nineteenth century's charged intellectual environment, the theory of evolution by Darwin was seen by some leaning towards atheism and agnosticism as a potential weapon against religion. Embraced and developed on materialistic lines, Darwinism aimed to undermine religious beliefs by suggesting that human existence resulted from chance, devoid of purpose, rendering spiritual and moral concerns obsolete. This ideology paved the way for moral relativism and liberalism, reducing humans to sophisticated beings with no higher purpose and discarding religious experiences as mere mental anomalies.

By the end of the twentieth century, Western secular modernity failed to deliver the envisioned utopia marred by world wars, mass destruction, environmental crises, hegemonic conflicts, and the rise of fascism, Nazism, and communism. The failures witnessed, including genocides and human suffering, led to a decline in atheism and agnosticism.

However, in the twenty-first century, these ideologies reemerged under the guise of "new atheism." Post-9/11 concerns about the rise of political Islam spurred this revival. New atheism evolved beyond mere disbelief into an ideology with its own beliefs and values (LeDrew, 2016). As it operates akin to a belief system, new atheism vehemently opposes religions and fervently propagates its own convictions, resembling the practices of organized religions.

Richard Dawkins' words paint a nihilistic view, emphasizing the absence of inherent purpose or morality in a universe governed by Darwinian evolution and natural processes. "In a universe of electrons and selfish genes, blind physical forces and genetic replication, some people are going to get hurt, other people are going to get lucky, and you won't find any rhyme or reason in it, nor any justice. The universe that we observe precisely has the properties we should expect if there is, at bottom, no design, no purpose, no evil, no good, nothing but pitiless indifference" (Dawkins, 2008). However, amidst this perspective, when we observe the grand tapestry of existence, we witness the intricate laws governing celestial bodies, harmonious ecosystems, and precise biological processes sustaining life.

These manifestations of order and purpose suggest a Divine plan intricately woven throughout the universe. Contemplating this cosmic design allows for a deeper connection to a Merciful God, recognizing His wisdom and compassion in the elegant balance of the cosmos. The Qur'an alludes to this interconnectedness, stating, *"Do you not see that to Allah prostrates whoever is in the heavens and whoever is on the Earth..."* [Qur'an 22:18].

CHAPTER 3

Does God Really Exist?

"Indeed, in the creation of the heavens and Earth, and the alternation of the night and the day, and the [great] ships which sail through the sea with that which benefits people, and what Allah has sent down from the heavens of rain, giving life thereby to the Earth after its lifelessness and dispersing therein every [kind of] moving creature, and [His] directing of the winds and the clouds controlled between the heaven and the Earth are signs for a people who use reason." ~ *(Qur'an 2:164)*

Islam teaches that not only God exists, but there is no doubt about His existence. Allah says in the Qur'an, *"...Can there be any doubt about God, the Creator of the heavens and Earth? He calls you to Him to forgive you, your sins and let you enjoy your life until the appointed hour..."* [Qur'an 14:10].

Islam also teaches that believing in God is ingrained in human nature and was never an invention or achievement of the human mind. Belief in God is intrinsic to the human soul, a profound realization that the soul did not create itself but instead acknowledges the existence of its Creator.

According to Islam, the very first concept that humans had of God was of the oneness and unseen supreme entity who created and sustained the cosmos and all that could be seen or felt about and around it. That foundational thinking or knowledge gradually altered over time, resulting in beliefs in other deities, attributing partners with God, and eventually rejecting or denying God's existence altogether. Belief in the One real and All-Powerful God is "foundational," and it is both "natural" and "rational."

Much scientific research in various fields of study has proven that the concept of God is deeply embedded in human nature. Olivera

Petrovitch (Petrovich, 2021), Paul Bloom (Bloom, 2005), Justin Barrett (Barrett, 2004), and Deborah Kelemen (Kelemen, 2004/5) are a few examples of well-known researchers who have investigated and written on the cognitive science of religion. Their writings confirm that everyone is a born believer and has the experience of calling on God, especially in times of vulnerability, crisis, and sorrow.

Why are there still those who doubt or deny God's existence, despite the inherent capacity within humans to possess fundamental knowledge for recognizing the reality of a Divine entity? One typical reason is that individuals want to know whether there is a rational basis for their inner belief, sometimes in a quest for scientific evidence in support of their feelings.

However, because science focuses on what can be observed, it can only explain the physical world's reality. It has shied away from the invisible, higher spiritual, and supernatural realms. Furthermore, science cannot be used to disprove God's existence because of two reasons.

First, science is primarily concerned with explaining "contingent" phenomena (phenomena that need causes), and it does so within the paradigm of methodological naturalism, which focuses on natural explanations for natural phenomena. When science explains a phenomenon, it typically does so by referencing another contingent phenomenon. This is essentially an exposition of contingency; one event is contingent upon another, which is again contingent upon another. However, this leads to the issue of infinite regress. If each contingent fact is explained by another contingent fact, then one could keep tracing this chain of explanations back ad infinitum. Such a scenario raises the logical fallacy of not being able to explain completely the phenomenon.

Second, a scientific explanation of certain natural phenomena can sometimes contradict religious positions simply because science uses "scientific models" to explain natural phenomena in the physical world. However, these models do not claim to represent "absolute truth." They are probabilistic frameworks based on deductive inferences from a limited collected empirical data—a small sample is studied, and the findings are used to generalize the larger population. These models also come with a lot of assumptions and scholarly disagreements. Discussions and studies on these models continue within the scientific community, and experts' perspectives can shift in response to new data and findings.

To put it another way, "scientific truth" is not an "absolute truth" because it is based on inferential conclusions drawn from a limited collection of empirical data. New observations can alter previously held scientific truths, which is the beauty of science: "Truth is not set in stone." No objective scientist can assert that science explains everything or that scientific truth reflects absolute truth, or that scientific research is devoted to the quest for absolute truth. As a result, one must recognize that science can only provide a partial understanding of reality and can never be used to refute the existence of the Creator.

On the contrary, if approached objectively, science can lead to the idea of a Necessary Being—God.

CHAPTER 4

Science in the Qur'an

"Recite in the name of your Lord who created. Created man from a clinging substance." ~ (Qur'an 96:1-2)

God revealed the Qur'an to Prophet Muhammad (PBUH) as the 'Final Testament' for humanity, aiming to guide and offer ultimate wisdom for both this life and the Hereafter. While not primarily scientific text, the Qur'an holds numerous signs attesting to God's existence and contains references to various scientific phenomena across cosmology, geology, astrophysics, and embryology.

Maurice Bucaille, a French medical doctor and scientist, extensively studied the Qur'an's scientific references. His findings in 'The Bible, The Qur'an, and Science' (Bucaille, 2001) suggested the Qur'an's full alignment with modern scientific discoveries.

For instance, the Qur'an describes the initial state of the universe as a single entity before its expansion—a concept akin to the Big Bang theory. *"Have those who disbelieved not considered that the heavens and the Earth were a joined entity, and We separated them...?"* [Qur'an 21:30]. The Qur'an also mentions the universe's continuous expansion: *"And the heaven We constructed with strength, and indeed, We are [its] expander"* [Qur'an 51:47].

Regarding human embryonic development, the Qur'an details stages from conception to birth. *"And certainly, did We create man from an extract of clay; Then We placed him as a sperm-drop in a firm lodging... So blessed is Allah, the best of creators"* [Qur'an 23:12-14]. Professor Keith L. Moore, a specialist in Anatomy at the University of Toronto, affirmed the Qur'anic teachings about embryology align with contemporary scientific knowledge (Moore, 1986).

In the Qur'an, the Earth is described as a bed and mountains as pegs. Allah says in the Qur'an, *"Have We not made the Earth a resting place? And the mountains as pegs?"* [Qur'an 78:6-7]. Modern Earth sciences reveal that mountains possess deep roots beneath the ground's surface, exceeding their elevation above ground. Consequently, what's visible of mountains above the Earth is just the tip of the iceberg compared to what's buried below. This discovery aligns 'pegs' as an appropriate descriptor, akin to how most of a properly set peg is underground. Sir George Biddell Airy first proposed the concept of deep mountain roots in 1865 (El-Naggar, 2003).

The Qur'an also highlights mountains' vital role in stabilizing the Earth's crust and preventing seismic disturbances. Allah says, *"And He has cast into the Earth firmly set mountains, lest it shift with you, and [made] rivers and roads, that you may be guided"* [Qur'an 16:15]. Hence, mountains extend below the Earth's surface (pegs), stabilizing the Earth's outer surface (El-Naggar, 2003).

These scientific findings, along with many others in Islamic texts, strengthen the Qur'an's position as the holy book conveying God's word to guide humanity in all life aspects and aid in discovering truths about the one true God. Despite numerous scientific references in the Qur'an, scientists have yet to categorize its scientific miracles definitively. In the Qur'an, Allah promises, *"We will show them Our signs in the horizons and within themselves until it becomes clear to them that it is the Truth"* [Qur'an 41:53].

CHAPTER 5

The Islamic Concept of God

"Say, 'He is Allah, [Who is] One, Allah, the Eternal Refuge. He neither begets nor is born, nor is there to Him any equivalent.'" ~ (Qur'an 112:1-4)

It is critical to begin with the Islamic concept of God since new atheists and agnostics have a distorted image of God and His characteristics. Almost all religions recognize the existence of a single Divine supreme entity who has the power, will, and knowledge to create, sustain, and administer the universe. The Qur'an discloses the name of this supreme entity, along with His other beautiful names and attributes. The names (*'asmaa'*) and attributes (*'sifaat'*) of God are closely related, but they are not identical. While the names and attributes both aim to describe God, the attributes often describe how God is or acts, whereas the names are what God is called.

The One and Only Almighty God is Allah, who embodies all the perfect, majestic, and attractive qualities that His grandeur and majesty deserve. Belief in God is the foundational and self-evident truth that requires no proof; it is both rational and natural, as well as the default state of the mind and heart, according to Islam. Allah says in the Qur'an, *"So, direct your face toward the religion, inclining to truth. [Adhere to] the innate nature of Allah upon which He has created [all] people..."* [Qur'an 30:30]. The Prophet Muhammad (PBUH) also reiterated this point when he said, "No child is born except that he is upon innate nature (of acknowledging the Creator), but his parents make him a Jew, a Christian, or a polytheist..." [Sahih Bukhari].

Atheists' and agnostics' denial or doubt of God's existence is irrational, unnatural, and an acquired state of mind and heart—it did not come naturally as a default state. Allah asks in the Qur'an, *"...Can there be any doubt about God, Creator of the Heavens and Earth?..."* [Qur'an 14:10]. The cognitive scientists of religion, such as (Petrovitch, 2021),

(Bloom, 2005), (Barrett, 2004), and (Kelemen, 2004/5), have proven this point scientifically, in line with Islamic teachings.

Since there are numerous examples of basic notions that are taken for granted within the present modern secular worldview, the concept of a self-evident foundational belief that requires no proof should be easily accepted in Western philosophy and the scientific community. The actuality of the external world, nature's uniformity and intelligibility, the law of causality (cause and effect), the validity of human reasoning, and the belief that truth is worth seeking are a few examples. These fundamental beliefs are self-evident facts that cannot be verified or disproved in any way, scientifically or otherwise, yet we accept them with full conviction. Thus, faith in the transcendental God, the Creator and Sustainer of the universe, is a fundamental belief that is self-evident truth and requires no proof. It is both reasonable and natural to hold that belief. It is a default state of the mind and heart that neither requires special learning nor external information transfer, nor is it a product of a specific culture or social condition.

While various rational tools are used in the Qur'anic discourse to provide evidence, reinforce arguments, and encourage reflection and understanding of God's existence and the Afterlife, the primary role of prophets and Divine scriptures is to explain a complete understanding of God's nature and provide guidance on how to live a devotional life that ensures success and happiness in this life and the Hereafter, rather than proving God's existence. Humans are assumed to have primordial knowledge of God's existence. Given that the human intellect lacks full comprehension of itself, let alone the innumerable truths and marvels of the reality of the cosmos, it would be impossible to arrive at the complete truth of God's nature without the help of prophets and scriptures. Therefore, we can only learn about God and what He reveals about Himself to us—what He wants us to know about Him. Through the Divine revelations conveyed by His prophets and sacred scriptures, humanity gains insight into God's nature, the purpose of existence, the expectations set for this life, and the nature of the life to come. In studying the Qur'an, it becomes evident that Allah consistently features His magnificence, often referencing His esteemed names and attributes, highlighting His unparalleled grandeur.

There are various chapters in the Qur'an that explain who God is. For example, Chapter 112 of the Qur'an contains the most profound description of God. When Makkan polytheists challenged the Prophet Muhammad (PBUH) to explain about God, God Himself revealed, *"Say: He is Allah, (who) is One, Allah, the Eternal Refuge, He neither begets nor is born. And none is like Him"* [Qur'an 112:1-4]. There are many other passages in the Qur'an in which Allah describes and introduces Himself. A few examples are: *"That is Allah, your Lord; there is no deity except Him, the Creator of all things, so worship Him. And He is Disposer of all things"* [Qur'an 6:102]. An additional verse in the same chapter states, 'Vision perceives Him not, but He perceives [all] vision; and He is the Subtle, the Acquainted' [Qur'an 6:103]. Another major portrayal of God in the Qur'an is the "Verse of the Throne." It states, *"Allah - there is no deity except Him, the Ever-Living, the Sustainer of [all] existence. Neither drowsiness overtakes Him nor sleep. To Him belongs whatever is in the heavens and whatever is on the Earth. Who is it that can intercede with Him except by His permission? He knows what is [presently] before them and what will be after them, and they encompass not a thing of His knowledge except for what He wills. His Kursi extends over the heavens and the Earth, and their preservation tires Him not. And He is the Most High, the Most Great"* [Qur'an 2:255].

In Islamic theology, Allah is not conceived as a mere abstract energy or impersonal force but exhibits agency. He is understood to possess power, will, knowledge, and intentionality. This concept is deeply rooted in various foundational texts and the broader philosophical discourse within the Islamic tradition. In the Qur'an, the Muslims' holy book, which is regarded as the verbatim word of Allah revealed to the Prophet Muhammad (PBUH), Allah is depicted as possessing the qualities of a conscious being with the total capacity to will, intend, and enact. The ninety-nine beautiful names of Allah (*Asma-ul-Husna*) signify various attributes that manifest agency, delineating His active involvement in the universe. Some of the names, such as *Al-Khaaliq* (The Creator), *Al-Razzaq* (The Provider), and *Al-Hakeem* (The Wise), explicitly indicate a Being with purpose and direction, not a passive or impersonal force.

Allah says in the Qur'an, *"And to Allah belong the best names, so invoke Him by them. And leave [the company of] those who practice deviation concerning His names. They will be recompensed for what they have been doing"* [Qur'an 7:180]. In another passage, Allah says, "Say, *Call upon Allah or call upon the Most Merciful. Whichever [name] you call - to Him belong the best names..."* [Qur'an 17:110]. *In another passage, "Allah - there is no deity except Him. To Him belong the best names"* [Qur'an 20:8]. In the Hadith, the recorded sayings, and actions of the Prophet Muhammad (PBUH), Allah's agency is affirmed through narrations that describe Allah's actions, decisions, and responses to human activities. Muslim philosophers and theologians have extensively elaborated on the concept of Divine agency.

The notion of *Tawheed*, the Oneness of Allah, stresses not only the unity of God but also His active role as the sustainer and governor of the universe. It is crucial to differentiate the Islamic concept of Allah from pantheistic or deistic views, which often conceive the Divine as an impersonal force pervading the universe. It is also crucial to differentiate the Islamic concept of Allah from the Christian Trinitarian view, which often conceives God as both Divine and human. In Islam, Allah is distinct from His creation, maintaining a transcendental nature while having a personal and intimate relationship with His creatures through His mercy, guidance, and sustenance. Islamic teachings encourage believers to foster a personal relationship with Allah, approaching Him with prayers (*salat*), supplications (*dua'as*), and remembrance (*dhikr*), seeking His guidance, mercy, and forgiveness. This personal relationship with Allah inherently recognizes His agency, as it is built on the understanding that Allah listens, responds, and actively engages with His creation. Allah says in the Qur'an, *"And when My servants ask you, [O Muhammad], concerning Me – indeed I am near. I respond to the invocation of the supplicant when he calls upon Me. So let them respond to Me [by obedience] and believe in Me that they may be [rightly] guided"* [Qur'an 2:186]. In another passage, Allah says, *"And We have already created man and know what his soul whispers to him, and We are closer to him than [his] jugular vein'* [Qur'an 50:16]. Allah also says in the Qur'an, *"We are near to it (the soul) than you, but you do not see"* [Qur'an 56:85].

In conclusion, logical arguments and scriptural support corroborate the idea of Allah's agency, a central doctrine in Islamic theology. It envisions Allah as a Being with will, knowledge, and the power to act, guiding the happenings of the universe with wisdom and purpose. This belief in Allah's agency fosters a dynamic and personal relationship between Allah and believers, based on reverence, trust, and seeking His guidance and grace. It stresses Allah's active, conscious, and intentional involvement with the cosmos and the lives of individuals, steering clear of depicting Allah as an abstract, impersonal force devoid of will and intentionality.

Below is the detailed list of the ninety-nine beautiful names of Allah (Asma-ul-Husna), each explaining an aspect of the diverse attributes of Allah, reflecting His greatness, generosity, and benevolence, among other characteristics. Understanding and pondering these names can enhance one's understanding and connection with the Divine. It showcases the multifaceted nature of Allah, highlighting His might, wisdom, mercy, justice, and boundless magnanimity that assist in guiding believers in their journey to faith.

Ar-Rahmaan (الرَّحْمَـٰن): The Most Merciful – Signifies the utmost and inclusive mercy that encompasses all beings.

Ar-Raheem (الرَّحِيم): The Most Compassionate – Denotes Allah's special mercy towards the believers.

Al-Malik (الْمَلِك): The Sovereign – Refers to Allah's sovereignty over the universe, possessing authority and kingship over everything.

Al-Qudduus (الْقُـدُّوس): The Holy – Reflects Allah's purity from any imperfection, mistake, or shortcomings.

As-Salaam (السَّلَام): The Peace and Blessing – Signifying the source of peace and safety, and who secures and fosters goodness.

Al-Mu'min (الْمُؤْمِن): The Giver of Faith – The one who is instilling faith, security, and tranquility in the hearts of believers.

Al-Muhaymin (الْمُهَيْمِن): The Protector – Reflects the role of Allah as the one who observes His creation with a watchful and protective gaze.

Al-'Azeez (الْعَزِيـزُ): The Mighty - Allah's might and honor, which is unattainable for anyone else.

Al-Jabbaar (الْجَبَّارُ): The Compeller – The one who restores and reforms, compelling things to be the correct and intended way.

Al-Mutakabbir (الْمُتَكَبِّرُ): The Majestic – The one who is great and superior over His creation.

Al-Khaaliq (الْخَالِـقُ): The Creator – Referring to Allah's attribute of creating everything from nothing.

Al-Baari (الْبَارِئُ): The Maker – The one who creates with a plan, deciding and determining the measures and functionalities of everything created.

Al-Musawwir (الْمُصَوِّرُ): The Fashioner, Designer – The one who shapes and forms His creation with distinct features and characteristics.

Al-Ghaffaar (الْغَفَّارُ): The Forgiver – The one who forgives extensively.

Al-Qahhaar (الْقَهَّـارُ): The Subduer – The one who has the ability to do anything and everything, overpowering all His creation.

Al-Wahhaab (الْوَهَّـابُ): The Bestower – The one who continually, magnanimously, and lavishly bestows blessings and favors upon His creation.

Ar-Razzaaq (الـرَّزَّاقُ): The Provider – The one who provides sustenance and all that is necessary for the livelihood of His creation.

Al-Fattaah (الْفَتَّـاحُ): The Opener – The one who opens up the paths to goodness, success, and truth.

Al-'Aleem (الْعَلِيـمُ): The All-Knowing – Encompassing all knowledge, seen and unseen, known and unknown.

Al-Qaabid (الْقَابِـضُ): The Constrictor – The one who constricts and restricts the sustenance and life of His creation, exhibiting control overall.

Al-Baasit (الْبَاسِـطُ): The Expander – The one who expands and enhances the blessings, sustenance, and lives of His creation.

Al-Khaafid (الْخَافِض): The Abaser – The one who lowers and humiliates whoever He wills.

Ar-Raafi' (الرَّافِع): The Exalter – The one wo elevates the status of His believers and dignifies them.

Al-Mu'izz (الْمُعِزُّ): The Giver of Honor – The one who grants respect and honor to whom He wills.

Al-Mudhill (الْمُذِلُّ): The Giver of Dishonor – The one who can also degrade and diminish the status of whom He wills.

As-Samee' (السَّمِيع): The All-Hearing – The one who hears all things; nothing is hidden from Him, emphasizing His knowledge.

Al-Baseer (الْبَصِير): The All-Seeing – The one who sees all things, evidencing His complete awareness and knowledge of all matters.

Al-Hakam (الْحَكَمُ): The Judge – The one who is the arbitrator, judging between His servants with justice.

Al-'Adl (الْعَدْلُ): The Just – Reflecting Allah's attribute of being just in His rulings, not oppressing anyone.

Al-Lateef (اللَّطِيف): The Subtle One – Denoting Allah's kindness towards His creation, His awareness of the finest details.

Al-Khabeer (الْخَبِير): The All-Aware – Reflecting Allah's deep awareness and understanding of the inner states of all things.

Al-Haleem (الْحَلِيمُ): The Forbearing – The one who is forbearing, showing self-restraint, not hastily punishing the wrongdoers.

Al-'Adheem (الْعَظِيمُ): The Magnificent – Reflecting the grandeur and magnificence of Allah.

Al-Ghafuur (الْغَفُور): The Forgiving – Denoting Allah's encompassing forgiveness for His creation.

Ash-Shakuur (الشَّكُور): The Appreciative – The one who recognizes and appreciates the efforts and good deeds of His creations, rewarding them abundantly.

Al-'Ali (الْعَلِـــيُّ): The Highest – Signifying Allah's transcendence above His creation, being the most high.

Al-Kabeer (الْكَبِيرُ): The Great – Reflecting the greatness of Allah in all aspects.

Al-Hafeedh (الْحَفِيظُ): The Preserver – The one who preserves and protects His creation, guarding them from harm and maintaining the order of the universe.

Al-Muqeet (الْمُقِيتُ): The Nourisher – The one who sustains and nourishes all His creations, taking care of their needs.

Al-Haseeb (الْحَسِـــيبُ): The Reckoner – The one to whom all will be accountable; He who takes account of every single deed.

Al-Jaleel (الجَلِيـلُ): The Majestic – The one who possesses great and majestic attributes, being noble and honorable.

Al-Kareem (الْكَرِيـمُ): The Generous – The one who is generous, giving without expecting anything in return.

Ar-Raqeeb (الرَّقِــيبُ): The Watchful – Reflecting the ever-watchful attribute of Allah, being aware of all that happens.

Al-Mujeeb (الْمُجِيـبُ): The Responsive – The one who responds to the prayers and needs of His creations.

Al-Waasi' (الوَاسِـــعُ): The All-Encompassing – Signifying the vastness of Allah's attributes and His knowledge.

Al-Hakeem (الْحَكِيمُ): The Wise – The one who is wise in His creation and command, full of wisdom in all His actions.

Al-Waduud (الــوَدُودُ): The Loving – Denoting the loving nature of Allah; the one who loves His believing servants and is loved by them.

Al-Majeed (الْمَجِيـدُ): The Glorious – Reflecting the glory and nobility of Allah, being magnificent in all aspects.

Al-Baa'ith (الْبَاعِثُ): The Resurrector – The one who will resurrect all of His creation on the day of judgment.

Ash-Shahheed (الشَّــهِيدُ): The Witness – The one who witnesses everything; nothing escapes His knowledge.

Al-Haqq (الْحَــقُّ): The Truth – Signifying that Allah is the ultimate truth; all that He says and does is the truth.

Al-Wakeel (الوَكِيلُ): The Trustee – The one upon whom the believers rely and entrust all their affairs.

Al-Qawiyy (الْقَــوِيُّ): The Most Strong – Reflecting the might and power of Allah, being the strongest.

Al-Mateen (الْمَتِينُ): The Firm – The one with firmness in all His actions, a reflection of His strength and stability.

Al-Waliyy (الوَلِــيُّ): The Protecting Friend – The one who is a friend and protector, guiding and supporting His believing servants.

Al-Hameed (الْحَمِيدُ): The All-Praiseworthy – The one who is praised and praiseworthy due to His perfection and goodness.

Al-Muhsiy (الْمُحْصِــي): The Accounter – The one who knows the count of everything, highlighting His knowledge.

Al-Mubdi' (الْمُبْــدِئُ): The Originator – Reflecting Allah's attribute of originating and commencing the creation.

Al-Mu'eed (الْمُعِيدُ): The Restorer – The one who will restore and resurrect His creation on the Day of Judgment.

Al-Muhyiy (الْمُحْيِي): The Giver of Life – The one who grants life, creating living beings.

Al-Mumeet (الْمُمِيــتُ): The Taker of Life – The one who takes away life, determining the end of every living being.

Al-Hayy (الْحَيُّ): The Ever-Living – Signifying that Allah is eternal, never dying, the source of all life.

Al-Qayyuum (الْقَيُّــومُ): The Self-Existing – The one who sustains and maintains His creation, needing no support from anyone.

Al-Waajid (الْوَاجِدُ): The Perceiver – The one who perceives and finds everything; nothing is absent from Him.

Al-Maajid (الْمَاجِدُ): The Noble – Reflecting Allah's nobility and generosity, being worthy of all honor and praise.

Al-Waahid (الْوَاحِدُ): The Unique – The one who is unique in His essence, attributes, and actions, having no partner or equal.

Al-Ahad (الْأَحَدُ): The One – The sole and indivisible entity in His essence, attributes, and actions. He is singular and unparalleled, having no rival or counterpart. He is the ultimate in oneness, beyond human comprehension in His singularity.

As-Samad (الصَّمَدُ): The Eternal – The one who is eternal, perfect, and complete, not needing anything from His creation.

Al-Qaadir (الْقَادِرُ): The Capable – The one who has the power to do anything and everything, being able to accomplish whatever He wills.

Al-Muqtadir (الْمُقْتَدِرُ): The Powerful – Reflecting Allah's great power and authority over everything.

Al-Muqaddim (الْمُقَدِّمُ): The Expediter – The one who brings forward, advancing and promoting what He wills.

Al-Mu'akhir (الْمُؤَخِّرُ): The Delayer – The one who delays what He wills, holding back and postponing.

Al-Awwal (الْأَوَّلُ): The First – Signifying that Allah is the first, there was nothing before Him.

Al-Akhir (الْآخِرُ): The Last – Denoting that Allah is the last; there will be nothing after Him.

Adh-Dhahir (الظَّاهِرُ): The Manifest – Reflecting that Allah is apparent and manifest through the signs in the creation.

Al-Baatin (الْبَاطِنُ): The Hidden – The one who is hidden and cannot be comprehended by human senses.

Al-Waaliy (الْوَالِي): The Governor – The one who governs and administers the affairs of the universe.

Al-Muta'ali (الْمُتَعَالِي): The Supreme – The one who is above and beyond all of creation, being exalted and high.

Al-Barr (الْبَرُّ): The Beneficent – The one who is kind, generous, and beneficial, showing goodness to His creation.

At-Tawwaab (التَّوَّابُ): The Accepter of Repentance – The one who accepts the repentance of His servants and forgives them.

Al-Muntaqim (الْمُنْتَقِمُ): The Avenger – The one who avenges and takes retribution from the wrongdoers.

Al-'Afuww (الْعَفُوُّ): The Pardoner – The one who pardons and forgives the sins of His creation, overlooking their faults.

Ar-Ra'uf (الرَّؤُوفُ): The Compassionate – The one who is full of compassion and mercy for His creation.

Maalik-ul-Mulk (مَالِكُ الْمُلْكِ): The Owner of All Sovereignty – Reflecting that Allah is the owner of everything, having dominion over all things.

Dhu-l-Jalaal wa-l-Ikraam (ذُو الْجَلَالِ وَ الْإِكْرَامِ): The Lord of Majesty and Bounty – Denoting Allah's great majesty and generosity, being the source of all bounties.

Al-Muqsit (الْمُقْسِطُ): The Equitable – The one who is just and fair in His judgments, dealing equitably with all.

Al-Jaami' (الْجَامِعُ): The Gatherer – The one who will gather all His creation on the day of judgment, assembling them together.

Al-Ghaniyy (الْغَنِيُّ): The Rich – Reflecting that Allah is free of all needs, being rich and independent.

Al-Mughni (الْمُغْنِي): The Enricher – The one who enriches and satisfies the needs of His creations.

Al-Maani' (الْمَانِــعُ): The Withholder – The one who withholds and prevents harm from reaching His creation.

Ad-Darr (الضَّــارُ): The Creator of The Harmful – The one who creates harm and hardship, testing His creation.

An-Naafi' (النَّافِعُ): The Creator of Good – The one who creates good and beneficial things, granting benefit to His creation.

An-Nuur (النُّــورُ): The Light – Reflecting that Allah is the light of the heavens and the Earth, guiding through darkness.

Al-Haadiy (الْهَــادِي): The Guide – The one who guides, leading His creation to the right path.

Al-Badiy' (الْبَدِيــعُ): The Incomparable – The one who is unique and incomparable, creating with no previous example.

Al-Baqiy' (الْبَاقِي): The Everlasting – The one who remains forever, never perishing or coming to an end.

Al-Waarith (الْــوَارِثُ): The Inheritor – The one who inherits, to whom all returns after the death of His creation.

Ar-Rasheed (الرَّشِيدُ): The Rightly Guided – The one who guides rightly, leading to the correct path.

As-Sabuur (الصَّبُورُ): The Patient – The one who is patient, not rushing to punish the wrongdoers, giving them time to repent.

Based on the attributes mentioned above, one can conclude that God is free of constraints, limitations, flaws, failures, and any resemblance. He is indivisible and has no parts, companions, or rivals. Nothing is like Him, and He is not like anything. Allah says in the Qur'an, *"Nor is there to Him any equivalent"* [Qur'an 112:4]. He is not subject to idleness, sleep, slumber, fatigue, lethargy, languor, disease, death, or change. Everything in this universe is under His power, and He is above everything else. Nonetheless, He possesses a complete and comprehensive understanding of everything, examining the most profound depths.

God is near—nearer to a person than his or her own jugular vein. Allah says in the Qur'an, *"And We have already created man and know what his soul whispers to him, and We are closer to him than [his] jugular vein"* [Qur'an 50:16]. Allah exists beyond the confines of space and time. He is Eternal, All-Powerful, All-Knowing, All-Seeing, and All-Hearing. He created the entire universe and rules over it. His knowledge is limitless and without fault, and He knows everything. Allah says in the Qur'an, *"Say, If the sea were ink for [writing] the words of my Lord, the sea would be exhausted before the words of my Lord were exhausted, even if We brought the like of it as a supplement"* [Qur'an 18:109]. Elsewhere, *"And if whatever trees upon the Earth were pens and the sea [was ink], replenished thereafter by seven [more] seas, the words of Allah would not be exhausted. Indeed, Allah is Exalted in Might and Wise"* [Qur'an 31:27].

He holds knowledge over all that unfolds between the deepest abysses of the Earth and the loftiest reaches of the heavens. He can comprehend the smallest atom in the universe or heaven. He is aware of everything, both visible and hidden. He can hear and see everything. Nothing can escape His hearing, no matter how little, and nothing can escape His sight, no matter how subtle. Distance has no effect on His hearing or vision. He is unconcerned with distance or proximity. Darkness, too, cannot block His vision. As He says in the Qur'an, *"Vision perceives Him not, but He perceives [all] vision; and He is the Subtle, the Acquainted"* [Qur'an 6:103].

Nothing comes into being without His power, will, and knowledge, no matter how small or large, good or evil, beneficial or harmful, known or unknown. Whatever He wills comes to pass, and what He does not will does not happen. Nothing, not even a glance of the eye or a stray thought in the human mind, is beyond His control. He can do whatever He wants. There is no one who can overturn His decisions. There is nothing that can stop Him. There is no shelter but in Him. His orders and His wills are the only ones that are carried out. All creations will be unable to dislodge even one atom from its proper location unless He wills it. There is no precedence or subsequence of any event from the designated time established by Him. There is no originator of actions, including human activity, apart from Him. He molds and refines all into their ultimate states of perfection, and no configuration surpasses His Divine craftsmanship. He is wise in His actions and just in His decisions. His justice is unlike any creature's or human's. Everything He does is driven by a sense of justice, never by oppression or injustice. His creative power is responsible for everything in the cosmos. For all of eternity, He stands alone, an everlasting presence beyond the bounds of time and existence. He was neither preceded nor will be superseded by non-existence. That is, nothing preceded Him, and nothing will surpass Him. He originated everything from nothing (ex-nihilo). He performed miracles and communicated His commands and prohibitions to all humanity through His prophets and messengers. He is the one who will resurrect humanity and assemble them on the Day of Judgement. He shall meticulously reckon them for their deeds and conduct in their Earthly journey, bestowing generous rewards or just punishments in accordance with their actions and His mercy.

CHAPTER 6

Why is God the Only Deity Worthy of Worship

"Allah - there is no deity except Him, the Ever-Living, the Sustainer of [all] existence. Neither drowsiness overtakes Him nor sleep. To Him belongs whatever is in the heavens and whatever is on the Earth. Who is it that can intercede with Him except by His permission? He knows what is [presently] before them and what will be after them, and they encompass not a thing of His knowledge except for what He wills. His Throne extends over the heavens and the Earth, and their preservation tires Him not. And He is the Most High, the Most Great." ~ (Qur'an 2:255)

If there is one ultimate truth and reality, the only way to attain it is to reject all false assumptions first. This is precisely the aim of the Islamic "testimony of God" or "testimony of faith." The Muslim spiritual journey to God commences with the rejection of all false gods and the affirmation of the One true almighty God, the Absolute. Allah's declaration in the Qur'an, *"Indeed, I am Allah. There is no deity except Me, so worship Me and establish prayer for My remembrance"* [Qur'an 20:14], serves as the cornerstone of the Islamic faith. Within it lies the spiritual, intellectual, and moral emancipation of the heart, mind, and soul, freeing them from incorrect dogmas, misbeliefs, and non-beliefs. Essentially, the testimony liberates individuals from the personal prison of spiritual struggles, an experience shared by many, including new atheists and agnostics.

Nothing merits or is truly worthy of worship except the One and Only Almighty God—Creator and Sustainer of the universe—referred to in the Qur'an and other sacred texts as Allah. There is no deity except for the One true Creator. Everything that has ever existed, exists currently, or will come into existence in the future is the creation of this singular, genuine Creator.

In his work, "Ancient Beliefs and Modern Superstitions," Martin Lings elaborates on the innate human inclination toward worship. He articulates, "Equipped as he is by his very nature for worship, man cannot not worship; and if his outlook is cut off from the spiritual plane, he will find a god to worship at some lower level, thus endowing something relative with what belongs solely to the Absolute. The profound longing for freedom is fundamentally a yearning for God, with absolute freedom epitomizing a quintessential attribute of Divinity" (Lings, 1965). Thus, worshiping God merely frees the soul from the clutches of numerous lords. Allah illustrates this concept in the Qur'an, *"Allah presents an example: a slave owned by quarreling partners and another belonging exclusively to one man - are they equal in comparison? Praise be to Allah! But most of them do not know"* [Qur'an 39:29]. That is, if God is not the object of worship, ultimately, one ought to be worshiping something else—idols, creatures, science, evolution, philosophy, ideas, money, sex, desires, whims, and so on. Atheists and agnostics are not exempt from this rule. Allah states in the Qur'an, *"Have you seen the one who takes as his god his own desire? Then would you be responsible for him?"* [Qur'an 25:43].

Why is God worthy of worship? The right of God to be worshipped is an inherent fact of His Being because existence itself is owed to Him. In the Qur'an, Allah says, *"Indeed, I am God. There is no god but Me; therefore, worship Me and establish prayer for My remembrance"* [Qur'an 20:14]. Therefore, God is deserving of our prayers, supplications, remembrance, adoration, obedience, love, petitions, praise, and gratitude. He is the One and Only God worthy of worship, and all acts of worship are specifically designated and dedicated to Him alone.

Additionally, God deserves praise because He is the creator and sustainer of all things. Allah asks rhetorically in the Qur'an, *"O mankind, remember God's favor upon you. Is there any creator other than God who provides for you from the heavens and the Earth? There is no deity except Him, so how are you deluded (away from truth)?"* [Qur'an 35:3]. Ultimately, God deserves our praises as He showers us with innumerable blessings and favors. Allah emphasizes in the Qur'an, *"And He gave you from all you asked of Him. And if you should count the favor of Allah, you could not enumerate them. Indeed, mankind is [generally] most unjust and ungrateful"* [Qur'an 14:34].

CHAPTER 7

What are the Atheist Arguments Against God's Existence?

"Blessed is He in whose hand is dominion, and He is over all things competent. [He] who created death and life to test you [as to] which of you is best in deed - and He is the Exalted in Might, the Forgiving." ~ Qur'an 67:1-2

To establish the existence of something, positive proof is necessary, which entails simply pointing to signs of its existence. Conversely, proving the non-existence of something requires negative proof, which is far more challenging due to the exhaustive search and verification needed for its non-existence. For instance, to confirm someone's presence in a building, we hunt for indications such as their coat, umbrella, parked car, or belongings. These may indicate the person's presence. However, proving someone is not present is arduous, requiring a thorough search of every space, room, store, and restroom. Only after such a search can one conclude, "I searched everywhere and couldn't find the individual. He or she is absent."

The Qur'an urges us to seek positive proof or evidence of God's existence in nature and within ourselves. In the Qur'an, Allah says, *"Then do they not consider the camels, how they are created; the sky, how it is raised; the mountains, how they have established; and the earth, how it is spread"* [Qur'an 88:17-20]. Additionally, Allah states, *"Soon we will show them our signs in the horizons and in themselves until it becomes clear to them..."* [Qur'an 41:53]. The Study Qur'an (Nasr et al., 2015) extensively discusses these verses. The desert environment depicted in the passage illustrates contemplating God's evidence in the created order, highlighting the significance of camels, mountains, sky, and earth. The camel's survival traits, seen in Arabic commentaries and Islamic literature, demonstrate God's wisdom and strength. The text could also allude to yielding to divine guidance, paralleling how camels yield to their leader.

God's might, understanding, intelligence, and mercy are shown through various natural elements sustaining life. Atheists, requiring negative proof for their denial of God's existence, face an impossible task. How can one demonstrate God's non-existence? The vastness of the universe renders proving God's non-existence not just difficult but impossible. It's more honest for nonbelievers to acknowledge, "I found no evidence for God's existence in my experience. He may exist." Such openness qualifies as "agnosticism" - admitting uncertainty about God's existence but remaining open to possibilities.

CHAPTER 8

I Exist, and Therefore, God Must Exist

"It is He who created the heavens and earth in six days and then established Himself above the Throne. He knows what penetrates into the earth and what emerges from it and what descends from the heaven and what ascends therein; and He is with you wherever you are. And Allah, of what you do, is Seeing." ~ (Qur'an 57:4)

Everyone, including atheists and agnostics, is unequivocally certain of their own existence. If God's existence seems a mystery due to His lack of observability, then so is every human being's actuality concerning their "self" or "soul." A person is not merely what appears on the surface but also the intangible 'I,' which remains unseen. A person's "self" or "soul" encompasses their personality, individuality, consciousness, free will, and intellect. It amalgamates the concepts of "soul" and "self." This notion is reflected in the philosopher René Descartes's statement (d. 1650 CE), where he didn't assert, "I am an observable material body, and thus, I exist," but rather, "I think, therefore I am."

Certainly, humans have a tangible material existence, yet their existence is at the level of consciousness or spiritual comprehension, surpassing mere physical observation. Similarly, God's essence remains unobservable, but His beautiful names and attributes are perceptible. All of God's creations are manifestations of God's beautiful names and attributes, and therefore, embody His beautiful names and traits. Hence, one can perceive God using the same logic Descartes employed to understand himself. That is, if we comprehend our own existence, we can infer the existence of God. Denying God would consequently entail denying our own existence. Anyone who acknowledges their existence is likely to affirm, "I exist; therefore, God must exist." In essence, "I comprehend God's existence as I am part of His creation." Allah states in the Qur'an, *"Soon we will show them our signs in the horizons and in themselves until it becomes clear to them..."* [Qur'an 41:53].

CHAPTER 9

How Can One Know God Without Seeing Him?

"And to Allah belongs the East and the West. So wherever you [might] turn, there is the Face of Allah. Indeed, Allah is all-Encompassing and Knowing." ~ (Qur'an 2:115)

One of the most prominent objections to God's existence that atheists and agnostics raise is, "If God exists, why can't we see Him?" or rather, "Why doesn't God reveal Himself?" Unable to directly observe God, they posit that the material cosmos constitutes the entirety of existence, with nothing existing beyond its bounds. Those who subscribe to such a perspective would find it challenging to understand the profound realities of the hidden universe. Coming to terms with the fact that sensory perceptions are the result of coherence between the sensory organs and the substances to be sensed or perceived is critical. Each of our senses perceives a distinct material manifestation that corresponds to a specific sensation, contingent upon various conditions. Similarly, one cannot expect the ears to have a sense of sight or the eyes to have a sense of sound. Since God is non-corporeal, non-material, and beyond time and space, our senses cannot perceive the actuality of the Almighty God. The restrictions are in our human nature, not in God's. Due to the limitations of the human eye, we cannot see God. An eye can only see what it directly encounters, which has dimensions and occupies space. As previously said, God has no bodily reality, which means He has no dimensions, nor does He occupy any space. God has flawless and limitless properties; therefore, He cannot be perceived by any of the five human sensory organs due to their own limitations.

However, God invites us to recognize Him by His signs and has made it necessary for us to ponder and reflect on His creations as a means of recognizing Him. His works are manifestations of His beautiful names and attributes. In the same way, one can identify the sun by examining its beams, sunlight, warmth, or even capturing its solar energy. Some individuals are open to God's signs and sense God's work all around them, while others disregard everything as meaningless and arbitrary. Every human has a natural innate knowledge of God's existence and desire to know Him, believe in Him, and surrender or submit to His will. This intrinsic proclivity, however, can be encouraged or suppressed. Indeed, God guides those who are earnest in their search for the truth and open to receiving His direction. Allah states that He will not change the condition of a people until they change what is in themselves, *"For each one are successive [angels] before and behind him who protect him by the decree of Allah. Indeed, Allah will not change the condition of a people until they change what is in themselves. And when Allah intends for a people ill, there is no repelling it. And there is not for them besides Him any patron"* [Qur'an 13:11]. In other words, those who continue to seek Him and seek His guidance will be led. Those who refuse to believe in Him and do not seek His guidance will be led astray. Allah says in the Qur'an, *"God guides to Himself whoever turns to Him"* [Qur'an 13:27]. Allah also says in the Qur'an, *"And say, 'The truth is from your Lord, so whoever wills – let him believe; and whoever wills – let him disbelieve...'"* [Qur'an 18:29]. To believe in God requires objectivity and an unbiased attitude to the possibility of God's existence, which can be quite confronting and humbling for some, especially the new atheists and agnostics. However, without this genuine openness and willingness, no facts or arguments can convince someone of God's reality. God cautions us that those who approach His signs with arrogance and pride will only find justification for their unbelief. Allah says in the Qur'an, *"I will turn away from My signs those who are arrogant upon the earth without right; and if they should see every sign, they will not believe in it. And if they see the way of consciousness, they will not adopt it as a way, but if they see the way of error, they will adopt it as a way. That is because they have denied Our signs, and they were heedless of them"* [Qur'an 7:146].

CHAPTER 10

Is It Necessary to Prove God's Existence to Have Faith in God?

"Allah does not charge a soul except [with that within] its capacity. It will have [the consequence of] what [good] it has gained, and it will bear [the consequence of] what [evil] it has earned..." ~ (Qur'an 2:286)

It is reasonable to have a strong belief in God based solely on one's natural disposition or fitrah, without the need for any proof. The Qur'an reveals instances of prophets seeking clarification or affirmation from God, not because they lacked belief but to increase their faith. Notable examples include Prophet Abraham (PBUH) and Prophet Moses (PBUH) in the Qur'an, displaying their curiosity to understand the Divine, reflecting the broader human quest for knowledge and certainty.

The story of Prophet Abraham involves him asking God to demonstrate how He gives life to the dead. Allah responds, asking if Abraham does not yet believe. Abraham replies, *"Yes, but [I ask] only that my heart may be satisfied"* [Qur'an 2:260-261]. Allah instructs him to take four birds, train them to come to him, and then place pieces of them on different mountains. Calling them, the birds come flying back to him. This event showcases divine power, affirming Allah's absolute control over creation and resurrection.

Prophet Moses also seeks to see God but is told that God cannot be seen as he wishes. Allah states, *"You will not see Me, but look at the mountain; if it should remain in place, then you will see Me." The mountain crumbles to dust upon God's manifestation, causing Moses to faint. Upon regaining consciousness, he reaffirms his unwavering faith and seeks God's forgiveness for his request"* [Qur'an 7:143-144]. These stories provide profound theological and high spiritual lessons. Despite their spiritual status, the Prophets express questions and yearnings akin to ordinary individuals, interpreted not as doubt but as a quest for spiritual enlightenment and certainty.

Regarding the necessity of proving God's existence to have faith, if doubts burden one's intellect and heart, evidence becomes vital in eradicating skepticism and boosting confidence. Moreover, individuals aiming to convey Islam's truth to non-believers or defend Islamic theology must resort to proof of God's existence. The Qur'an contains essential evidence for God's existence, and classical Muslim theologians and philosophers presented convincing arguments during the Islamic civilization's classical period.

CHAPTER 11

What are the Rational and Philosophical Arguments for God's Existence?

"Say, 'Travel through the land and observe how He began creation...'" ~ (Qur'an 29:20)

In the intellectual history spanning diverse cultures and schools of thought, the existence of God emerges as a universal focus of rigorous inquiry and passionate debate. This discourse spans theology, philosophy, and comparative religion, showcasing interdisciplinary engagement. According to Graham Oppy (2012), contemporary academia presents a robust debate shaped by scholars with varying worldviews. Notably, Western philosophers like Edward Fraser, Alvin Plantinga, and Robin Collins ardently defend theistic viewpoints, while Jordan Howard Sobel, Graham Oppy, and Michael Martin provide atheistic counterarguments (Kikanovic, 2021). Moreover, renowned Muslim thinkers such as al-Farabi (d. 950 CE), Ibn Sina (d. 1037 CE), al-Ghazali (d. 111 CE), Ibn Rushd (d. 1198 CE), Fakhr al-Din al-Razi (d. 1210 CE), and Mulla Sadra (d. 1636) have significantly contributed to this discourse through Islamic philosophical and theological perspectives.

Evans and Bagget (2014) emphasize that arguments for God's existence transcend mere matters of belief or disbelief; they involve intricate intellectual frameworks, relying on rationality, logic, and analytical scrutiny. This section aims to explore a diverse array of arguments concerning God's existence, from Islamic traditions to contemporary Western thought, offering a comprehensive scholarly examination of this perennial and universally resonant question.

The Contingent Argument

In Islamic tradition, the contingent argument for God's existence delves into metaphysical necessity and contingency, employing a logical analysis of existence and causality. Esteemed figures like al-Farabi, Ibn Sina, al-Ghazali, Ibn Rushd, Fakhr al-Din al-Razi, and Mulla Sadra have advocated this argument within the Islamic intellectual tradition. It operates within a nuanced framework of metaphysical contingency and necessity, resonating with theological axioms found in the Qur'an.

This argument stems from empirical observation, noting that certain entities or beings exhibit contingent properties—characteristics that might or might not exist and are dependent on an external principle for their existence. Consequently, the argument posits that such contingent beings rely on something beyond themselves for their existence. This external basis could be either another contingent being or a Necessary Being—a self-sufficient entity not reliant on any other for existence. Here arises a crucial question: Can there be an infinite chain of contingent beings, each depending on the other? This would lead to an infinite regress, a logical paradox, and an untenable proposition regarding existence. To resolve this, the argument concludes that a Necessary Being must terminate this endless chain. This Being embodies independence, self-existence, and self-sufficiency. In Islamic exegesis, this Necessary Being is identified as God or Allah, the ultimate grounding for all contingent beings.

The Qur'an presents verses that can be interpreted to support the argument from contingency. For instance, Qur'an 3:190 encourages believers to contemplate the intricacies of the heavens and the earth, implying a purposeful Creator necessary for the contingent world's existence. Allah states, *"Indeed, in the creation of the heavens and the earth and the alternation of the night and the day are signs for those of understanding"* [Qur'an 3:190]. Similarly, Qur'an 76:2 suggests the presence of a purposeful Creator behind the intricate biological systems in humans, pointing towards a Necessary Being. Allah states, *"Indeed, We created man from a sperm-drop mixture that We may try him; and We made him hearing and seeing"* [Qur'an 76:2].

These Qur'anic verses prompt a reflective approach to understanding divine signs in nature, implicitly reinforcing the argument from contingency. Within this argument, contingency serves as an initial point leading to inquiry into the nature and origins of contingent entities. Subsequently, the concept of a Necessary Being offers resolution, serving as the ontological grounding for all existence.

While the contingent argument explores the dependency and potential non-existence of beings, the notion of a Necessary Being emphasizes its self-sufficiency, independence, and eternal nature. Together, they form a complex philosophical discourse aiming to elucidate the concept of a self-subsistent, necessary being as the originator and sustainer of all existence.

The Qur'an further supports this concept by portraying God as the *"Eternal Refuge"* [Qur'an 112:1-2], reinforcing the notion of God's independence and self-sufficiency. It critically questions the possibility of a universe without a creator, implying the necessity of a Necessary Being [Qur'an 52:35-36]. The Qur'an describes God as *"the First and the Last,"* highlighting His eternal and omniscient nature, fitting attributes for a Necessary Being [Qur'an 57:3]. Moreover, it confirms God's capability as the creative force behind all existence [Qur'an 36:81]. These Qur'anic verses thus serve as theological support for the philosophical premises in the argument from contingency.

The concept of a sequence of dominoes leaning on each other can illustrate the contingent argument for God's existence based on the interplay between contingent and necessary beings. Imagine an endless row of dominoes, each relying on its predecessor for support, extending ad infinitum. Such an arrangement prompts scrutiny about its origin. Does this sequence of contingent entities extend perpetually into the past without a starting "first domino" standing upright, self-supported, and stable, the foundational underpinning for all subsequent elements to remain stable? In this scenario, each domino symbolizes a contingent being whose existence is not self-explanatory but reliant on prior causes or entities. In the metaphysical realm, the "first domino" symbolizes a Necessary Being, self-sufficient and independent, unaffected by external factors. This "first domino" offers foundational stability to the chain of contingent beings while maintaining inherent stability without external support. Within a theistic worldview, this Necessary Being is not merely an ontological concept but the Divine—God. Unlike contingent beings, God's existence is autonomous – free from external conditions and preexisting causes. This distinction differentiates the Divine from contingent entities, resolving the logical problems of an infinite regress. In summary, the domino analogy crystallizes the essence of the contingency argument, resolving the philosophical paradox of a universe of contingent entities without an origin or sustaining force.

To conclude, the argument from contingency in Islamic philosophy and theology represents a comprehensive intellectual pursuit. It amalgamates rational analysis with Qur'anic teachings to establish the existence of a Necessary Being identified as God in Islamic tradition. This argument offers a logically coherent and theologically robust path, leading to the recognition of God as the ultimate cause and sustainer of all contingent existences. By synthesizing rational inquiry with scriptural exegesis, it provides a holistic understanding of the subject matter within an Islamic framework.

The Cosmological Argument

The cosmological argument is rooted in traditional philosophical viewpoints, aiming to substantiate God's existence based on the presence and nature of the universe. The term "cosmos" refers to the order or arrangement of things, while "logos" pertains to the study of something (Pecorino, 2015). Therefore, cosmological arguments seek to elucidate why things are as they are to demonstrate the existence of God. Within this realm, "Kalam's cosmological argument," originating from Islamic intellectual tradition, holds significant prominence. This particular version, as per Nowacki (2007), is fervently debated in philosophy and widely discussed among numerous cosmological arguments, such as the first-cause argument. Being grounded in Islamic intellectual tradition, Kalam's cosmological argument infers God's existence from an Islamic perspective, positing that God is the underlying reason for the universe's existence (Nowacki, 2007).

This aligns with the Muslim belief in God's role as the creator of the universe. As stated in the Qur'an, *"Indeed your Lord is Allah, who created the heavens and the earth in six days (six periods) and then established Himself above the Throne..."* [Qur'an 7:54]. Hence, the cosmological argument supports this Islamic concept by asserting that the universe, with its distinct origin, necessitates a solid cause-and-effect link to exist. It affirms that God possesses the ability—power, will, and wisdom—to bring the universe into being. In essence, the cosmological argument, rooted in Islamic tradition, underscores God's role as the originator and sustainer of the universe, echoing aspects of the contingent argument.

The Kalam's cosmological argument is based on three fundamental premises. First, anything that begins to exist has a cause. Second, the universe begins to exist. Third, thus, the universe has a cause (Nowacki, 2007). The first premise asserts a cause-and-effect relationship in the universe, assuming a causal factor for finite things to exist. The finite nature of the cosmos, marked by its inception, inherently requires a causal factor.

Conversely, the second premise aligns with both philosophical and empirical evidence indicating the universe's origin *(Reichenbach, 2004)*. For instance, the Big Bang Theory posits the universe's emergence from a singularity approximately 13.8 billion years ago (*Ikpendu & Ahmed, 2020; Manson, 2009*), supporting the idea that the cosmos commenced its existence at a precise point in time. Consequently, the third premise of Kalam's cosmological argument concludes that the cosmos has a cause, identified as God within the Islamic context. This argument offers a compelling framework, affirming Muslims' belief that God is the ultimate source of all creation [Qur'an 21:30; 21:33; 41:11].

In Islamic theology, God is referred to as "Qadim," signifying "ancient" or "eternal," illustrating His transcendence beyond place, time, or circumstances (Denova, 2022). This portrayal correlates with the description in the Muslim holy book, stating, *"There is nothing like him, and he is the One who hears and sees [all things]"* [Qur'an 42:1]. The Qur'an further corroborates the conclusion of the Kalam's cosmological argument. The cause behind the universe's existence must be spaceless and timeless, predating the existence of space and time. Additionally, this cause must possess immense power to bring about the cosmos's existence. Muslims believe that God, possessing supreme power over everything and unrestricted by any limitations, is the cause of the universe's existence. Allah states in the Qur'an, *"Whatever is in the heavens and whatever is on the earth is exalting Allah. To Him belongs dominion, and to Him belongs [all] praise, and He is over all things competent"* [Quran 64:1]. Thus, within the Islamic context, this argument serves as an intellectual and rational foundation affirming God as the ultimate cause behind the universe's existence. Supported by scientific evidence, this argument underscores God's eternal, powerful, knowledgeable, and creative nature, thereby affirming His existence.

The Teleological Argument

The teleological argument, commonly known as the design argument, asserts that the intricate details, designs, and purposes observed in the world indicate the existence of a creator (Pecorino, 2015). It contends that the remarkable intricacy and sophistication found in nature are not products of mere coincidence. According to Philips (1997), the intricate complexity and diverse, sophisticated systems shaping human existence strongly suggest the existence of a supremely intelligent entity responsible for its creation.

The teleological argument rests on two premises. Firstly, "human artifacts are products of intelligent design, and they serve a purpose" (Pecorino, 2015). This notion emphasizes the complexity, intricate order, and purpose evident in the natural world. These characteristics encompass the fine-tuning of the universe (Collins, 2012) and the intricacy of living organisms (Dembski, 1998). In the Islamic context, these attributes are perceived as the wonders of God's creations or designs, as described in the Muslim holy book. Allah describes Himself in the Qur'an as *"Originator of the heavens and the Earth. When He decrees a matter, He only says to it, 'Be,' and it is"* [Qur'an 2:117]. Secondly, "it is more plausible that the universe is a product of intelligent design and has a purpose" (Pecorino, 2015). This premise asserts that the order, complexity, and purpose of the natural world are unlikely to have arisen by chance or solely through natural processes. Consequently, the intricate balance and precise conditions required for life to exist can imply an intentional design rather than random chance. Drawing upon the creation narrative expounded in numerous passages of the Qur'an, Muslims staunchly uphold the omnipotent might of God and His Divine intentions as the catalyst behind the inception of the universe and the natural world.

Based on these two premises, the argument suggests that a powerful and intelligent designer created the cosmos (Pecorino, 2015). The Islamic framework aligns with this conclusion, affirming the existence of God as the universe's intelligent designer. Within Islamic teachings, Muslims learn that God is the Creator of all things—a lesson emphasizing how the natural world beautifully reflects the design of the Divine. Philips (1997) argued that the presence of a designer behind an existing design was a valid point; every design must have a designer. Hence, the teleological argument resonates with the Islamic teaching that God is the designer of the cosmos. It asserts that the myriad intricate orders and complexity of the world cannot be simply attributed to natural processes or chance (Williams, 2012). This affirmation establishes the presence of a conscious and intelligent Creator. Furthermore, Muslims are taught that God created the world so that people could know and glorify Him (WAMY, 2014). This teaching demonstrates that the universe was created for a purpose, which supports the conclusion of the teleological argument by attributing order and purpose in the universe and the natural world to an intelligent being, God. It is consistent with the Islamic belief in God as the Creator (WAMY, 2014), whose knowledge, purpose, and intentionality are mirrored in the complexities of creation, which would not have existed had God not been present.

The Fine-Tuning Argument

(Manson, 2009) defines the fine-tuning argument as a variation of the teleological argument regarding the existence of God. Philosophical discussions within fine-tuning arguments typically revolve around the fine-tuning of the universe for life. According to (Friederich, 2017), several scientists acknowledge that the universe's ability to support life is intricately woven into numerous fundamental characteristics, such as the values of certain natural constants, the structure of natural laws, and specific conditions in the early phases of the cosmos. Therefore, the fine-tuning argument asserts that God's existence is rooted in the intricate and delicate balance of the universe's fundamental constants and conditions that allow life to exist (Chan, 2017).

Within the Islamic worldview, the fine-tuning argument validates

God's existence as the universe's fine tuner. It underscores the precision and delicacy involved in balancing the underlying constants and conditions necessary for life. As part of their beliefs and teachings, Muslims hold that God is the Creator and Sustainer of the universe, with the ability to control every aspect of existence. Fine-tuning supports this belief by suggesting that the finely tuned constants and conditions required for life cannot be adequately explained by chance or mere physical requirements.

The fine-tuning argument focuses on crucial universal constants seemingly adjusted to allow for the emergence of life (Barnes, 2012). For instance, the strong nuclear force, if absent, would prevent the existence of atoms and chemical bonds, thereby eliminating the building blocks of life (Mufti, 2014). Other vital constants include the cosmological constant, describing the universe's expansion acceleration, the ratio of electromagnetic force to gravity, mass density, proton to neutron mass ratio, and quantum fluctuations. These are a few among many physical constants and conditions invoked in the fine-tuning argument, suggesting that even slight variations in these constants would drastically alter the universe. This argument aligns with the Islamic faith's belief in God as the Designer or Creator, finely tuning these constants to reflect His purposeful design.

Moreover, the fine-tuning argument proposes that the chance of these fundamental constants falling within the life-permitting range alone is relatively low, if not impossible (Barnes, 2012). This proposition is grounded in arguments emphasizing the narrow range of values required for life compared to the potential spectrum of values. This strongly resonates with the Muslim belief that God, the Designer, deliberately crafted the universe, showcasing the precise calibration necessary for life.

Furthermore, the fine-tuning argument considers both individual fundamental constants and their interrelationships in physics (Chan, 2017). This notion reveals the intricate correlation among these constant values, illustrating their profound interplay. Based on this assertion, (Chan, 2017) suggests that the absence of any one of these parameters would make the existence of complex life impossible. The Islamic faith concurs with this argument, holding that what God created operates in perfect order and harmony (Yaran, 2003). This fine-tuning emphasizes the belief in God as the ultimate Designer of the universe. Hence, the precise calibration of these parameters enabling life's emergence and sustenance showcases God's work and wisdom. Based on the assertions of the fine-tuning argument and drawing from the Islamic perspective, God is the fine-tuner of the universe, and the existence of the universe affirms the existence of God, its Creator, and Fine-Tuner.

The Intelligent Design Argument

The intelligent design argument asserts that the intricacies of the cosmos and life suggest the presence of an intelligent Designer and Creator. It primarily stems from the inadequacy of natural processes to sufficiently account for certain features of reality. For instance, proponents of the intelligent design argument contend that biological systems exhibit irreducible complexity, contradicting the principles of evolution (Morrison, 2019). According to this viewpoint, if specific sections of these systems are separated, they remain non-functional. Consequently, concepts such as Darwinian and neo-Darwinian evolution, as well as natural selection, are deemed irrelevant or obsolete. Moreover, the precise calibration of physical constants and principles that sustain life implies a deliberate design and designer rather than mere chance (Yaran, 2003). This argument also highlights the complexity and specificity of genetic information in living organisms, proposing an intelligent designer over natural processes. The challenge is compounded by the lack of viable natural explanations for the origin of life, potentially indicating the presence of a transcendent designer (Morrison, 2019). Scientific theories such as Darwinism, Newtonian physics, and Leibnizian philosophy, for instance, imply the existence of a supreme creative intelligence to explain the primordial beginning of existence and natural laws (Shanks & Green, 2011).

Islamic doctrine aligns with the concepts presented in the intelligent design debate. Firstly, the Qur'an portrays God as the sole Creator and Designer of the cosmos. Amongst creation, God emerges as a wise, knowledgeable, intelligent, and highly skilled Creator, orchestrating a harmonious balance that invokes profound awe. Numerous verses in the Qur'an evoke a sense of wonder and reverence for the inherent beauty in God's creation. For example, Allah is praised as the *"Cherisher and Sustainer of the Worlds"* [Qur'an 1:2-4], highlighting God as the supreme designer of creation. Another passage emphasizes, *"Indeed, in the creation of the heavens and the Earth... are signs for a people who use reason"* [Qur'an 2:164], acknowledging the signs of God's creation as evidence of His existence.

Moreover, the Islamic intellectual heritage delves into various philosophical and scientific studies of creation, demonstrating its complex yet ordered and seamless nature, signifying an intelligent designer (Hussaini, 2016).

Islamic studies recognize the human capacity to comprehend and relate to a Deity. For instance, studies on Islamic positivism and scientific truth based on the Qur'an by Dupret and Gutron (2016) assert that science supports religion and affirms God's existence. Referred to as scientific creationism, their research highlights intriguing insights into the historical Muslim heritage. Firstly, while the Qur'an does not explicitly reference science, it remarkably anticipates scientific truths such as the expansion of the universe, continental drift, and the greenhouse effect, suggesting a supernatural origin. This argument aligns with the assertions of the French physician Maurice Bucaille (Dupret & Gutron, 2016). Secondly, archaeology contributes to the discovery and validation of truths mentioned in the Qur'an, such as Moses' crossing of the Red Sea (Dupret & Gutron, 2016). These findings establish a consistent pattern wherein science discovers and aligns with truths already outlined.

The Moral Argument

The moral argument posits that every individual possesses an inherent ability to discern between right and wrong. This shared moral compass among humans suggests an origin external to themselves. According to Johnson (2021), this argument suggests that God is the most plausible explanation for the existence of objective moral truths and responsibilities. Thus, God is perceived as the fountainhead of moral guidance. Evans and Bagget (2014) concur with Johnson's viewpoint, asserting the clear link between religion and morality, indicating that objective moral truths and duties require a religious foundation. These might be attributed to God's existence, Divine interventions, or intrinsic attributes. Consequently, moral arguments shed light on the essence of genuine moral standards and obligations.

The moral argument for God's existence strongly resonates with the teachings and beliefs of Islam. Al-Bar & Chamsi-Pasha (2015) regard God as the ultimate source of moral instruction and guidance within Islamic teachings. Muslims consider moral standards and duties as Divinely ordained and immutable, integral to the Islamic moral and ethical system. Moreover, the Qur'an provides an elaborate system of moral and ethical precepts believed to be rooted in Allah's Divine nature. For instance, Allah's beautiful name, "*al-Haqq*," embodies "Truth," and the Qur'an emphasizes the importance of honesty and truthfulness in multiple verses [Qur'an 2:42, 3:135, 4:135, 22:30]. It also underscores the significance of kindness and compassion toward parents [Qur'an 17:23, 31:14] and the wider community [Qur'an 2:267, 90:14]. Recurring themes in the Qur'an emphasize charity and aiding those in need [Qur'an 2:261, 2:267, 9:60], highlighting the moral and ethical obligation to alleviate suffering and promote well-being. Additionally, the Qur'an stresses the value of justice [Qur'an 4:135], integrity [Qur'an 5:1], humility [Qur'an 7:55], forgiveness [Qur'an 42:40], and tolerance [Qur'an 49:13]. It promotes principles of fairness and equity, urging believers to stand up for justice even when it contradicts their interests [Qur'an 4:135]. The wrongness of hoarding wealth and the virtue of sharing it equally are recurring themes [Qur'an 92:18; 9:103; 63:9; 102:1]. Al-Bar & Chamsi-Pasha (2015) further demonstrate that the five pillars of Islam - *shahadah* (testimony of faith), *salat* (prayers), *zakat* (compulsory charity), *sawm* (fasting), and hajj (pilgrimage to Makkah) - embody high moral qualities. Hence, Muslims believe that their objective moral and ethical standards and duties derive from Allah, corroborating the argument for God's existence as expounded in the moral argument's premises.

The moral argument comprises two key premises that bolster the conclusion of God's existence. The first premise indicates the existence of objective moral ideals and obligations (Kikanovic, 2021), suggesting genuine and universal moral truths and obligatory duties regardless of personal or cultural beliefs. This insight implies the existence of moral ideals objectively beyond human subjectivity. People believe in objective moral principles solely because they believe in God (Chong, 2005), aligning with the Islamic belief that Allah embeds moral precepts within the universe's fabric. Muslims perceive objective moral and ethical standards and duties as crucial in seeking God's pleasure (Ali, 2015), shaping their character, guiding their actions, and highlighting their responsibilities towards others, as Allah commands justice [Qur'an 4:135], honesty [Qur'an 2:188], kindness [Qur'an 17:23], charity [Qur'an 2:261], truthfulness [Qur'an 9:119], compassion [Qur'an 2:177], equality [Qur'an 49:13], integrity [Qur'an 5:1], tolerance, and forgiveness [Qur'an 25:63]. The second premise of the moral argument posits that without God's existence, objective moral and ethical values cease to exist (Chong, 2005). This premise assumes that moral and ethical standards depend on a Divine being enforcing them, implying that God's existence best explains the objective existence of moral and ethical values and obligations. This premise is consistent with the Islamic concept of God's attributes, including justice, wisdom, mercy, compassion, kindness, forgiveness, love, and others.

The Human Brain Argument

The argument for the existence of God, based on the human brain, posits that the inherent rational capacities within the human mind serve as evidence for the existence of a Divine being. The ability for rational and logical reasoning inherently suggests the presence of a source characterized by rationality and logic. Reason seeks to comprehend the world in its pursuit of ultimate understanding. Human abstract reasoning and logical thinking support the notion of intelligent design in creation, indicating the existence of a rational and intelligent designer. Consequently, the functionality of the human mind transcends mere natural processes and possesses an abstract quality. Exploring a higher, non-physical reality becomes crucial to fully explaining how the human mind operates, suggesting the existence of a transcendent entity. However, the rejection of God and the supernatural world in the scientific naturalism worldview undermines the validity and trustworthiness of the human mind, intellect, and power of reasoning. These faculties are considered elements of the soul (*nafs*), interconnected with the supernatural realm. We place trust in our minds, intellect, and reasoning abilities because they originate from beyond the material world—they emanate from God. Yet, if our minds, intelligence, and reasoning have evolved from mindless apes, the question arises: Why should we rely on them?

Numerous passages from the Qur'an support the assertion that human beings can rationally employ their minds to discern the world, forming the basis for their responses to matters of faith and guidance. For instance, Allah states in the Qur'an, "*So then they turned (in thought) back to themselves and said, 'Surely you are the ones who are doing wrong deeds.' They were then confounded with shame (and said), 'You know full well that these (idols) do not speak!'*" [Qur'an 21:64-65]. The foundation of Islam relies on reflection and reason to establish an understanding of God and inspire rational thought. Furthermore, as the Qur'an is rooted in God's revelation to Prophet Muhammad (PBUH), it requires intellectual engagement to grasp its principles and applications (Yaran, 2003) (Bladel, 2007). Practices such as meditation, research, and prayer, which engage the mind, contribute to developing faith in God. The Qur'an portrays God as an intelligent entity, The Wise (*al-Hakeem*). Therefore, comprehending Him requires the utilization of the mind to pursue knowledge.

Ibn Tufayl, a classical Islamic philosopher, contends that intuition not only provides a better understanding of God than traditional proofs but also supports other acknowledgments of the Divine (Hawi, 1975). He fervently maintains that both intuition and reason offer a direct intellectual conduit to fathom the reality of God's existence and the underlying rationale for creation (Mihirig, 2022). Building upon this claim, Mihirig (2022) separates inferential and non-inferential claims, using the rich Islamic Kalam (theology) tradition to counter Erlwein's position. He suggests that Islamic philosophy and the effort to prove God's existence are distinct. The Islamic Kalam tradition stresses the essential role of reason in doctrinal matters. Moreover, the Islamic intellectual tradition includes the concept of "*istidlal*" (inference), signifying knowledge derived from careful consideration and logical reasoning (Yaran, 2003).

Influential Islamic scholars like Al-Farabi, Ibn Sina, and Ibn Rushd strongly supported this notion, believing that rationalism could facilitate understanding God.

The Human Consciousness Argument

The central assertion in the argument for God's existence based on human consciousness is that naturalism, a worldview positing that physical processes can explain everything without invoking supernatural beings, fails to adequately describe the subjective experience of consciousness. Human consciousness constitutes a profoundly enigmatic phenomenon, encompassing thoughts, emotions, self-awareness, and the capacity to perceive the world. From a naturalistic standpoint, consciousness is generally viewed as an emergent property of complex neural networks in the brain. However, this explanation faces the challenge of addressing the fundamental nature of consciousness itself. Philosopher David Chalmers famously coined "the hard problem of consciousness" (Chalmers, 2010), asserting an intrinsic, subjective quality to conscious experience that defies reduction to physical processes. For instance, why does neural activity in the brain lead to sensations such as seeing the color red or experiencing emotions like love? Naturalism struggles to offer a satisfying explanation for this question.

Conscious experience encompasses myriad raw, subjective qualities—such as the distinct taste of chocolate or the profound sensation of joy associated with eating it. These intimate aspects of consciousness are termed "*qualia*" (Chalmers, 2010). Unlike objective and quantifiable phenomena, which naturalism primarily addresses, *qualia* remain deeply personal and inherently subjective. Their existence hints at a facet of reality transcending the confines of the physical realm. The argument posits that consciousness, especially its subjective and qualitative aspects, suggests the existence of a transcendent source—often conceptualized as God or a higher spiritual reality. This proposition suggests that such a transcendent source provides the metaphysical basis for consciousness, elucidating why naturalism fails to explain its qualities.

From an Islamic theological perspective, this argument aligns with the belief that God is not solely the creator of the physical world but also the source of consciousness and the human soul. It implies that consciousness in human beings constitutes evidence of a Divine plan or purpose. In the Qur'an, Allah says, *"Truly, We did offer the trust (Amanah) to the heavens and the Earth, and the mountains, but they declined to bear it and were afraid of it. But the man bore it. Verily, he was unjust (to himself) and ignorant (of its results)"* [Qur'an 33:72]. Qur'anic scholars interpret the term *"Amanah"* or *"God's Trust"* as referring to human self-awareness (*consciousness*) and human freedom of choice (*free will*), enabling human beings to develop morally, intellectually, and spiritually, pursuing perfection and excellence. While all other creatures declined, humans accepted it, leading to observable distinctions such as birds not striving to enhance their nest structures across generations, while human endeavor has progressed from modest dwellings to skyscrapers and the exploration of extraterrestrial realms.

The argument regarding human consciousness stands as a testament to divinity, affirming the existence of a supreme being through the profound depth of our consciousness—an emblem of spiritual enlightenment and intellectual elegance. This argument compellingly asserts the undeniable reality of consciousness since people clearly possess and intentionally utilize it. Consequently, it suggests that the subjective experience of consciousness defies natural explanation, hinting at its origin as the product of an intentional supernatural agent (Kimble, O'Connor, & Kvanvig, 2011). This source would require a higher level of consciousness, indicative of transcendence. Moreover, purely naturalistic and scientific explanations of consciousness fail to address its subjective aspects, such as intentionality, self-awareness, and reasoning ability. This argument enables us to discern a profound truth: the existence of a higher reality from which consciousness emanates. Within the broader framework of existence, consciousness serves a specific Divine purpose, intricately woven by Allah, the One and Only Creator, who has instilled intentionality and purpose into the very fabric of our being.

Furthermore, the belief in the concept of the soul is deeply rooted in Islam and recognized to possess the capacity to operate within the spiritual realm (Latifa, Hidayat, & Sodiq, 2019). According to Islamic teachings, humans consist of more than mere physical matter, possessing an immaterial essence that allows engagement in conscious activities, such as self-awareness and purpose-finding (Mihirig, 2022). The deliberate and purposeful engagement of consciousness enables connection with and comprehension of God. Faith in God and religious discourses are perceived as an influence of divinity on human consciousness, guiding their actions, a viewpoint supported by the texts of the Qur'an. For instance, Allah says in the Qur'an, *"And (by) the soul and He who proportioned it; And inspired it (with discernment of) its wickedness and its righteousness; He has succeeded who purifies it; And he has failed who instills it (with corruption)"* [Qur'an 91:7–10]. Consequently, it offers a plausible explanation for the existence of a Deity. According to (Hawi, 1975), intuition and consciousness can assist in shifting the debate on God's existence from mere conceptual understanding to lived reality. He asserts that because intuition is based on abstraction, it necessitates the use of logic and reasoning. Abstractness allows a wide range of possibilities, among which is the existence of a Deity. However, as conceptions can only move away from a source and not towards one, the actuality of consciousness and intuition can only imply the existence of a source of awareness—God (Hawi, 1975).

As a prerequisite for knowledge and comprehension, Islamic philosophy and theology underscore the significance of self-awareness as a constituent of consciousness. Al-Farabi and Ibn Sina, who argue that God's knowledge originates first from His knowledge of Himself (Yaran, 2003), advance this argument, indicating that God's understanding of His own nature reflects consciousness as an active element of reality. Consequently, God's boundless consciousness serves as evidence of His existence. In summary, the argument for God's existence based on human consciousness relies on the notion that naturalism alone fails to sufficiently explain the subjective, qualitative nature of consciousness, proposing the existence of a transcendent source—God—to account for the depth and richness of conscious experience.

The Human Free Will Argument

In essence, the argument for God's existence based on human free will can be summarized through four premises. The first asserts that individuals have the capacity to make decisions and choices independently of external influences, assuming genuine, autonomous agency in their actions. The second contends that with free will comes moral responsibility, suggesting that humans, by making choices, bear moral accountability for the consequences of those choices. The third premise implies the existence of objective moral values and duties – moral truths that transcend individual beliefs or cultural norms, forming a framework for determining right and wrong. The fourth and pivotal premise posits that for the existence of objective moral values and human moral responsibility, there must be a source or foundation for these values. This source is identified as God, a Divine being who establishes and upholds the moral order. The argument ultimately concludes that human free will and objective morality point to God as the ultimate moral lawgiver and sustainer of the moral framework.

According to the human free will argument, the very existence of human free will implies the existence of a being that allows autonomous decision-making. It asserts that naturalistic or deterministic theories cannot solely explain free will. Several premises underpin this argument. Initially, human judgments are asserted to be independent of external forces or physical rules, and moral responsibility is inherently connected to free will, necessitating accountability. Furthermore, the existence of free will, unconstrained by physical rules, indicates a world beyond the physical universe. The human free will argument challenges determinism by positing that events like free will cannot be predicted, suggesting the existence of a non-physical aspect of reality. The explanation for these non-physical elements, points to the existence of God.

Following this argument, the Islamic faith points to God as the Creator of all things. The bedrock of religion is the unwavering belief in God (Yaran, 2003). As highlighted in the previous section, the term "*Amanah*" or "God's Trust" in the Qur'anic passage [Qur'an 33:72] is translated by scholars as referring to human self-awareness (consciousness) and human freedom of choice (free will), enabling human beings to develop and grow morally, intellectually, and spiritually, and to pursue perfection and excellence. It implies that God is the one who grants humans free will. Additionally, in the Qur'an, human beings are presented as having the ability to exercise free will. According to the Muslims' holy book, humans can make decisions without being predetermined. Allah says in the Qur'an, *"Indeed, this is a reminder, so he who wills may take to his Lord a way; And you do not will except that Allah wills. Indeed, Allah is ever Knowing and Wise"* [Qur'an 76:29-30]. In another passage, *"And say, 'The truth is from your Lord, so whoever wills - let him believe; and whoever wills - let him disbelieve…'"* [Qur'an 18:29]. The moral responsibility for free will choices necessitates accountability and judgment. The three essential beliefs out of the six pillars of faith in Islam are belief in one God, belief in the Prophet Muhammad (PBUH), and belief in the Day of Judgment (Hussaini, 2016) (Yaran, 2003). Muslims believe in the Afterlife, in which every person will be accountable for their actions in the worldly life and are rewarded or punished based on the choices they make throughout their lifetime on Earth.

The concept of human free will is intricate, particularly when juxtaposed with the foundational tenet of the Islamic faith—the belief in Divine predestination. The omnipotent nature of God bestows upon Him an unerring knowledge of all events, past, present, and future. Consequently, while God possesses foreknowledge of human actions, He does not impose these actions upon them. This notion can be analogized with an astronomer's capability to predict and document a solar eclipse years before its occurrence. The prediction, grounded in extensive scientific understanding, does not cause the eclipse to transpire; it merely foresees it. Similarly, believing in Divine predestination should not be misconstrued as negating human free will. It rather explains that the outcomes of our choices invariably align with "God's laws" and "God's decrees." Humans are endowed with the privilege of free will, bearing the onus for their decisions and deeds. Nonetheless, it's imperative to discern that while humans can make choices, realizing these choices is not independent. It is, in fact, Allah who manifests them. The "human will" is a prerequisite, setting the stage for realizing the "Divine will." Allah says in the Qur'an, *"While Allah created you and that which you do?"* [Qur'an 37:96]. In another passage, Allah says, *"He to whom belongs the dominion of the heavens and the Earth and who has not taken a son and has not had a partner in dominion and has created each thing and determined it with [precise] determination."* [Qur'an 25:2]. Here is another verse that indicates Allah is the originator of everything, *"[He is the] Originator of the heavens and the Earth. How could He have a son when He does not have a companion and He created all things? And He is, of all things, Knowing."* [Qur'an 6:101].

Islamic theology, as encapsulated in the doctrine of *Tawheed*, asserts the existence of one absolute Creator singularly responsible for the genesis and governance of all that exists. In Islam, there is no dichotomy of divine forces governing good and evil; there is only Allah, the singular, All-powerful, and All-Knowing Deity. This contrasts with some interpretations of Christian thought, where the presence of a benevolent God is sometimes paralleled by a malevolent adversary, often referred to as Satan or the Devil, seen as a potent force of evil with a certain autonomy. The Qur'an addresses the issue of evil not as a separate creative force but because of human free will and the whisperings of Satan, who, unlike in dualistic systems, has no independent creative power. Satan's role is limited to that of a tempter, one who whispers into the hearts of humans, inviting them to sin. However, the ultimate control and sovereignty remain with Allah, who is the source of all good and permits trials and tribulations as a test of faith or as a means of spiritual growth for human beings.

Therefore, Allah is the creator of all that exists, and while He allows the existence of evil, it often manifests through human decisions to act against divine guidance. Allah permits actions and their subsequent outcomes to unfold; He does not compel individuals to act in malevolent ways. For instance, when one chooses to drive irresponsibly at excessive speeds or under the influence of alcohol, they bear the responsibility for their actions, including any accidents that might occur. However, God's Divine will govern the specifics of such accidents, such as the victims, the nature of their injuries, and those who escape harm. The mere existence or permission of evil does not inherently make it wicked. It is the human choice to embrace the evil that defines it as such. God does not endorse or commit evil deeds in His perfection — humankind does. The Qur'an echoes this sentiment: *"What comes to you of good is from Allah, but what comes to you of evil, [O man], is from yourself. And We have sent you, [O Muhammad], to the people as a messenger, and sufficient is Allah as Witness"* [Qur'an 4:79].

Islamic thought supports the concept of free will, according to which God gave humans the ability to make their own moral decisions (Yaran, 2003). God, in His limitless power and transcendence, does not interfere with free will, allowing humanity to act independently. Given this ability to choose, humankind cannot blame God for their decisions (Rizvi & Terrier, 2021). Hick, a Christian philosopher, says that the foundation of moral freedom (free will) is to allow humans to achieve spiritual and moral maturity (Rizvi & Terrier, 2021). Muslim philosophers and theologians argue that free will and its relevance to the concept of good and evil indicate that human beings are imperfect and limited. Hence, they must draw from a supreme source to overcome their existential frailties. Furthermore, humans can only discover their purpose if they consider morality and choice objectively (Yaran, 2003). These assertions point to an entity that is full of actualization and perfection. In general, the Islamic faith acknowledges the existence of God as the source of all things, including human free will. God permits humans to behave freely by allowing free will rather than utilizing His Divine will to control human decisions. It also adheres to the philosophy of human moral responsibility and accountability for their choices.

The Religious Experience Argument

The religious experience argument is founded on a person's contact with religious belief and practice. It is largely considered by some as a subjective argument because it is founded solely on the contact between the individual and the Divine. The idea derives its substance from the narratives of individuals on their encounters with:

1)   divinity and supernatural power

2)   religious experiences and their transformative outcomes

3)   the consistency of transcendent experiences across religions and cultures

4)   the general belief that existing experiences are credible and authentic

5)   the general belief in the existence of a transcendent entity (Al-Faruqi I. R., 1973).

These interactions can happen in a variety of ways. Some people, for example, have claimed visions, profound feelings, and mysticism. As a result, tying the substance of this argument to philosophy or science is difficult because they cannot be measured, confirmed, or objectified. They function only on trust and belief. This experience points to the existence of an entity beyond the natural and physical realms based on surpassing scientific and philosophical evidence.

In Islamic theology and philosophy, there exists a compelling argument rooted in the profound religious experiences of individuals. This argument suggests that the personal encounters and spiritual revelations that believers undergo serve as substantial evidence for the existence of God. These experiences, held in high regard within the Islamic tradition, are considered by many to be a significant aspect of the broader discourse on the existence of the Divine. The Islamic religion, like all other religions, rests upon Divine encounters, rooted in wavering faith and profound beliefs. The belief in the Qur'an as the ultimate authority of the Islamic faith is the most important of them all. Muslims believe that the Qur'an is the literal word of God, divinely revealed to the Prophet Muhammad (PBUH), through which God conveyed knowledge about His names and attributes and delineated His directives for humanity (Saleh, 2019). Belief in the Qur'an and the Prophet (PBUH) is inextricably linked to belief in Allah (Bladel, 2007). Furthermore, practicing Islam entails seeking an experience with the Divine. These encounters can range from everyday actions like prayer, teaching, studying the Qur'an and Shari'ah regulations, charity, pilgrimage, and fasting to more profound and dramatic encounters like the *Mi'raj*, the night miraculous journey to the heavens, which the Prophet Muhammad (PBUH) is said to have experienced. The *Mi'raj* denotes being awake and brought to the presence of God (Yaran, 2003). The Prophet Muhammad (PBUH) relates to this notion by explaining that the Muslims' regular canonical prayer is the *al-Mi'raj* of a believer. It means that religious experience occurs at various degrees for different people depending on the purity of their intentions and their skills (Yaran, 2003). Muslims regard this as the pinnacle of religious experience. Similarly, Islam defines belief as the awareness of truth, stating that God is more than a theory but a fact and reality. *Tasdiq* (ratification) is a notion that contends that knowledge of God is necessary for faith (Yaran, 2003). Thus, belief in God, coupled with a deep understanding of His presence, not only reaffirms His existence but also derives its profound validation from the remarkable and universal impact of religious experiences on the lives of individuals across all cultures.

The Ontological Argument

Evidence for God's existence falls into two categories: a priori (before the fact) evidence that starts from the cause (the Creator) and a posteriori (after the fact) evidence that starts from the effect (the creation). Most of the arguments discussed so far fall under the second category of a posteriori. That is, by observing the effects (creation), it can be clearly indicated that the cause (Creator) of these effects exists. For example, in Kalam's cosmological argument, God's existence is proved as the cause of the universe's existence. A priori argument also referred to as an ontological argument, claims to start from the Creator Himself and not from the creation. Thus, an ontological argument attempts to prove God's existence from the concept of "existence" itself. The terms "ontology" and "existence" can be synonymous.

Ibn Sina (d. 1037 CE), a distinguished Muslim philosopher, advanced an ontological argument by defining existence into two primary categories. Firstly, there is the "necessary existence" (or *wajib al-wujud*), an entity that intrinsically contains its own reason for its existence, independent of external causes. "Contingent existence," on the other hand (or *imkan al-wujud*), refers to something that does not have its own reason for its existence, but instead depends on external causes (Meisami, 2013). For example, plants, animals, and people are contingent beings because their existence depends on outside factors and does not come from themselves. In contrast, a Necessary Being is self-sufficient and unbounded by external causes. Under this self-sufficiency, a Necessary Being must have always existed, free from the constraints of temporality or dependence. In sum, Ibn Sina's ontological argument suggests that "contingent beings," lacking inherent reasons for their existence, necessitate the presence of a "Necessary Being" that contains the rationale for its existence within itself and is thereby eternal. This "Necessary Being" is identified as God. An identical concept was used when discussing the contingent argument for God's existence.

The notion of an infinite regress of contingent beings is a critical element in Ibn Sina's ontological argument, as it plays a vital role in justifying the necessity of a "Necessary Being" or God. Ibn Sina contends that while contingent beings rely on external factors for their existence, it would be logically untenable to postulate an infinite chain of such beings. An infinite regress would mean that each contingent being depends on another contingent being ad infinitum, leading to a situation where any being in the sequence remains unexplained. If every being were contingent and thus dependent on something else for its existence, then an infinite regress would imply that nothing could ever come into existence in the first place. In such a scenario, the existence of any being would be perpetually deferred, and existence itself would become unknowable. Therefore, Ibn Sina argues that this infinite regress must terminate with a "Necessary Being" that provides a foundational explanation for the existence of contingent beings. A "Necessary Being" must exist that serves as the ultimate cause and ground of all existence (Meisami, 2013). This "Necessary Being" is one whose existence is self-explanatory and independent of external factors. Under its necessity and self-sufficiency, this Being is eternal, meaning it has always existed and is not subject to the constraints of temporality or dependence. Ibn Sina identifies this "Necessary Being" as God, the ultimate cause that brings contingent beings into existence and sustains them, thereby resolving the paradox of an infinite regress of contingent beings. In summary, Ibn Sina's ontological argument for the existence of God differentiates between "necessary" and "contingent" beings and introduces the untenability of an infinite regress of contingent beings as a critical premise. This logical impasse necessitates the existence of a "Necessary Being"—God—as the ultimate cause and foundation of all that exists. This Necessary Being must possess the attribute of necessity, meaning it exists in and of itself, not contingent upon anything else for its existence. The Qur'an supports this proof when Allah says, *"Will it not suffice that your Lord is Witness to everything?"* [Qur'an 41:53].

The ontological discourse surrounding the existence of God found a notable advocate in Mulla Sadra (d. 1635 CE), an eminent Muslim philosopher from Persia. Dissatisfied with Ibn Sina's framework, which hinges on the notion of "contingent existence," Mulla Sadra articulated his ontological reasoning rooted in pure "philosophy of existence." Several foundational principles emerged from this intellectual endeavor, serving as the scaffolding for his broader philosophical system.

Firstly, Mulla Sadra introduced the concept of *"gradation of existence,"* postulating that existence is not a uniform notion but rather exists hierarchically organized. At the pinnacle of this hierarchical structure, according to Sadra, lies a supreme, flawless, perfect entity. Secondly, he emphasized the principle of causality, asserting that every event or entity emanates from a cause. The logical result is that an infinite causal chain would be untenable. Within the parameters of a temporal sequence, each cause precedes its effect. Therefore, in Sadra's view, God serves as the *"Prime Mover"* or the inaugural cause in this chain. Thirdly, which is the cornerstone of Sadra's argument, is the principle of *"fundamental motion,"* which suggests that entities are intrinsically inclined towards perfection and self-actualization. This principle breaks from traditional static unchanging conceptions of existence to introduce a dynamic element that inherently seeks to attain higher degrees of existence and perfection. Lastly, Sadra introduced the principle of *"unity of existence,"* which suggests that all existents are interconnected through a singular, overarching source. The rationale for this is that all existence emanates from and is sustained by this standard, uniting source. Hence, this source becomes an indispensable underpinning for the existence of anything at all.

In Islamic theology, God is conceived as the orchestrator and harmonizer of all entities, an understanding that fits together seamlessly with Mulla Sadra's philosophy. Classical Islamic thinkers like Asha'ri (d. 936 CE) corroborated the legitimacy of the causality principle as evidence for a Creator. Other early scholars, including Al-Kindi (d. 873

CE) and Al-Farabi (d. 950 CE), contended that God's existence is a prerequisite for the existence of the created world. Islamic doctrines also stress the incomprehensibility and supreme nature of God, resonating with Sadra's concept of a graded hierarchy of existence, while other sources indicate that, in Islam, God is not merely an abstract concept but an objective reality (Yaran, 2003). The Qur'an does not simply enumerate God's attributes but presents them as a holistic composite that forms His identity. Mulla Sadra's ontological argument suggests that a singular source emanates, unifies, and upholds existence. This source is perfect, absolute, and immutable, making it a transcendent intelligence. In Islamic theology, this supreme source is identified as God. As a result, the ontological presumptions closely coincide with Islamic teachings to affirm that an intelligent, transcendent being—whom Muslims believe to be God—sovereignly orchestrates the entirety of existence.

The Origin of Life Argument

The complexity and intricacy of life are central to the origin of life debate. Supporters argue that it can only be explained by the existence of a Divine provider of life—God. The complexities range from intricate biological systems to the intelligence hypothesis. Other challenges include explaining the origin of life's building components from molecules, the structure of DNA, the fine-tuning of the universe to allow life's sustenance, and the possibility of abiogenesis (the idea that life arose from nonlife more than 3.5 billion years ago on Earth) (Yaran, 2003). According to the origin of life argument, all these delicate yet perfectly balanced complexities can only indicate the existence of an omnipotent and supreme being. Furthermore, such a dynamic existence of things cannot be attributable to randomness or chance, adding weight to the case for God's existence.

The Islamic faith supports the view and inclination that life originates from God. To begin with, the Qur'an is explicit about God originating life. Allah says in the Qur'an, *"[He] who created death and life to test you [as to] which of you is best indeed - and He is the Exalted in Might, the Forgiving"* [Qur'an 67:2]. The creation of life, according to the Qur'an, is miraculous, pointing to an omnipotent being. For example, Allah says in the Qur'an, *"Verily, we created man from a sperm-drop mixture (nutfa amshaj), in order to try him: so, we gave him, of hearing and sight"* [Qur'an 76:2]. In this context, there is an originator of life. In another verse, *"It is He who forms you in the wombs however He wills. There is no deity except Him, the Exalted in Might, the Wise"* [Qur'an 3:6]. Islam advocates for the concept of monotheism, and according to the Qur'an, Allah is the single giver and source of life as He proclaims, *"Say: He is Allah, the One; Allah, the Eternal, Absolute; He begets not, nor is He begotten; And there is none like Him"* [Qur'an 112:1-4]. The Qur'an also uses the understanding of creation to instill faith and belief in people by using creation as evidence of God's power, will, and knowledge. For example, in this verse, *"What is the matter with you that you are not conscious of Allah's majesty, seeing that it is He who created you in various stages?"* [Quran 71:13-14]. Islamic teachings also demonstrate God's matchless capacity to create a seamless balance in which all His creations, no matter how dynamic or complicated, can exist and function on Earth. For example, in his explanation of the fine-tuning of creation, Al-Ghazali (d. 111), a leading Muslim scholar, refers to a ''well-ordered system'' that reflects the "original and flawless designer" (Yaran, 2003). Allah says in the Qur'an, *"That is Our established way for those We had sent before you of Our messengers; and you will not find in Our way any alteration,"* [Qur'an 17:77] to demonstrate creation's original orderliness. A supreme system of laws that allows for life's sustenance on Earth demonstrates the existence of an original designer and designer of things rather than mere chance and natural occurrence (Yaran, 2003). In general, life exists in complexities, but all these complexities and nuances are perfectly structured to run seamlessly, flawlessly, and efficiently, hinting at the existence of a supreme being, the designer and controller. Therefore, God has an essential role in the remarkable and ordered fine-tuned universe to support life.

The Revelation Argument

The revelation argument for the existence of God is rooted in the idea that human knowledge and understanding are inspired through Divine revelation. Here, compelling evidence for the existence of

God can be found in the tangible revelations that God has conveyed to humanity through His prophets, serving as a Divine compass to guide humankind. This argument asserts that God has revealed His existence and His nature to human beings via inspirational/sacred sources (Pecorino, 2015). These sources include sacred religious texts, prophecy, miracles, and personal encounters. For example, in the Qur'an, God reveals Himself on every page as much as He wants us to know about Him. The revelation may stem from several factors. For example, there is the claim of personal spiritual experience with Divinity. These experiences are purely subjective and are based on faith and belief spawned from personal conviction. However, their credibility has been argued based on two main factors. Firstly, there is consistency, coherence, and reliability in sources of Divine revelation across cultures and throughout history. Secondly, revelation may result in the evident transformation of the persons involved. The argument also asserts that revelation is not limited to human frailties or natural constraints, suggesting a transcendent entity exists.

The revelation argument can be related to the Islamic faith in several ways. To start with, the Qur'an stands as a sacred text, serving as an indispensable source that unveils insights into God, as well as God's instructions and Divine will for humanity (Saleh, 2019). Additionally, the Islamic faith is founded on the belief in the Prophet Muhammad (PBUH) as a communicator of God's will and guidance (Saleh, 2019). Since these instructions and interactions between the Prophet (PBUH) and God are documented in the Qur'an, it becomes a credible and reliable source for posterity. The Islamic faith strongly teaches that humanity has witnessed a long chain of prophets who have been sent as messengers of God to people and nations (Saleh, 2019). Another factor is the belief of Islam in the presence of one Supreme Being, which is the source of all revelations that can be communicated directly to a person or through appointed messengers (Imamoglugil, 2020).

Al-Ghazali, a renowned classical Islamic scholar, described God by saying, "Praise be to God, the Creator, the First, the Last, the Doer of whatever He wills, who guides His servants towards the true path, who makes Himself known to men that He exists by Himself without any partner, He is singular without any associate, the Eternal without any before Him and without any beginning, the Everlasting without an end. He is the first, the Last, the External and the Internal, the all-knowing" (Keith, 2003). The text contains a consensus that inferential knowledge requires reflection and thinking from which revelation is birthed (Mihirig, 2022). This argument is supported by Hussaini's statement on the strength over deism, where revelation is essential in explaining God's existence (Hussaini, 2016). Additionally, philosophers and theologians such as Abu Al-Wafa Ibn Aqil (d. 1119 CE) concur that reason is required to understand revelation, which is a pure form of knowledge (Imamoglugil, 2020). Therefore, using revelation to prove God's existence is credible and acceptable in Islam. Additionally, the Islamic faith is practiced through constant devotion. Muslims seek to experience God's revelation through prayer, meditation, and other ways, such as studying the Qur'an and pilgrimage, pointing to the acknowledgment of God's transcendence. While this argument can generally vary between people owing to its subjective nature, there is a strong proposition for the argument in the Islamic context since Islam is based on interaction and communication with the Divine through various means.

Why is the Qur'an the true word of God?

Ten reasons are highlighted here to answer that critical question. The Qur'an is free from errors, contradictions, and imitations. It has been preserved (in the book form and memorized) letter-for-letter and word-for-word in its original language (Arabic), and it is incorruptible. It is a "revelation," not an "inspired" book. It has a simple, pure, and universal message that appeals to human intellect, reason, and inherent beliefs about the almighty God and the Hereafter. It has been divinely facilitated to be memorized easily, even among non-Arabic speakers. It has been transmitted not only as a written book but as a memorized book, as well. It has a very deep, moving, and transformative effect on readers. It describes many natural phenomena that are in line with today's science. It was revealed to and bestowed upon the Prophet (PBUH) who was unable to read or write, yet it stands as a masterpiece of both eloquence and brilliance. It contains many historical facts unknown before and many predictions that were fulfilled.

Why the Qur'an?

The Qur'an describes this worldly life as only a portion of our total existence. It's a life of trials and tribulations with ups and downs for everyone. The real life is eternal bliss in the Hereafter. There is no doubt that every person will experience trying times in their life where they might feel empty, confused, depressed, unsure why they exist, and yearning to understand what their purpose and place in this life is. During this time, it's not uncommon to question what will happen to them beyond this life and how to prepare for the next, if there is one. Man is not born knowing exactly how to live, but because of God's unbounded mercy and love, He equipped man with rational tools to learn, and He sent us an instructional manual, the Qur'an, that can guide us on our journey traversing this life, helping us fill those voids deep within our hearts.

Why must everyone, including disbelievers, read the Qur'an?

The Qur'an is the last or final testament from God to mankind. The Qur'an claims to have come to confirm what has rightly been conveyed from previous scriptures, correct what has been misunderstood or misrepresented if not fabricated, and complete the previous scriptures sent to previous prophets. The Qur'an also claims that God took it upon himself to protect His book. Therefore, according to Muslims, it is God's only pristine revelation on Earth. It is a complete source of Divine guidance. It is a source to understand the purpose of existence and what is expected of humanity. The Qur'an reveals profound truths about Islam, God, and the very essence of the self. It imparts wisdom on the mysteries of existence, shedding light on the journey beyond mortality. Within its verses, the seeker unearths the wonders of scientific, linguistic, and numerical miracles, as well as glimpses into the origins of life and the vast material cosmos. Examining deeper, one can navigate the terrain of the unseen realm, in which the soul transcends Earthly boundaries. Ultimately, the Qur'an guides the heart towards moral virtues, firmly anchored in knowledge, power, will, wisdom, and unerring Divine justice.

Why do Muslims keep reciting the Qur'an regularly?

Reciting the Qur'an regularly is a Divine command. The meaning of the word "Qur'an" itself is to "Recite!" Reciting the Qur'an is an act of worship; there is a ten-fold reward for each letter recited, and the best person among people is the one who learns and teaches the Qur'an. The Qur'an will intercede on the Day of Judgement for the one who recited it during their earthly life. Reciting the Qur'an is a medicine for the heart and removes anxieties and worries, filling the heart with peace and tranquility: "The man who has nothing of the Qur'an in him is like a ruined house" (Tirmidhi). Furthermore, it strengthens one's faith and brings one closer to the Creator while also creating a shield from all types of evil and facilitating guidance for those who are lost. A reader of the Qur'an is introduced to nations of past civilizations—the prophets and their people, the believers and disbelievers, the oppressors and the oppressed, the ones who were elevated, and the ones who were cursed. The more one reads the Qur'an, the better one recognizes not only one's own character but also the characteristics of the people described in it. Be it man or woman, in riches or in poverty, with wisdom or in innocence, nobility or commoner, leader or follower, youngster or in age's embrace, across all races, ethnicities, and nations, one shall find their reflection in the profound persona depicted within the sacred verses of the Qur'an.

Within the Qur'an, the intricacies of the human experience unfold – from the depths of greed, envy, and hatred to the heights of generosity, love, and compassion. It traverses the realms of death, loss, and sacrifice, emerging into the radiant realms of joy and triumph. It unveils stories of those who surrendered to the Divine will despite countless adversities. It touches on the lives of those who arrogantly turned away from the signs of God. In its verses, one encounters those who are faithful, ignorant in their beliefs, deceptive, or hypocritical. It paints pictures of both the obedient and the defiant. In its sacred text, everyone—both weak and strong—find their place in humanity. In the Qur'an, a sincere seeker will find not just a mirror to reflect upon their essence but also a compass that will guide them to their higher self.

CHAPTER 12

Arguments for God's Existence in the Qur'an

"Indeed, it is Allah who causes the seed grain and the fruit stone to split and sprout. He brings the living out of the dead and brings the dead out of the living. That is Allah; so how are you deluded?" ~ (Qur'an 6:95)

Faith in a higher power bears a compelling influence on the heart, intuition, and experience, as well as the rational mind. In addition to the contingent argument for God's existence that has already been discussed in detail in the previous chapter, the Qur'an eloquently advances a complex argument in favor of God's existence, drawing from the wellspring of religious experiences, Divine revelations, the intricacies of creation and design, and the profound moral foundations of existence.

Religious Experience

In general, all human beings sense God's existence—or what they perceive as a higher power—by pure instinct, with or without a prophetic revelation to guide them. Expressions of this *sensus divinitatis* have appeared in cultures and religions all over the world despite them being widely separated by time, geography, and language (Paul, 1998). This notion of faith in God being the "foundational belief," as previously discussed, resonates with the Qur'anic concept of *fitrah*, which embraces the innate disposition within each soul, recognizing God as the Creator. Allah says in the Qur'an, *"So [Prophet Muhammad], as a man of pure faith, stand firm and true in your devotion to the religion. This is the natural disposition God instilled in mankind—there is no altering God's creation—and this is the right religion, though most people do not realize it"* [Qur'an 30:30]. Thus, *fitrah* is the natural, original state of human beings at birth. It's a state of intrinsic goodness, pureness, and sinlessness, recognizing God deeply in one's soul and longing for Him. It sheds light upon the Islamic view of man's essential nature in which God is the reality and the only one worthy of worship.

The nature of *fitrah* is such that it does not require external factors to make a person believe in God and act righteously, but it needs external factors to cause a person to deviate from *fitrah* or to grow to the full potential of the *fitrah*. If the *fitrah* of a person is nurtured and well-protected, human beings will find belief and virtues quite appealing to the heart and disbelief and vice abhorrent to the heart. Therefore, based on the Qur'anic concept of *fitrah*, it is reasonable to say that all people are born wired as believers in God, and the mission of the prophets and Divine revelations is simply to awaken the truth that exists within and reinforce the natural disposition that already exists within people.

Fitrah as goodness means that the spiritual, intellectual, and moral nature of human beings is designed in such a way that makes it necessary to believe in God, adopt a tendency to worship Him alone, and act righteously to maintain well-being if one chooses to do so. Even polytheists, who believe in multiple gods and deities, often subscribe to the idea of a higher power or a greater God over all their gods. Allah elaborates, *"If you asked them who created the heavens and Earth, they are sure to say, 'God.' Say, 'Praise belongs to God,' but most of them do not understand"* [Qur'an 31:25]. In addition, *"If you [Prophet Muhammad] ask them who created them they are sure to say, 'God,' so why are they deluded?"* [Qur'an 41:8].

The fact that all humans can sense a higher power suggests that they will instinctively turn to that higher power in times of danger. At some point in life, every person will have an intense experience that causes a natural reaction to turn to supplication toward the higher power. There are many cases of people who experience a sudden brush with death that causes them to recognize the Creator and call on Him or become more faithful to God and their religious tradition. Allah states, *"Whenever they go on board a ship, they call on God and dedicate their faith to Him alone, but once He has delivered them safely back to land, see how they ascribe partners to Him!"* [29:65]. Also, *"Say [Prophet Muhammad], Who is it that saves you from the dark depths of land and sea when you humbly and secretly call to Him [and say], If He rescues us from this, we should truly be thankful? Say, God rescues you from this and every distress; yet you still worship others besides him."* [Qur'an 6:63-64]. Similarly, *"When something bad happens to people, they cry to their Lord and turn to Him for help, but no sooner does He let them taste His blessing then—lo and behold! —some of them ascribe partners to their Lord, showing no gratitude for what We have given them."* [Qur'an 30:33-34]. Furthermore, *"When man suffers some affliction, he prays to his Lord and turns to Him, but once he has been granted a favor from God, he forgets the One he had been praying to and sets up rivals to God, to make others stray from His path"* [Qur'an 39:8].

According to *Imam Al-Ghazali* (d. 1111), one of the leading lights of Islamic scholarship in the early twelfth century, the innate natural disposition is the impulse for people to "seek knowledge of the reality of things" (Al-Ghazali, 1972). If this spiritual thirst for the discovery of the meaning and purpose of life is not quenched, it will create a void and emptiness in the heart and an uneasiness with existence. While reason is an important tool to achieve faith in God, it is still merely one step along the spiritual path. The "knowledge of God" resides primarily in the heart and is reinforced by reason, but it is not achieved and consolidated by reason alone (Parrott, 2022). There must be an authentic religious experience, the acknowledgment of a greater purpose and meaning to the universe, and the taste of spiritual fruits. The classical scholars of Islam defined the "knowledge of God" not as a collection of facts and arguments but rather as a light within the heart (Parrott, 2022). The "light" of the knowledge of God is found in the guidance, spiritual direction, and the sense of peace and tranquility that believers attain by practicing Islam. It can fill the spiritual void in all of humanity.

The greatest proof for the existence and lordship of God, therefore, is discovered in the intuitive experiences of the heart through which the believers find comfort, inner peace, moral education, and meaning in life—the spiritual fruits of true religion. Allah says in the Qur'an, *"A light has now come to you from God, and a Scripture making things clear, with which God guides to the ways of peace those who follow what pleases Him, bringing them from darkness out into light, by His will, and guiding them to a straight path"* [Qur'an 5:15-16]. In another verse, Allah says,

"Believers, be mindful of God and have faith in His Messenger: He will give you a double share of His mercy; He will provide a light to help you walk; He will forgive you—God is most forgiving, most merciful" [Qur'an 5:28]. Also, *"Truly, it is in the remembrance of God that hearts find peace"* [Qur'an 13:28].

In addition to the *fitrah*, God took a "primordial covenant" with the souls of all the children of Adam before their material existence, where they testified that God is their Lord. Allah says in the Qur'an, *"[Prophet] when your Lord took out the offspring from the loins of the Children of Adam and made them bear witness about themselves, He said, 'Am I not your Lord?' and they replied, 'Yes, we bear witness.' So, you cannot say on the Day of Resurrection, 'We were not aware of this"* [Qur'an 7:172]. From this verse, it is understood that the progeny of Adam had a spiritual existence in the spiritual realm before coming to this material world, where they took the first covenant and testified that God is their Lord. Thus, human beings possess a primordial awareness of God, which constitutes part of human nature, prior even to their conception in the womb.

Further to the "primordial covenant," the Qur'an refers to when human beings accepted God's Trust while all other creatures refused to carry it. Allah says in the Qur'an, *"Truly, We did offer the Trust (al-amanah) to the heavens and the Earth, and the mountains, but they declined to bear it and were afraid of it. But the man bore it. Verily, he was unjust (to himself) and ignorant (of its results)"* [Qur'an 33:72]. The Qur'an commentators refer to this "trust" as human self-awareness (consciousness) and freedom of choice (free will), enabling human beings to develop and grow morally, intellectually, spiritually, and pursue perfection and excellence. Thus, Islam explains the source of human consciousness and free will. For many people, God seems to be far and unreachable, but He reassures us in the Qur'an that He is much nearer to us than our jugular vein or our own souls. This underlines our recognition of God, our complete dependence on Him, and our need to submit to His will. Allah says in the Qur'an, *"And We have already created man and know what his soul whispers to him, and We are closer to him than [his] jugular vein"* [Qur'an 50:16]. In another verse, Allah says, *"We are near to it (the soul) than you, but you do not see"* [Qur'an 56:85].

Only some achieve an authentic religious or spiritual experience or understanding in a proper theological framework. Human nature is not immune to alteration by misguided beliefs, doctrines, and philosophies that contradict healthy instincts. Prophet Muhammad (PBUH) said, "No one is born except upon instinct *(fitrah)*. Then his parents turn him into a Jew, Christian, or polytheists..." [Sahih al-Bukhari]. When human nature and intuitive belief in one God are corrupted, either by negative experiences or the influence of others, then rational arguments may be required for a person to return to their original natural state: "Our intuitive beliefs, which we gain from our natural disposition and experiences, serve to anchor and inform the beliefs that we gain through reflection and conscious, rational deliberation" (Barrett, 2011). In this way, reading and reflecting on the Qur'an builds upon intuitive experiences of the heart by appealing to the mind and the power of reason.

Islam teaches that the belief in God as the Creator and the only one who deserves to be worshiped has been ingrained in human nature as primordial knowledge. Every child is born with the ability to recognize the one God and the tendency to submit to His Will. This view resonates with some modern philosophy, cognitive science, and anthropology. For example, what should be made of the idea that believing in God is an essential part of the human psyche? It is already fundamental to the believer. This belief doesn't require acquisition over time; it simply exists. It's intrinsic, requiring no explanation to anyone about conviction in God's existence. In essence, belief in God's existence is a foundational, self-evident truth—natural, rational, default state, and devoid of the need for proof as Allah asks rhetorically, *"Can there be doubt about God, Creator of the Heavens and Earth?"* [Qur'an 14:10].

One of the principles of Islamic law is "Certainty cannot be overturned by doubt." This principle is referred to as "belief conservation" and is quite relevant in the preservation of one's faith in God's existence. For instance, when one knows and regards John as a friend, the absence of this knowledge in someone else does not negate John's existence. There is no obligation to provide proof of John's existence to anyone;

the relationship is a personal reality, a complete story. For the believer, God exists. Period. A Muslim reads God's Qur'an, visits God's house of worship (mosque) to pray to Him, fasts in the month of Ramadan, pays charity, and makes the pilgrimage to Makkah to obey His command. In all these experiences, they realize that God is present in their life. He is the reality to whom believers are speaking to and the one watching over them. No reason further than this is required.

A renowned philosopher, Tom Morris, explains in his book, "Philosophy for Dummies" (Morris, 1999) a similar principle of belief conservation in philosophy, signifying that we generally hold beliefs for which we do not require proofs. It is expedient to maintain our beliefs. Consider the things you believe in—the things for which you do not need an explanation. For example, the man I know to be my father is my father, and the woman I know to be my mother is my mother. I don't have any tangible proof for this, except my lifelong experience that they are my parents. I do not doubt it and have never been required to prove it. This is something I have accepted without absolute proof. We have accepted many other things in our lives without conclusive evidence. We accept things based on science, indications, history, reporting, narrations, or circumstantial evidence. When we are convinced of something, we believe in it, and according to this principle, we should not give up that belief.

We should conserve these beliefs unless someone proves the contrary. Of course, we must confirm these beliefs are correct through truth searching. If another person doubts our faith, they must prove they believe otherwise. So, the burden of proof for God's non-existence is on the atheists and agnostics. In other words, if believers believe that God exists, and atheists and agnostics think God doesn't exist, atheists and agnostics must prove God's non-existence—which they have not been able to do so far. Why? Because positive proof is easy, but negative proof is not only tricky but it's impossible.

Divine Revelation

The evidence for God's existence can be the actual revelation that God sent to mankind through His Prophet (PBUH) as Divine guidance for humanity. One of the primary purposes of the Qur'an is to invite people to reflect on and appreciate God's creation as a way of believing in Him. Throughout the Qur'an, God calls attention to His marvelous designs and complexities in the universe and within His creation, which are sufficient to indicate that the universe and everything in it is a product of an intelligent, powerful, and merciful Creator. For example, God says in the Qur'an, *"Indeed, in the creation of the heavens and Earth, and the alternation of the night and the day, and the [great] ships which sail through the sea with that which benefits people, and what Allah has sent down from the heavens of rain, giving life thereby to the Earth after its lifelessness and dispersing therein every [kind of] moving creature, and [His] directing of the winds and the clouds controlled between the heaven and the Earth are signs for a people who use reason"* [Qur'an 2:164]. There are many passages like that in the Qur'an that invite readers to think, ponder, contemplate, reflect, and search for the signs of God. Everything in the universe is a sign pointing toward the Divine.

Atheists and agnostics often question, "How is the Qur'an the authentic word of God?" Numerous clear signs affirm that the Qur'an is indeed the exact word of God. Many scholarly works have expounded on this topic. In summary, some of the top reasons why the Qur'an is considered the exact word of God are as follows:

1)   It is free from errors or contradictions. This fact is also confirmed in the Qur'an itself. Allah says, *"Will they not think about this Qur'an? If it had been from anyone other than God, they would have found much inconsistency in it"* [Qur'an 4:82].

2)   Unlike other scriptures, it has been preserved, word-for-word, since it was revealed over fourteen hundred years ago in its original Arabic language, confidently affirms in no uncertain terms, *"We have, without doubt, sent down the Message and We will assuredly guard it (from any corruption)"* [Qur'an 15:9].

3)   It has a simple, pure, rational, universal message and inherent beliefs about the Almighty God, which appeals to the human heart and intellect.

4)   It is Divinely facilitated for memorization. Millions of people across the globe who don't necessarily speak Arabic but can read the Qur'an in Arabic have learned and memorized it cover-to-cover.

5)   It has a deep, moving, and transformative effect on people.

6)   Considering the state of ignorance at the time of its revelation over fourteen centuries ago, it contains a considerable number of amazingly scientific facts unknown then but have only recently been discovered by scientists facilitated by enormous technological advances. A few examples include water being the origin of all living things [Qur'an 21:30], the expanding universe [Qur'an 51:47], the individual uniform orbits of the sun, moon, and other celestial objects [Qur'an 21:33], and many more.

7)   It also contains many historical facts unknown to the people at that time.

8)   It spells out numerous predictions and prophecies that have proven to be correct.

9)   It was revealed to Prophet Muhammad (PBUH), who could neither read nor write, yet its unique style is universally accepted as the pinnacle of Arabic eloquence and linguistic beauty.

The most rational explanation for the Qur'an's various unique and miraculous aspects is that it can only come from God. No human being can produce such work. The Qur'an asserts its Divine origin and unparalleled eloquence. As part of this assertion, the Qur'an challenges humankind to produce a similar text as a testament to its Divine source. This challenge is presented in verse, *"And if you are in doubt about what We have sent down upon Our Servant [Muhammad], then produce a surah the like thereof and call upon your witnesses other than Allah, if you should be truthful. But if you do not—and you will never be able to—then fear the Fire, whose fuel is men and stones, prepared for the disbelievers"* [Qur'an 2:23-24] and in verse, *"Say, If mankind and the jinn gathered in order to produce the like of this Qur'an, they could not produce the like of it, even if they were to each other's assistants"* [Qur'an 17:88]. The challenge in these verses is clear, and it has not been fulfilled yet. The Qur'an asserts that neither humans nor jinn (spirits) can produce a text equivalent in its eloquence, profundity, and guidance. The challenge is not just about linguistic beauty but also encompasses its guidance, prophecies, consistency, and the impact it has on its readers. It invites those who doubt its Divine origin to attempt to produce something similar, but it simultaneously asserts that such an endeavor will inevitably fail. By positioning the Qur'an as inimitable, it establishes its authority and Divine origin for believers.

Examining the Qur'an's discourse unveils its intriguing approach. It weaves a narrative, drawing inspiration from God's signs manifested in His creations, reinforcing the argument for God's existence as the Creator and Sustainer of the universe. The Qur'anic appeal is that the workings of the universe could not regulate itself in such a way that everything contributes to life and growth and provides for every situation and every condition. This should instinctively raise the conviction that there exists an entity who is the source of life for the entire universe, looks after it, and possesses attributes without which such a complete and flawless machinery of existence would never have arisen.

The Qur'an questions whether man's instinct can ever compel him to believe that all this machinery of life has come into existence by itself, devoid of any aim or purpose. Is it possible that this machinery of reality, as it is, has no designer? Does this entire order of life owe its existence to just a blind and deaf "nature," a lifeless matter, or an insensitive electron, and not to a being possessing a will of its own and a direct intellect? If this were the case, the situation would unfold as follows: intricate patterns and designs emerge without an obvious creator, and mercy and order pervade without a clear giver or director. Everything exists, yet it's challenging to understand what makes it exist. This perspective challenges our understanding of human nature, as actions are difficult to imagine without someone doing them, order without someone maintaining it, plans without planners, structures without builders, designs without designers, art without artists, and existence without a clear source.

The very instinct of man will cry out that such cannot be the case. The Qur'an points out that it is against the nature of humanity to ponder over the workings of the universe and then deny God's existence. We can deny everything under the stress of indifference or arrogance, but we cannot deny our own nature. We can go against everything but cannot go against ourselves. When we look around and find that the power of God is at work everywhere, our very nature will proclaim that what we behold cannot exist without God.

The Qur'an addresses human nature itself and invites it to answer from its sheer depth. Some verses appeal to man's instincts and aptitudes: *"Who provides for you from the sky and Earth? Who controls hearing and sight? Who brings forth the living from the dead and the dead from the living? And who governs everything?"* [Qur'an 10:31]. Also, *"That is God, your Lord, the Truth. Apart from the Truth, what is there except error? So how is it that you are dissuaded?"* [Qur'an 10:32]. Moreover, another verse states, *"In this way, your Lord's word has been proved to those who defy [the Truth]—that they do not believe"* [Qur'an 10:33]. In another set of verses states, *"...who created the heavens and Earth? Who sends down water from the sky for you—with which We cause gardens of delight to grow you have no power over the trees that grow in them. Is it another god beside God? No! But there are people who take others to be equal with God. Who is it that made Earth a stable place to live? Who made rivers flow through it? Who set immovable mountains on it and created a barrier between two bodies of water? Is it another god beside God? No! But most of them do not know. Who is it that answers the distressed when they call upon Him? Who removes their suffering? Who makes you successors in the Earth? Is it another god beside God? Little notice you take! Who is it that guides you through the darkness on land and sea? Who sends the winds as heralds of good news before His mercy? Is it another god beside God? God is far above the partners they put beside Him! Who is it that originates creation and reproduces it? Who is it that gives you provision from the heaven and Earth? Is it another god beside God? Say, Show me your evidence then, if what you say is true. Say, No one in the heavens and the Earth knows the unseen except God. They do not know when they will be raised from the dead: their knowledge cannot comprehend the hereafter; they are in doubt about it; they are blind to it"* [Qur'an 27:60-66]. Finally, *"Let man consider the food he eats! We pour down abundant water and cause the soil to split open. We make grains grow, and vines, fresh vegetation, olive trees, date palms, luscious gardens, fruits, and fodder: all for you and your livestock to enjoy"* [Qur'an 80:24-32].

The Qur'an illuminates the truth that one might close their eyes to all aspects of the world, seeking signs of God, yet cannot avert their gaze from the channels of their sustenance. Allah says in the Qur'an, *"It is God who sends water down from the sky and with it revives the Earth when it is dead. There truly is a sign in this for people who listen. In livestock, too, you have a lesson - We give you a drink from the contents of their bellies, between waste matter and blood, pure milk, sweet to the drinker. From the fruits of date palms and grapes, you take sweet juice and wholesome provisions. There truly is a sign in this for people who use their reason. And your Lord inspired the bee, saying, 'Build yourselves houses in the mountains and trees and follow the ways made easy for you by your Lord.' From their bellies comes a drink of different colors in which there is healing for people. There truly is a sign in this for those who think"* [Qur'an 16:65-69].

The Qur'an frequently invokes the intricacies of the natural world as evidence for the existence of God as the Supreme Creator. It stresses the meticulous organization and development found within the universe as a testament to the presence of a guiding intellect. The Qur'an suggests that the flawless and comprehensive nature of this cosmic order is indicative of the perfection of the mind that orchestrates it. One can quickly notice that everything in this world needs sustenance and is provided with it. Indeed, someone must give it, but who could that be? Certainly not the one who himself needs nourishment. Allah cajoles, *"It was We who created you: will you not believe? Consider [the semen] you eject—do you create it yourself, or are We the Creator? We ordained death to be among you. Nothing could stop Us if We intended to change you and recreate you in a way unknown to you. You have learned how you were first created: will you not reflect? Consider the seeds you sow in the ground—are you making them grow, or We? If We wished, We could turn your harvest into chaff and leave you to wail, 'We are burdened with debt. We are bereft.' Consider the water you drink—was it you who brought it down from the raincloud or We? If We wanted, we could make it bitter: will you not be thankful? Consider the fire you kindle—are you making the wood for it to grow, or We? We made it a reminder and useful to those who kindle it, so [Prophet] glorify the name of your Lord, the Supreme"* [Qur'an 56:57-75].

Origin of the Universe

More evidence in the Qur'an that points to the existence of a Creator relates to the understanding of the origin of the universe or what caused the universe to come into existence in the first place. Imagine walking in a desert and finding a smartphone. We know a smartphone is made of glass, plastic, and metal. Glass comes from sand, plastic from hydrocarbons, and metal from the ground. Even if you disregard all the software, programming, networking, and communication that make up a smartphone, would you believe that the smartphone manufactured itself? That the sun shone, the wind blew, the lightning struck, the oil bubbled to the surface and mixed with the sand and metal, and over millions of years, the smartphone came together by random natural coincidences? Nobody who has the ability to reason would ever believe that!

Modern science, religion, and common sense inform us that the universe is finite and has a beginning, but where did the universe ultimately come from? Human experience and simple logic note that something that has a beginning does not simply come from nothing, nor can something create itself. We can reason that a higher "being" created the universe. This higher being must be powerful and intelligent to have brought the whole universe into existence and made the natural laws that govern it. One can also reason that this higher being must be timeless, space-less, and matter-less because time, space, and matter came into existence only with the creation of the universe. All these attributes make up the basic concept of God, the Creator of the universe.

Some people have argued, "If the universe needs a Creator, who then created the Creator?" This is a common objection from the new atheists and agnostics: "Who created God?" This objection can be found in Richard Dawkins' famous book, *The God Delusion* (Dawkins, 2006). Dawkins' assumption that the mode of existence of the Creator is similar to that of the creation indicates his own delusion in his understanding of the reality of God. It is essential to understand the difference in the modes of existence between God, the "necessary existent," and His creations, the possible or "contingent existents." A necessary existent does not require a cause because it exists by itself (by its essence), but a contingent existent requires a cause because it is an effect of a cause or dependent on one. Thus, God does not need a cause, but all creations do. Since the necessary existent is the first cause, the absolute cause, or the no-cause cause, therefore, "Who created God?" is an illogical question—an oxymoron. God is not created; He has always existed. He has no cause. If He were created, He would not have been God because one of the attributes of God is the Creator. If God is created, He is no longer a Creator but a creation or creature. Thus, God is neither created nor did He create Himself because that would also be logically absurd. Therefore, God, the Creator, is different from His creation. Unlike the universe and the rest of creation, God is absolute and eternal, which means He has always existed and has no beginning and end. He is not preceded by non-existence; there was never a moment in the past in which He did not exist, nor will there ever be a moment in the future in which He will not exist.

Today, atheists and agnostics are putting forth many dubious arguments to explain the origin of the universe, avoiding the simple, natural, and rational theistic answer that God created the universe. The three most popular atheistic explanations of the origin of the universe include the arguments that

1)   the universe was created by a Big Bang,

2)   the universe came from nothing

3)   the universe was born out of the multiverse.

However, all these arguments have been proven to be flawed. Allah provides a powerful logical argument for His existence in the Qur'an, addressing atheists and agnostics through elegant rhetoric, *"Or were they created by nothing? Or were they the creators [of themselves]? Or did they create the Heavens and Earth? Rather they are not certain"* [Qur'an 52:35-36]. The Qur'anic argument in these verses cites four possibilities to explain how something can come into being, but only one is correct. First, could nothing create it? (*"Or were they created by nothing?"*) Second, could it be self-created? (*"Or were they the creators [of themselves]?"*) Third, could a possible or contingent existence create it? (*"Or did they create the Heavens and Earth?"*). This implies that a created thing is ultimately created by something else. Finally, it is made by a necessary existent (*"Rather they are not certain"*). This implies that the denial of God as the Creator is baseless. The Qur'an asserts the existence of an uncreated Creator or the first cause.

Clearly, the universe truly exists. It is hard to believe that anyone would deny that the universe's existence is a reality. I exist, and you exist, and we all believe in a world that exists. The question is, "How did the universe come into existence?" The philosopher Keith Ward says in his book 'God, Chance, and Necessity' that there are only three possibilities for how the universe could come into existence. One is the possibility that it comes naturally to the believer to think that God created the universe. The two other options are either that the universe came into existence by chance (a random process) or it came into existence by necessity (Ward, 2001).

Does the universe exist by necessity? Is there anything that dictates the universe must exist? Believers cannot imagine that God does not exist because for a possible or contingent existence to exist, it must have a cause. However, if the cause is also contingent, it will also need a cause. An endless chain of causes will make it impossible to bring a contingent existence into existence. Thus, a chain of causes must end with the "first cause" to complete the chain of causes. Therefore, God must exist. But there are no believers who say the universe must exist. Considering that modern science, religion, and common sense inform us that the universe is finite and has a beginning, we can comfortably conclude that there is no reason to believe that the universe must necessarily exist, leading us to the possibility that the universe came into being by some random process or chance, as new atheists and evolutionists hypothesized, but what we call a random process or chance or coincidence is part of a larger scheme that we may not understand fully. There is no random chance or coincidence with the Creator.

If you say, "I bumped into this person by chance at the supermarket," it's not really by chance just because you might be unaware of a larger cosmic plan. Things happen that you may not be fully aware of or in control of. For example, you happen to be there and meet this person, but because you didn't expect it, you said, "by chance." Similarly, you may say, "I won the lottery by chance," but of course, there are theories of numbers and probability behind the win. You also bought a ticket to begin with, which is necessary to win the lottery. The winning number you chose may appear random, but of course, it's part of a more elaborate mathematical probability scheme. What appears to be random is part of a more extensive process, which is not so lucky.

In a similar scenario, suggesting that the universe emerged into existence through a random process implies the existence of a certain process. In the same case, if you say that the universe came into existence by some random process, it means there is some process. Some process operates in such a way that occasionally, it will produce a sort of universe like the one we have now. But what this means is that the question has now shifted from "How does the universe exist?" to "How did that random process come into existence to give rise to something like our universe?" This still takes us back to the question, "How does something like our universe come into being?" Nobody can claim that it simply comes into existence without requiring an explanation. Instead, we are left with the only possibility that God created the universe.

We now have evidence for claiming that God exists. We know that the universe exists. It must have a cause for its existence, and the best explanation for that cause is that God is the one who created it. If we look around us, we can see the thought process behind various designs. The chair we sit on was designed to support the weight of a person's body. Everything around us has been designed for a particular purpose. So, what stops us from thinking that the universe itself, with all its designs, has a designer?

Consider solar and lunar eclipses. How do they happen? Think about rain. How does it come about? Snow, too—how does it appear? These natural phenomena have specific designs and reasons behind them. Take the solar eclipse as an example: The sun is much bigger and farther from us than the moon. This exact size and distance relationship means that when the moon moves between the sun and the Earth, it perfectly covers the sun's disk, leaving only the sun's outer light visible. We see a beautiful solar eclipse. This precise balance in nature shows us that the universe is planned and purposeful, and we attribute this design to God, the Creator.

Perfection of the Universe

Further Qur'anic evidence that attests to the existence of God, the Creator, lies in the intricate order and flawless equilibrium within the universe. Could such a large, complex, but ordered universe have coincidentally and randomly formed without design and supervision? Many features in the universe indicate being specially designed or fine-tuned to support life, such as the Earth's distance from the sun, the thickness of the Earth's crust, the speed at which the Earth spins around its own axis and revolves around the sun, the percentage of oxygen in the atmosphere, and even the degree of Earth's tilt on its axis. If these measurements were slightly different from what they are, life could not exist. In the same way that a watch has an intelligent maker to keep accurate time, shouldn't the Earth have an intelligent maker to keep exact time around the sun? Could this occur by itself? When reflecting upon the universe's order, the intricacies of natural laws, and the systems within, doesn't it make sense to think about a creator?

Consider Earth itself, along with its precise placement in relation to the moon and the sun. Scientists reveal that even a slight adjustment closer or farther would render our planet inhospitable. A slightly longer day, a fraction of a degree shift in the Earth's axis, or a minor alteration in the atmosphere's composition would extinguish life. Notably, the presence of Jupiter, a massive celestial guardian, resides in the ideal position to deflect asteroids and safeguard the planet from catastrophic collisions. All these lead to the existence of an intelligent and wise Designer.

Moral Anchor

If God did not exist, there would have been no objective moral values system simply because of the absence of a higher moral authority. Right and wrong or good and evil would be determined by a dominant group that would be subjective and potentially violent. If a society perceives its morals and ethical values as guardians of its continuity, should it contemplate another society's moral and ethical values? Quoting Richard Dawkins, who leads today's new atheism propaganda, "There is no good or evil. We are machines to propagate DNA" (Dawkins, 2006). This means new atheism teaches that even evil people could not be immoral because there is no absolute right or wrong—everything is socially constructed. What is moral or immoral for one community, may or may not necessarily be true for the other.

Atheists claim to rely on science to explain the universe and life, but science can neither prove nor deny moral and ethical values. For example, one cannot prove that murder is wrong or immoral through scientific methodology. All other metaphysical characteristics, such as love, hate, emotions, consciousness, memory, thought, and imagination, cannot be proved by science. Neither can science give us morality and ethics in general. Science is fundamentally amoral, and nothing in science compels anyone to be moral or ethical. You cannot extract charity, justice, selflessness, kindness, compassion, and altruism from a double helix or a chromosome. Those characteristics are derived from God per His commands and prohibitions through the authentic holy scriptures and prophetic teachings.

From an atheistic perspective, humans are perceived as advanced brutes, distant relatives to primates, and cousins to chimps. If animals bear no moral responsibilities, why, then, should humanity? Most atheists, however, would concede that we have moral and ethical responsibilities yet fail to explain why. What are the legal or philosophical underpinnings? Sitting on a beach while witnessing a child drowning may prompt a moral duty to attempt a rescue. However, the origin of this altruistic impulse raises intriguing questions. Did evolution drive humanity to place themselves in harm's way? Can anyone pinpoint a gene with this innate sense of responsibility? Theists contend that without the existence of God, concepts like good and evil, right and wrong, moral and immoral, and truth and falsehood would lose foundational reference points.

Attempting to redefine "good" as merely "that which enhances personal pleasure" raises profound concerns. After all, one person's pleasure could entail another's suffering, torture, or even death. Consider the disturbing scenario where an individual derives pleasure from harming innocent children or burying them alive in their backyard. From an atheistic standpoint, such actions might not be classified as immoral, though they remain socially unacceptable. But what if societies' norms shift to embrace such horrors? Think about slavery or the Ku Klux Klan (KKK) against Blacks in North America or the apartheid system against Blacks in South Africa, the Nazis in Germany against Jewish people, or any aggressive war for that matter. On what grounds would atheists condemn those crimes against humanity, child exploitation, or rape if society found it acceptable and conducive to their perpetuation? On what grounds can they say this is morally wrong? From a theistic perspective, the innate natural state (*fitrah*), God's revelation, and Prophetic teachings provide moral imperatives. Regardless of the moral values recognized—whether believed to be sourced from revelation, society, or inherent within the human essence—these values provide a framework for objective moral standards: abstain from murder, theft, and adultery; uphold respect for parents and neighbors; avoid oppression; and adhere to the truth, among others.

Richard Dawkins says, "Every single human interaction occurs because humans want to prolong their species or they want reciprocal advantage—I scratch your back, you're going to scratch mine because, at the end of the day, we are all apes" (Dawkins, The Selfish Gene, 1976). How, then, can atheists explain "good" acts? Consider, for instance, the act of offering one's seat to an elderly lady on a train. Is it driven by a desire to ensure the continuity of the species or to garner monetary rewards? Does it stem from a hidden agenda to exploit or gain something? The answer transcends such simplistic motives. Similarly, what motivates a person to anonymously donate blood to aid the sick, even without an audience? Can it be attributed to an innate virtuous drive or a quest for mutual benefit? That's why altruistic characters like Mother Teresa and many others rooted in different societies would be atheistic moral enigmas. Just like the issue of the presence of "evil and suffering" in the world bewilders atheists in understanding theism, the issue of "morality and ethics" perplexes theists in understanding atheism.

If the physical universe is all there is, and humans are accidental by-products of mindless and purposeless evolution—not intentionally designed or created but appearing on Earth by chance—life on Earth would have no objective meaning, purpose, or value. It would not matter what choices one makes. If God doesn't exist, there is no objective morality and personal accountability for the actions of all humanity. Therefore, living a moral and spiritual life or living an immoral and hedonistic life would be the same, creating a paradox in the atheistic worldview. One can proclaim to the world that he or she is an atheist, but one cannot live like one because to live by an atheistic worldview means to live a life with no objective meaning, purpose, or values. In reality, atheists and agnostics live a life of objective meaning, purpose, and values, which is essentially a theistic life based on a theistic worldview, despite the rejection of God.

CHAPTER 13

Arguments for the Afterlife

"Did you think that We had created you in play (without any purpose), and that you would not be brought back to Us?"
~ (Qur'an 23:115)

In Islam, Afterlife is a concept of life after death, both physical and spiritual. The Qur'an is clear about the physical and spiritual Afterlife; hence, a believer must adopt this proposition. There is a whole chapter in the Qur'an dedicated to resurrection and Afterlife, Chapter 75: *Al-Qiyamah* (The Resurrection). It starts with, *"I swear by the Day of Resurrection"* [Qur'an 75:1]. In Islamic tradition, death is the separation of the soul from one's body and the beginning of one's Afterlife.

In Islamic theology, the journey of the soul after death is characterized by several distinct phases. Immediately post-burial, the deceased enters the *"Questioning"* stage, where the angels *"Munkar and Nakir"* assess the individual's faith through a series of queries. Those steadfast in their beliefs will find solace, while those wavering in faith or non-believers will confront adversity. Following questioning is the *"Barzakh,"* an intermediary realm where souls linger, experiencing either tranquility or tribulation contingent upon their earthly actions and God's mercy. The subsequent phase, the *"Resurrection,"* signifies a momentous event where all souls are physically revived, as graphically explained in Chapter 75 of the Qur'an (The Resurrection). This precedes the *"Day of Judgment,"* a pivotal juncture where everyone is meticulously evaluated for their beliefs and actions during earthly existence. This Afterlife journey culminates in the *"Reward and Punishment"* phase. Here, one's balance of virtuous versus nefarious deeds determines one's eternal abode—paradise for the righteous and hellfire for the wicked. These stages underscore the profound significance of faith, deeds, and Allah's mercy in the Islamic worldview, as they permanently shape one's destiny in the Hereafter. Allah says in the Qur'an, *"Does man think that we shall not assemble his bones?"* [Qur'an 75:3].

The Qur'an emphasizes the importance of believing in the Afterlife as a fundamental aspect of Islam by repeatedly mentioning the existence of resurrection and the Afterlife. For example, *"Every soul will taste death. ... Then to Us will you be returned"* [Quran, 29:57]. In another passage, *"So consider the signs of God's mercy; how He gives life to the Earth after its death. Indeed, it is He Who gives life to the dead, for He is powerful over all things"* [Qur'an 30:50]. Thus, the renewal of the Earth after a severe drought presents an argument for resurrection and Afterlife.

In another passage, Allah argues about resurrection and the Afterlife, *"Has human not considered that We have created him from a drop of (seminal) fluid? Yet, he turns into an open, fierce adversary; And he puts forth for Us a parable and forgets his own creation. He says: 'Who will give life to these bones when they have rotted away and become dust? Say! He (God) will give life to them Who created them for the first time! And he it is the All-Knower of every creation! He Who has made for you fire from the green tree, and see, you kindle fire with it; Is not He Who has created the heavens and the Earth able to create (from rotten bones) the like of them? Surely, He is; He is the Supreme Creator, the All-Knowing; When He wills a thing to be, He but says to it "Be!" and it is; So, All-Glorified is He in Whose Hand is the absolute dominion of all things, and to Him you are being brought back"* [Qur'an 36:77-83].

Another passage in the Qur'an related to resurrection and Afterlife states, *"Does man think he will be left alone? Was he not only a drop of split-out sperm that morphed into a clinging form that God molded in proportion, fashioning the two sexes, male and female? Does He who can do this not have the capacity to resurrect the dead?"* [Qur'an 75:36-40]; Also, *"And certainly did We create man from an extract of clay; Then We placed him as a sperm-drop in a firm lodging; Then We made the sperm-drop into a clinging clot, and We made the clot into a lump [of flesh], and We made [from] the lump, bones, and We covered the bones with flesh; then We developed him into another creation. So blessed is Allah, the best of creators; Then indeed, after that you are to die; Then indeed you, on the Day of Resurrection, will be resurrected; And We have created above you seven layered heavens, and never have We been of [Our] creation unaware"* [Qur'an 23:12-17]. Additionally, *"You will advance from stage to stage. So why don't they believe?"* [Qur'an 84:19-20].

The question the Qur'an poses is, *"Why doesn't man trust that God can raise him up from the dead?"* Classical Muslim philosophers and theologians rigorously debated resurrection and the Afterlife. They contemplated the possibility of proving physical resurrection, questioning whether it is strictly a matter of faith. The Islamic arguments for the resurrection and Afterlife can be understood through various aspects, including Qur'anic references, logical reasoning, and the notion of Divine justice with reward and punishment.

The first reasoning suggests that the Divine Creator possesses immeasurable capabilities that could have theoretically deployed human beings directly into terrestrial existence without the intermediate stage of gestation within the womb. However, this is different from the course that has been taken. Instead, human beings undergo a complex developmental journey within their mothers' wombs, a period that serves as a crucible for physiological formation. Imagine a hypothetical dialogue occurring among unborn entities in this prenatal stage. Within this framework, the notion of "life beyond the womb" could be an object of profound skepticism. For these entities, the womb would represent the totality of their known universe, a cosmos in and of itself. Any speculation about an existence beyond this encapsulated realm would be challenging and implausible. Yet, the moment of birth serves as an empirical revelation, thrusting the individual into a broader context of earthly existence that was previously inconceivable. Drawing parallels from Islamic eschatological principles, one can consider earthly life similar to a gestational period on a grander scale. In this "macrocosmic womb," individuals undergo intellectual, spiritual, and moral maturation. This holistic development is not an end but a preparatory stage for the next, as-yet-unknown phase of existence—namely, the Afterlife.

The second reason - the notion that human existence lacks meaning or purpose in the absence of resurrection and an Afterlife - is a subject of profound theological import in Islamic thought. The Qur'an explicitly declares that human beings are endowed with a unique standing among God's creations: "*And We have certainly honored the children of Adam and carried them on the land and sea and provided for them of the good things and preferred them over much of what We have created, with [definite] preference*" [Qur'an 17:70], a distinction that serves to underscore their inherent worth and existential significance. This raises a crucial question: Would a Divine architect of such meticulous precision and grandeur create human beings only for them to lead transient lives devoid of ultimate consequence? The Qur'an confronts this existential dilemma, stating unequivocally that human beings are not fashioned in vain; instead, they are created with an express purpose and are destined to return to their Creator: "*Then did you think that We created you uselessly and that to Us you would not be returned?*" [Qur'an 23:115]. In another passage, the Qur'an further accentuates this point by challenging individuals to contemplate the cosmic order. It emphasizes that the heavens, Earth, and everything between them were not created without serious purpose and a designated temporal framework: "*Do they not contemplate within themselves? Allah has not created the heavens and the Earth and what is between them except in truth and for a specified term. And indeed, many of the people, in [the matter of] the meeting with their Lord, are disbelievers*" [Qur'an 30:8]. From this vantage point, the absence of resurrection and Afterlife would not only run counter to the Divinely ordained purpose of human creation but would also render life futile—a mere ephemeral flash without lasting significance. The inescapable conclusion, therefore, is that belief in resurrection and Afterlife is intrinsic to the significance and purpose of human existence, according to the Islamic cosmological and existential framework.

The third reason is that a final reckoning in the Afterlife is a compelling mechanism to inspire individuals to lead virtuous lives in the present world, intending to achieve celestial rewards in the future. Within the Islamic paradigm, earthly existence is understood as a transient phase where human beings undergo trials and tribulations to assess their devotion and submission to the Divine will. The ideas of resurrection and life beyond death are a poignant reminder of the enduring implications of one's earthly conduct. Consequently, certainty in Afterlife is intrinsically linked to Divine retribution and reward principles. Islamic doctrine stipulates that human beings will face judgment for their earthly actions, and their everlasting destiny in the Afterlife will be ascertained following their moral and ethical comportment. This eschatological viewpoint endows life with a profound sense of purpose and justice, galvanizing adherents to aim toward moral and ethical conduct and to avoid malevolence.

The fourth reasoning for the Afterlife is grounded in God's nature. The concept of God is understood through a set of Divine names or attributes, such as *Al-Kareem* (The Generous) and *Ar-Raheem* (The Most Compassionate). These names not only shed light on the nature of God but also delineate the ethical and metaphysical underpinnings of the cosmos. Within the Islamic paradigm, these Divine attributes are both descriptive and prescriptive, setting the gold standard by which concepts of generosity and compassion are gauged. The nature of God is understood as infinitely generous and compassionate, which forms the archetype for the embodiment of these virtues in our world. To delve deeper into these concepts, one can examine instances in the natural world that echo God's abundant generosity and compassion. Take, for instance, the phenomenon of symbiosis in biology. This is a process where organisms from disparate species forge mutually advantageous relationships. A prime example is the mycorrhizal association between fungi and plants: while fungi benefit from the carbohydrates provided by plants, they reciprocate by furnishing plants with vital nutrients from the terrain. Even at a microscopic level, such complex and delicate relationships demonstrate a system that is based on mutual sustenance and benefit, possibly reflecting Divine munificence, benevolence, and magnanimity.

Furthermore, nature is replete with systems designed to shield and nurture those who are fragile and susceptible. Take, for example, the role of a mother in various mammalian species, who often takes significant risks and burdens to care for her offspring. This can be seen as a manifestation of Divine mercy, as it ensures the continuity and well-being of otherwise powerless species in their nascent stages. Based on these observations, one might contend that if mortality and the absence of hope for Afterlife truncated the human experience, these Divine attributes would become insufficient or contradictory.

To elaborate, if suffering, injustice, and moral and existential predicaments comprised our human experience, then the Divine qualities of munificence and mercy would appear compromised. If the injustices of this life were never rectified, if suffering were never explained or made meaningful, if virtues were never rewarded beyond the ephemeral scope of our earthly existence, then one could argue that this would be incompatible with a God who is "The Generous" and "The Most Compassionate." Thus, the concept of Afterlife is a necessary extension of these Divine attributes. It offers a context in which Divine justice, mercy, and munificence can be fully realized in a way that is not constrained by the limitations and imperfections of our earthly lives. Without Afterlife, these Divine qualities would not fully express themselves and could be perceived as inconsistent with the observed phenomena of suffering and injustice. In that sense, belief in Afterlife harmonizes the Divine attributes with the human experience, resolving the existential questions and moral dilemmas that pervade our earthly existence.

The fifth reasoning for the existence of Afterlife stems from observations concerning the human existential experience on Earth. Certain facets of this experience appear to symbolize resurrection and life after death. Take, for instance, the daily human cycle of sleep, dreaming, and awakening. This recurring sequence can be interpreted as a metaphorical representation of death, the unseen realm, and resurrection. The Qur'an, which compares sleep and death to awakening and resurrection, supports this interpretation of Islamic theology. Allah says in the Qur'an, "*Allah takes the souls at the time of their death, and those that do not die [He takes] during their sleep. Then He keeps those for which He has decreed death and releases the others for a specified term. Indeed, in that are signs for a people who give thought*" [Qur'an, 39:42].

Moreover, an additional observation relating to the human existential condition that alludes to the Afterlife pertains to the remarkable surplus of human capabilities that seem to exceed the basic requirements for survival in this mortal existence. For instance, the state of an unborn child in the uterus with unutilized organs such as arms, legs, mouth, etc., serves as a precursor to the life that awaits it outside the womb, suggesting that we are conceived with an inherent orientation towards a life that extends beyond our current one. Additionally, neuroscientific research contends that the average individual utilizes merely a fraction of their brain's potential throughout their terrestrial existence. This underutilization of mental faculties suggests an alternative plane of existence wherein these capabilities will find their full expression.

Thus, the complexity and the latent potentials inherent within the human condition provide a compelling case for the existence of Afterlife, corroborating the theological insights offered by the Qur'an.

CHAPTER 14

Finding God Through Reason

"He is Allah, the Creator, the Inventor, the Fashioner; to Him belong the best names. Whatever is in the heavens and Earth is exalting Him. And He is the Exalted in Might, the Wise." ~ (Qur'an 59:24)

Unlike human existence, which is contingent and requires a cause to come into existence and continue in existence, God's existence must be a necessary existence that requires no cause for Him to come into existence or to remain in existence. Unlike human beings, whose lives are demarcated by the temporal boundaries in the mother's womb and death, God's existence is not delimited by the conditions of non-existence either prior to or after His being. The human experience is essentially a temporal interplay between existence and non-existence. As we endeavor to decipher the underlying rationale for human existence, we are confronted with the limitations of causality. An infinite regress of causes would not make sense from a logical or metaphysical point of view because it would not fully explain existence. To circumvent this epistemological impasse, it becomes important to entertain the notion of a "Prime Mover" or "First Cause." This entity, by definition, must be self-existent without an antecedent cause, transcending the conventional dimensions of time and space. It is posited as the Necessary Being that inaugurates the causal chain without itself being contingent upon any preceding causal factors.

This theoretical construct suggests a being of immense power, intelligence, and knowledge capable of ex nihilo creation—the capacity to bring all things, including humanity, from a state of nothingness into existence. This entity, commonly called God, is not only the initial impetus and the ultimate cause of all that exists but also the cause for remaining into existence all that exists. The existence of such a being is not merely a speculative postulate but rather a logical necessity that provides the foundational bedrock for the causal structure of reality.

In more accessible terms, God serves as the raison d'être for the entire cosmos, thereby making His existence a logical imperative and the wellspring of all existence. In simpler terms, everything exists because of God. Allah says in the Qur'an, "*And it is He who begins creation; then He repeats it, and that is [even] easier for Him. To Him belongs the highest attribute in the heavens and Earth. And He is the Exalted in Might, the Wise*" [Qur'an 30:27].

One can logically conclude the attributes of God from the concept of the necessary existence. This essential being, which has always existed and will always exist, lacks a beginning or end without ever experiencing non-existence. It is free from external demands and is not subject to division or annihilation. As a result, qualities associated with corporeality, such as transition, growth, and movement, do not apply to the necessary existence. Lastly, it remains unseen and imperceptible to human senses, which are inherently imperfect, while the necessary existent embodies perfection.

CHAPTER 15

Is It True That Religion Depends on Faith, But Science Does Not?

"And it is He who gives life and causes death, and His is the alternation of the night and the day. Then will you not reason?" ~ (Qur'an 23:80)

According to "naturalism," there are no supernatural forces or laws that interfere with any of the phenomena in the universe (Languages, 2023). In other words, "Naturalism not only denies the existence of supernatural or metaphysical realities; it also excludes or dismisses any supernatural, religious, or spiritual explanations" (Stefon, 2009). The new atheist and agnostic scientists who favor naturalism subscribe to a fallacy relating to religion and science: "Religion is dependent on faith, but science is not," and a corollary to that fallacy, "Science is dependent on reason, while religion is not." To dispel this fallacy, we must first examine the dictionary definition of "faith," and we shall soon discover that both atheism and science necessitate a much higher level of faith than religion.

Most English dictionaries define "faith" as "loyalty" or "trust," and in common language, these words signify "the demand of some evidence." When no evidence is given, it is qualified as "blind faith" or a "leap of faith." As a result, many individuals, including new atheists and agnostics, are confused about the difference between "faith" and "blind faith" or "leap of faith," which leads many people, including new atheists and agnostics, to believe that atheism and science involve no faith in their conceptions, while religion requires faith. The irony is that atheism is also "a belief system," and science "cannot do without faith."

Many atheists and scientists believe (or have faith) in the philosophy of naturalism, as well as in the reality of the external world, the uniformity of the natural world, the rationality and intelligibility of the physical universe, and the rules of causation. Naturalism philosophy connects the scientific method to philosophy by asserting that all things and occurrences in the cosmos are natural, and so all knowledge of the universe falls under the jurisdiction of scientific research. Naturalism also assumes, in principle, that nature is entirely knowable. Nature has a regularity, a pattern, unity, and wholeness that suggests objective laws, without which the pursuit of science and scientific knowledge would be ridiculous.

Scientists conduct scientific research and draw conclusions using their minds and the power of reason. While we can improve our rational faculties and reasoning power by using them, we are aware that we did not create or originate them. How is it possible that the thoughts and perceptions within the mind can offer even a resemblance of an accurate representation of reality? Is it necessary to analyze our cognitive abilities? Where do they come from? Why should we trust these minds if they came about through Darwinian evolution and natural selection of mindless, purposeless, and unguided processes? Would trust be placed in a computer, for instance, if there were suspicions that it originated from an unguided and mindless process? "Modern humanism is the faith that through science, humankind can know the truth—and thus be free," writes John Gary, a well-known atheist, "but if Darwin's theory of natural selection is true, this is impossible" (Gary, 2002). Gary continues, "The human mind serves evolutionary success, not truth" (Gary, 2002). As a result, science cannot be used to refute God's existence.

To summarize, atheists, agnostics, and scientists who believe in naturalism require a higher level of belief or faith that radically exceeds religious faith. In contrast to religious faith, which is founded on intellectual axioms, rational arguments, and intuitive self-evident undeniable realities that we see with our eyes, atheistic and scientific faith is built on unrealistic premises and inaccurate imaginations. For instance, atheists, agnostics, and scientists who adhere to naturalism must contend with a minimum of these five enigmatic aspects:

1)   The universe emerged from nothingness to become a fantastic, marvelous universe that matches the most accurate measures and subtle limits;

2)   Coincidence produced the subtle limits and physical constants in which the universe was formed, which contradicts the fact that there are two conditions for coincidence: place and time. By claiming that the universe emerged from nowhere and no time, the concept of coincidence itself is negated;

3)   Randomness, along with the immediate environment of the Earth, produced life, bacteria, species, and man, even though the human mind, with its now full development and might, can still not produce the simplest forms of life;

4)   All the moral and ethical values we deem valid mostly run counter to materialism since genuine morals and ethics represent a material burden and loss of worldly interest. These are the facts and the outcome of the material. It would be best to believe in all such intellectual impossibilities to start as an atheist;

5)   Hypothetically, in atheism no intellectual, philosophical, or material authority stops the annihilation of all humans on Earth because the material universe does not recognize right and wrong or moral and immoral; therefore, it makes no difference whether all humans on Earth are kept alive or exterminated, according to atheism, which is also predicated on faith but lacks any residue of knowledge, textual or intellectual proof, or ethics.

CHAPTER 16

Can Science Disprove God's Existence

"Indeed, in the creation of the heavens and the Earth and the alternation of the night and the day are signs for those of understanding." ~ (Qur'an 3:190)

The interplay between scientific investigation and the concept of a Divine entity remains an intricate and compelling subject for exploration. As an intellectual endeavor, science is primarily geared towards explaining empirical phenomena based on a framework of methodological naturalism, which prioritizes naturalistic interpretations for observable occurrences. However, it is critical to recognize that the limitations inherent within the scientific methodology not only leave space for the concept of a "Necessary Being," but it may offer supplementary layers of understanding bolstering such a metaphysical notion.

In its mission to dissect the universe's mechanics, science is proficient at explaining causal chains—how one event results from a preceding one within the parameters of the physical realm. Yet, it encounters epistemological and methodological limitations when answering more existential questions, such as "What is the ultimate cause of the universe?" At this point, the realms of philosophy and theology, through arguments like those concerning contingency, become essential in addressing inquiries that avoid scientific resolution alone. For instance, cosmological models like the Big Bang Theory may provide a scientific framework for the evolution of the universe. Yet, they still grapple with the ontological question: What caused the Big Bang to occur? What was before the Bing Bang? Why does existence occur?

Scientific explanations characteristically reference antecedent phenomena, revealing an inherent contingency within the natural world. This pattern, however, presents the problem of an infinite regress. If each contingent occurrence is attributable to another contingent event, one could ostensibly continue this retrogressive sequence ad infinitum, which engenders logical and metaphysical complications. Such dilemmas can only be resolved by philosophical and theological arguments for a "Necessary Being" or "Prime Mover," which is intrinsically not contingent and is the linchpin for the entire causal chain. Thus, scientific endeavors inadvertently accentuate the philosophical need for a non-contingent entity by highlighting the essential contingency within natural phenomena. This harmonious coexistence of science and the notion of a Necessary Being is a legacy advanced by Medieval Muslim thinkers to their European counterparts, "Of course, God rules over the universe, but we should still enquire into the natural world without harming religion."

Science expounds on the "How?" unraveling the laws governing the universe. In contrast, the concept of God as a "Necessary Being" provides the "Why?" furnishing an ontological basis for the universe and its inherent laws. The two paradigms supplement each other, paving the way for a more holistic comprehension of reality. Exploring the natural world's intrinsic complexity and order could signify the manifestation of purpose or design, traditionally ascribed to a Divine Entity or a Necessary Being in theistic doctrines.

In summary, the emphasis of science on elucidating contingent events through other contingent events and contingent circumstances should not be interpreted as a denial of the concept of a Necessary Being. Instead, this focus may bolster the philosophical and theological proposition for the existence of such a Being. By expounding the inherently contingent nature of the universe, science stresses the metaphysical necessity for an "Uncaused Cause" to preclude the logical fallacy of an unending chain of causation. Therefore, the scientific exploration of contingency and the metaphysical notion of a non-contingent, Necessary Being or God should not be perceived as either in competition or mutually exclusive. On the contrary, they enrich and supplement one another in the quest for understanding the nature of existence.

CHAPTER 17

Can Darwinian Theory of Evolution Disprove God's Existence

"And certainly did We create man from an extract of clay. Then We placed him as a sperm-drop in a firm lodging. Then We made the sperm-drop into a clinging clot, and We made the clot into a lump [of flesh], and We made [from] the lump, bones, and We covered the bones with flesh; then We developed him into another creation. So blessed is Allah, the best of creators." ~ (Qur'an 23:12-14)

The argument that the Darwinian Theory of Evolution is incompatible with Islamic theology has been rigorously examined within Islamic scholarly discourse. Nonetheless, the theory does not negate the existence of God; in fact, it may necessitate it. The claim is based on an essential principle in Islamic theology: the argument for existence of God from contingency.

In essence, the argument from contingency in Islamic thought suggests that the universe and all its constituents are dependent or "contingent" entities. They rely on something else for their existence and cannot persist indefinitely. Thus, according to Islamic teachings, a Necessary Being (God) is imperative to provide the foundation for these contingent beings. The Darwinian theory of evolution, with its principles of natural selection, mutation, adaptation, and genetic inheritance also relies on fundamental laws of nature. Therefore, the theory itself is contingent upon the basic properties and conditions of the universe. If one observes evolution through the Islamic lens of contingency, it is not a self-sufficient process that can completely explain the variety and forms of life on Earth, but itself is contingent upon the basic properties and conditions of the universe, a set of laws that hinge on the existence of a Necessary Being—God!

Moreover, from the Islamic perspective, God's role is not confined to the initiation of the universe; He is also its Sustainer. Consequently, whether life originated and evolved through natural processes or not, the conditions that permitted such processes to commence and those that continue to sustain them can all be construed as contingent phenomena that would require a Necessary Being or God.

To summarize, according to Islamic theology and employing the contingency argument, the Darwinian theory of evolution does not invalidate the concept of God. Instead, it provides a narrative that potentially explains the contingent processes through which God orchestrates and maintains the existence of life. This interpretive framework allows for the harmonious co-existence of belief in God as the Necessary Being and the acceptance of any scientific evidence, including that which supports the theory of evolution.

CHAPTER 18

Common Atheists' and Agnostics' Questions About God

"How can you disbelieve in Allah when you were lifeless and He brought you to life; then He will cause you to die, then He will bring you [back] to life, and then to Him you will be returned?" ~ (Qur'an 2:28)

Why did God create us?

Everyone would acknowledge that all parts of the body including limbs, skin, brain, eyes, ears, legs, hands, heart, and all other innards, serve a distinct purpose. If every individual part serves a distinct purpose, would it make any sense that an individual who is composed of these parts serve no purpose? God, The All Wise, did not create us to wander without any purpose or to simply fulfill basic instincts and desires. Instead, God created humanity to worship Him—that is, to be subservient to Him. He describes this life as full of trials and tribulations as an examination. The real blissful, everlasting life is in the Hereafter. This life stands as a testament for everyone, discerning those who recognize God and adhere to His directives. Allah says in the Qur'an, *"Indeed, We created man from a sperm-drop mixture that We may try him; and We made him hearing and seeing. Indeed, We guided him to the way, be he grateful or be he ungrateful"* [Qur'an 76:2-3]. In another verse, *"And We will surely test you with something of fear and hunger and a loss of wealth and lives and fruits but give good tidings to the patient"* [Qur'an 2:155].

For a significant number of people, the underlying issue of rejecting God is not about believing in Him, but rather about the implications of believing in Him. Acknowledging God implies being answerable for one's deeds, potentially disrupting the lifestyle one desires. Therefore, the true challenge of this life lies in surrendering to God—in order to fulfill the purpose of our creation, rather than being governed by one's whims, arrogance, and self-importance.

Why does God need to test us?

Atheists and agnostics often challenge the theistic assertion that God possesses perfect knowledge of both the seen and the unseen within the universe by questioning the necessity of divine trials and tribulations for humanity. If God is omniscient, what remains obscured from His view that necessitates the tests of human beings? Human's tests and God's tests are not similar. Human tests are meant for exhibiting knowledge, whilst divine trials and tribulations are means of developing man's hidden abilities (physical, spiritual, moral, and intellectual) from potentiality into actuality—just as iron, for acquiring greater strength, is put into a furnace of fire to make it tempered, similarly human being is also nurtured within the furnace of adversities in order that he or she becomes steadfast. Moreover, God's relationship with humanity is not one of dependency or need. He is inherently transcendent, unaffected by human allegiance or defiance. Human piety does not benefit or augment Him in any way, nor does human impiety detract anything from Him. If all human beings choose to obey Allah, they will not add anything to His Kingdom; and if all human beings choose to disobey Allah, they will not reduce anything from His kingdom.

In His infinite wisdom and benevolence, God has blessed humanity with faculties for introspection, moral and ethical judgment, and spiritual longing. The trials and tribulations, adversities, and decisions fundamental in human life fulfill diverse Divine intents. One significant purpose of these trials and tribulations is to forge avenues for individuals to evolve morally and spiritually. Encountering challenges and navigating ethical dilemmas offer irreplaceable moments for personal growth and spiritual ascension. Importantly, these tests don't enhance God's knowledge—He is, after all, The All-Knowing—but rather guide humans toward a deeper self-realization and a more profound relationship with the Divine. Moreover, God's assurance of unparalleled rewards in the Afterlife—enveloping perpetual serenity and spiritual enrichment—is a testament to His generosity and equity. It is not that universal obedience would enlarge His dominion or universal disobedience would diminish it; instead, these challenges distinguish individuals by their moral and spiritual resolve.

In summary, the Divine trials and tribulations that permeate human life are not to God's advantage or improvement. They are beacons, providing humanity with a framework for moral and spiritual evolution, leading to a deeper, more enriched connection with the Divine.

Why would God create human beings with free will?

In the Qur'an, Allah states that the temporal worldly life serves as an arena of trials and tribulations for humanity. We cannot be tested without free will, and this is implied in verses: *"Indeed, We created man from a sperm-drop mixture that We may try him; and We made him hearing and seeing. Indeed, We guided him to the way, be he grateful or be he ungrateful"* [Qur'an 76:2-3]. The narrative of Adam's creation in the Qur'an portrays God talking to the angels, revealing His plan to create a human being as His vicegerent on Earth and endow him with intellect and the ability to make free choices, distinguishing him from other beings. Allah charted the righteous path for mankind (through His revelations and messengers); adherence to which leads to paradise, while negligence can lead to hellfire: *"When your Lord told angels, I am putting a vicegerent on Earth, they said, How can you put someone there who will cause corruption and bloodshed, when we celebrate Your praise and proclaim Your Holiness?"* [Qur'an 2:30]. The angels, in perpetual worship and unwavering obedience to God, struggled to comprehend the inauguration of a human being capable of both allegiance and defiance towards the Divine. They reasoned that such a being, possessing the ability to choose, could instigate disorder and violence. Concerning the profound matter of why God endowed humans with free will, allowing them the potential to err and commit transgressions, the Divine response, while not explicitly detailing the intricacies of His wisdom, is apparent in emphasizing His knowledge: *"I know things you do not know"* [Qur'an 2:30]. In a demonstration of the distinct position of humanity, God imparted to Adam the knowledge of the names of all entities. When He subsequently posed a challenge to the angels to identify these entities, they could not do so. Acknowledging their limitations, they responded, *"We know only of what You have taught us. You are The All-Knowing and The All-Wise"* [Qur'an 2:32].

God's rationale behind human creation is profound. He has equipped humans with cognition, a moral compass, free will, and the intellect to discern virtue from vice. However, this also means God must have accounted for the possibility that some individuals may misuse their endowed faculties, engaging in transgressions instead. The fact is that some misdeeds happen in the universe, not because God wants it or desires it, but because that is desirable as part of His grand scheme, which entails freedom of choice for human beings. One can argue that the very presence of such misdeeds in the universe attests to the unbridled freedom of choice humans exercise in their earthly lives.

At the heart of Western thought lies the conviction that individuals possess an innate capacity for self-determination. This is the foundational premise upon which the pillars of personal liberty and democracy are erected. Individuality presupposes that each person harbors a unique set of desires, preferences, and intentions that guide their actions. The celebration of individuality is predicated on the belief that one has the freedom to shape one's identity and destiny, which is inextricable from the concept of free will. Without the fundamental assumption that individuals can freely make choices, individuality would be devoid of substance and meaning. Personal liberty further exemplifies the assumption of free will. The liberties of thought, expression, association, and movement are regarded not merely as societal privileges but as intrinsic human rights. These freedoms are based on the idea that people are free to think, speak, gather, and move around their surroundings without being forced to. The fact that these freedoms are protected and promoted shows that most people agree that people have the choice to use these freedoms, which is a direct confirmation of the existence and importance of free will.

What is the point of human beings having freedom of choice?

The distinction lies between innate obedience and conscious obedience. Angels, lacking free will, remain perpetually engrossed in the worship of God, unwavering and consistent in their devotion. The Qur'an praises the angels as noble and righteous, emphasizing their steadfast obedience to Allah's commands. In contrast, human beings possess the gift of choice, which naturally results in a spectrum of faith and deeds.

Depending on their actions and faith, humans can rise in stature, surpass even angels, or, conversely, fall below the moral standard of animals. But what distinguishes innate obedience from voluntary obedience? Innate obedience can be likened to a robot, which operates precisely as it's programmed, without deviation. However, voluntary obedience is exemplified when a child adheres to the wishes of parents, even when unobserved. Consider a scenario where a child resists the temptation of cookies, despite his or her parents' absence, solely because they were instructed against it. Such a child becomes exemplary, having the capacity for defiance yet opting for obedience. This intentional act of devotion is particularly cherished, epitomizing the very essence of what God desires from humanity.

The theological framework in Islam offers a unique perspective on the issue of human free will and the existence of evil. In Islamic thought, human freedom is closely related to moral and spiritual testing and is undergirded by a profound belief in Divine justice, wisdom, and mercy. The Almighty Allah grants human beings the freedom of choice not as a concession but as a Divine plan rooted in His wisdom. This freedom serves multiple purposes, including establishing a moral framework where obedience to Allah is not forced but chosen, thus giving it greater spiritual value. Allah does not merely expect blind obedience; instead, He provides guidelines through the Qur'an and the Sunnah (the teachings) of the Prophet Muhammad (PBUH) for human beings to follow their own volition. This capacity for voluntary submission to the Divine will allows for the possibility of developing authentic faith (*iman*) and God-consciousness (*taqwa*).

In this Divine schema, the unfortunate reality of evil and suffering exists not because Allah wills malevolence but because these are analogies of a world where free will exists. They serve as tests, allowing for distinctions to be made between those who uphold virtue and those who falter. So, the fact that evil exists does not go against Allah's omnipotence and mercy; instead, it is something that Allah allows to reach higher spiritual and moral goals. The Islamic worldview rejects the frequently advanced argument by atheists and agnostics that the existence of evil rules out the possibility of a loving and all-powerful Creator. Such a viewpoint fails to consider the nuanced balance between human free will, Divine predetermination, and the overarching purpose of life as a test, as explicitly mentioned in the Qur'an. In Islamic theology, earthly life is a transient stage, a moral and spiritual testing ground, leading to an eternal life where ultimate justice is realized.

In summary, according to Islamic theology, Allah's allowance for human free will and the subsequent existence of evil are not indicative of Divine fallibility or malevolence. Instead, they are integral aspects of a grand cosmic plan aimed at the spiritual maturation of human souls, underpinned by Allah's boundless wisdom and mercy. The existence of suffering and evil is, therefore, not a valid argument against the existence of God but is a dimension of the complex moral and spiritual tapestry that human life is meant to be.

Why doesn't God reveal Himself?

As physical entities, human beings may mistakenly ascribe physicality to the Creator, which is incongruent with the Divine nature that transcends time and space. In the infinite wisdom of Allah, He has willed to remain beyond the realm of human perception, yet He manifests His Divine names and attributes through the signs He has placed in creation. In this transient life, every individual is endowed with the solemn responsibility to utilize the capabilities bestowed upon them by the Divine to recognize His existence. It is the privilege of those who exhibit sincerity, humility, and profound contemplation to discern and profess faith in Him. Upon reflection, the question, "Why doesn't the Divine manifest Himself directly?" unveils a more profound wisdom. The demand for such a revelation is misguided, for the omnipresence of God is manifestly evident through the intricacies and wonders of His creations.

Stephen Hawking wrote "A Brief History of Time" and is a proponent of the idea of "Black Holes" (Hawking, 1998). When he studied the universe's density, he noticed that the universe is far denser than what was visible. He could not reconcile mathematically that massive discrepancy in the numbers concerning the density of the galaxy compared to what was visibly measurable. He knew there was dark matter that could not be visible, and that light could not penetrate it, which he called the "Black Hole." Suppose Hawking has reached this conclusion without seeing this dark matter, yet it is acceptable in science. In that case, it means we derive scientific understanding without having to see something tangibly, but we know the effect of that thing hidden through that which is seen. In science, we derive so many things without seeing them tangibly. For example, Michio Kaku, a Japanese physicist (and many others) who studied "String Theories" and "Super String Theories," talks about two-digit dimensions that no science in the world today can experiment with. Still, it can be derived indirectly, and we can try to see its effects (Kaku, 1995). We can't see electrons around a proton, but we know they are there. Why are we rejecting belief in a Deity that we cannot see or measure if we can derive Him by observing His creations and His effects on us?

An excellent example in the world of science and mathematics is that of a function referred to as "infinity." Not only is the whole world of science and mathematics driven by "infinity," but without "infinity," nothing makes sense. However, infinity can't be touched or measured. So, what is infinity? Infinity is the idea of something that has no end. Nothing in this world is infinite. One can discuss and apply concepts to it, but one can never truly feel it—something constantly approaching infinity but never reaching the infinite. The moment it becomes indefinite, it becomes indescribable. The question of why God has not visibly revealed Himself to human beings is a complex and multi-faceted inquiry that intertwines theology and philosophy. The explanation we offered so far is an intricate tapestry of scientific and metaphysical perspectives, illuminating parallels between scientific theories like black holes, abstract mathematical concepts like infinity, and theological ideas regarding God's invisibility.

To summarize the core ideas from the given explanation:

1)   **Existence through Evidence:** Even in science, many concepts, such as black holes or dark matter, are accepted despite not being directly observable. These concepts are inferred from the observable effects they have on their surroundings.

2)   Test of Faith: In religious thought, the lack of a visible deity is often considered a test of faith, sincerity, and reflection. The belief is that God reveals Himself through the signs and patterns in the natural world and human life.

3)   The Abstract: Mathematical ideas like infinity are widely accepted despite being abstract and not directly observable. This further validates the idea that "unseen" doesn't mean "nonexistent."

However, we can offer some other more simplified non-scientific explanations:

The Wind: We cannot see the wind but feel its effects, like leaves rustling on a tree or a flag flapping. Similarly, while one might not be able to see God directly, the belief is that His existence can be inferred through the natural world and personal experiences.

Parent Behind a Curtain: Imagine a parent playing peek-a-boo with a child behind a curtain. The parent is hidden but gives clues to their presence, such as making sounds or moving the curtain. This can be likened to God giving signs or clues to His existence without fully revealing Himself.

Invisible Ink: Consider a message written in invisible ink. While you can't see the message directly, applying heat or a special light reveals it. According to the faithful, God's presence is similar; it might not be immediately visible but can be 'seen' by those who know how to look.

Recipe of a Cake: If you are presented with a cake, you don't see the ingredients—flour, sugar, eggs—but you know they must exist for the cake to be there. Similarly, the "cake" of our universe suggests to believers that there must be a "recipe" or divine power, will, and knowledge, even if that power, will, and knowledge is not directly observable.

Magnet: Magnets attract metal objects without being seen to do so. The force is invisible but real. This can be an analogy for divine influence—unseen yet potent.

Bank Account: You can't see the money in your account, but a positive balance allows you to make transactions. It's evidence that the money exists. Similarly, the "positive balance" of beauty, order, and morality in the world can be seen as evidence of a higher power for those who believe.

By simplifying the concepts, we can make them more accessible while preserving the essence of your argument: that the visible effects or signs in the world can point to an invisible, yet potentially existing, God.

Why does God choose destiny for us? And if He doesn't, then how can He be All-Knowing?

Islam teaches that God is All-Knowing, and there is no doubt about that. God's knowledge is complete, while human knowledge needs to be completed and is subjected to time. Time is an element that controls the quantity and quality of human knowledge. God is not bound by time; He created time, so His knowledge is not bound by time.

An atheist asks: "How does God know the future?" This is a question outside the parameters of God since God is outside time and is not bound by it. All of creation is subjected and bounded by time, but God isn't. How does He know the future? God's view and response is instant, and His knowledge is instantaneous—everything to Him is perpetual now! Even the word "instantaneous" is time-bound because of "where," "how," and "when." These are "time" sentences and cannot be escaped by any creation. Hence, God's knowledge is beyond instantaneous!

God's knowledge is infinite and absolute; therefore, that is a condition. The question is, "Does God know where we will end up in the hereafter, even before we exist?" The answer is "Yes, at all times," since God is All-Knowing.

We may also ask, "Since God knows where I'm going to be in the hereafter, why did He create me on this Earth?" Knowing something does not imply interjecting in it. Knowing that it will rain tonight because the weather report predicts it will does not mean the meteorologist brought the rain. Knowledge does not imply interjection of it.

Muslims believe in the absolute good God. Islam doesn't teach the divine duality of a "good God" and a "bad God." Does evil exist? Yes, it does. Do people do wrong things? Of course, they do. An atheist would say, "Then, who's doing it? If God is doing everything, how can He do anything evil?" Islam teaches whatever evil is performed is not because of God; God would never intend to do evil. When a person chooses to do any action, good or bad, God creates the action based on the person's choice. God allows the power to carry out those actions based on free will. Thus, God's knowledge does not imply He interjected in it but knows our intentions. He knows the essence of our choices. He creates the power to carry out the actions but does not negate the individual's liability for their actions.

If God exists, why is there evil and suffering in the world?

Many atheistic arguments against the existence of God have been formulated in response to Christianity. The modern world, shaped by the European Renaissance, partly stems from Christian dogma and the influence of the Catholic Church. Numerous proponents of atheism are former Christians critiquing their religious teachings and responding with atheistic arguments.

Christianity emphasizes the love of God, a positive aspect. However, atheists argue that if God is All-Loving, He would not want anyone to suffer. Both Muslims and Christians share the belief in an All-Powerful God. Atheists, therefore, reason that if God is All-Loving and All-Powerful, He has the capability to eliminate suffering, and His love would drive Him to do so. The persistence of suffering, according to atheists, disproves God's existence.

However, a logical flaw emerges in the atheists' argument. They lack definitive proof that God does not exist because there might be reasons for God to permit suffering. God is not only All-Loving and All-Powerful, but He is also All-Wise. God may have valid reasons for allowing some suffering to persist, and it is for these reasons that suffering might be permitted. The atheist's argument, seemingly deductive, is not rational due to the possibility of unconsidered reasons for God's allowance of suffering.

Are there good reasons for God to allow suffering in the world?

Muslims acknowledge some reasons for God permitting suffering. For instance, the idea that God is testing humanity in this world implies a range of suffering experiences. The wisdom of God determines the width of this variety. The spectrum will exist between good and evil, prosperity and economic hardship, health and illness, joy and suffering.

Minor inconveniences may prompt complaints, but what appears deficient in one situation may be beneficial in another. The Qur'an acknowledges this balance, *"Fighting has been enjoined upon you while it is hateful to you. But perhaps you hate a thing, and it is good for you, and perhaps you love a thing, and it is bad for you. And Allah Knows, while you know not"* [Qur'an 2:216]. God balances and sustains the world as He wills.

Trials and tribulations serve as God's tests for mankind, providing opportunities to elevate faith. Muslims believe in the hereafter, where inconveniences in this life may be compensated. The Prophet Muhammad (PBUH) states, "Amazing is the situation of the believer. If a thorn pokes the believer and he praises God, it gets stored up as a reward in a life hereafter" [Sahih Muslim].

The believer's outcome is ultimately good, as God considers the entire big picture. Most of humanity, preoccupied with the evils and sufferings of this world, often fails to see beyond it. Those who have served God or been wronged are generously rewarded in paradise. The overarching result is that, ultimately, good prevails.

Why believe in God when Darwin's natural selection theory can explain all life mysteries?

The reconciliation of Darwinian evolution with Islamic thought, specifically the belief in God, is a multifaceted subject that Islamic theologians, philosophers, and scientists have approached in various ways. The question posed—the apparent tension between belief in God and the explanatory power of Darwin's theory of natural selection—is not trivial and is best addressed through careful analysis.

Firstly, it is crucial to note that Darwinian evolution is a scientific theory or model that attempts to explain biological diversity and the process of speciation through natural mechanisms, primarily natural selection acting upon random genetic mutations. Notably, the theory is framed within the paradigm of methodological naturalism, which means it seeks natural explanations for observed phenomena without making any claims about supernatural entities or occurrences. However, the model itself doesn't represent an "absolute truth" because any scientific model is deductive or based on probability. The scientific model also involves many assumptions and technical disputes regarding its correctness. There is always a possibility of future modification of the model or abandoning it altogether when new findings or new data are discovered.

From an Islamic perspective, the belief in God (*Tawheed*) is foundational and encompasses far more than just the explanation of biological life. The Islamic worldview argues for the necessity of a Creator not only for the existence of life but also for the universe itself, its finely-tuned properties, and the moral and spiritual dimensions of human experience. The Sustainer and Governor of all things (*Rabb al-'Alamin*) are attributes of God that Darwinian evolution does not address, according to Qur'anic narratives.

It should also be emphasized that the Qur'an provides a teleological view of creation, wherein every entity has a purpose. This notion extends to human beings' moral and spiritual development, which is beyond the scope of what Darwinian theory seeks to explain. In Islamic thought, the ultimate objective of human life is to worship God and to achieve a state of moral and spiritual excellence, goals that are transcendent and not explicable by natural selection, which is amoral and lacks foresight.

Moreover, some Islamic scholars argue that Darwinian theory could be compatible with Islamic teachings. This line of reasoning posits that the mechanisms of natural selection and genetic mutation could be how God brings about the diversity of biological life. In this interpretation, natural laws and processes are not independent of God but are the very expressions of God's will and creative power. Scholars who hold this viewpoint often point to Qur'anic verses that encourage the study of the natural world to understand signs (*Ayat*) of God's existence and attributes.

However, it is worth noting that not all Islamic scholars or lay Muslims agree with the compatibility of Darwinian evolution and Islamic teachings, particularly when it comes to the creation of human beings. Traditionalist scholars may emphasize a more literal interpretation of the Qur'anic account of creation and may be skeptical that humans share a common ancestry with other life forms.

In summary, from an Islamic standpoint, the explanatory power of Darwin's theory of natural selection is not seen as mutually exclusive with belief in God. Instead, the approach can be understood as explaining one facet of the natural world, which manifests God's creativity and governance. The Islamic worldview encompasses the origins and diversity of life and moral, spiritual, and cosmological dimensions, which go beyond the scope of natural selection and evolutionary biology.

Why could it not be that all of life was generated from an extremely simple and primitive single-celled organism?

In the Islamic intellectual tradition, several philosophers and theologians have deeply engaged with questions regarding the existence of God and divine intervention, blending scriptural exegesis with philosophical reasoning. Two prominent figures in this respect are al-Farabi and Ibn Sina. According to al-Farabi's "Political Regime," the world emanates from a single, necessary First Cause, identified by Muslims as Allah (God). He argued that everything originates from this First Cause in a hierarchical order, reaching down to the physical world. This emanation is seen as a divine act that accounts for the world's existence and maintenance, thereby attributing life's complexity and diversity to divine orchestration (McGinnis & Reisman, 2007). In his "The Book of Healing," Ibn Sina's argument from contingency remains one of the most famous arguments for the existence of God within Islamic and Western philosophy. He argued that everything in the universe is contingent, meaning it could exist or not exist. For the universe to exist, there must be a necessary being upon which all contingent beings depend. This necessary being must be uncaused and possess the reason for its existence. In Islamic thought, this necessary being is identified as Allah (Peterson, 2009). Both al-Farabi's and Ibn Sina's arguments can be considered philosophical grounds for divine intervention in the creation and sustainment of the world, including the complexity of life forms. While they may not directly address modern debates about the origin of life as a single-celled organism, their arguments have been used by contemporary Islamic scholars to highlight the notion of divine orchestration as an alternative or complementary explanation to naturalistic accounts of life's origins.

Many other theists (Muslims and Christians) have formulated critiques or alternatives to prevailing scientific theories. Theistic arguments collectively propose that divine creation and sustenance best account for the complexity, purpose, and very existence of life. For example, critics often point to the gaps and unproven aspects in the theory of "abiogenesis," which attempts to describe how life could have originated from non-living matter (Wells, 2000). Research reports from institutions like the J. Craig Venter Institute suggest a minimum threshold of genes necessary for life (minimum gene set concept), challenging the idea of life originating from simplicity (Glass et al., 2005). Another interesting critique from Michael Behe's famous book, "Darwin's Black Box," with his notion of "irreducible complexity," posits that specific biological systems are too complex to have evolved naturally from simpler precursors (Behe, 1996).

Finally, although more commonly discussed within Christian circles, the concept of "theistic evolution" has also been explored in the Islamic context. In Islamic thought, the notion that God could use natural processes like evolution as a means of creation is not entirely at odds with Islamic teachings, although it remains a point of debate since there is nothing explicit in the Qur'an or Prophetic teachings that references the idea that different kinds of living organisms have developed from earlier forms. Examples of contemporary Muslim scholars who exhibit reconciliatory views are Nidhal Guessoum (b. 1960 CE) and Israr Ahmed (d. 2010 CE). Nidhal Guessoum, an astrophysicist and Islamic scholar, is one of the contemporary figures who have explored this idea. Guessoum argues that belief in evolution can be compatible with the Islamic faith.

He contends that while the Qur'an describes the creation of life forms, including human beings, it does not go into scientific detail, leaving room for interpretation and reconciliation with scientific theories like evolution. His book "Islam's Quantum Question: Reconciling Muslim Tradition and Modern Science" extensively discusses this matter (Guessoum, 2011). Some scholars, such as Israr Ahmed, have posited that Islam accepts "micro-evolution" (within species) but is skeptical of "macro-evolution" (from one species to another), particularly concerning human beings, because it may conflict with the Qur'anic narrative of the unique creation of Adam (Ahmed, 2013). Theistic evolution as a reconciliatory view between faith and science exists within Islamic discourse, although it is not universally accepted. The debate often revolves around how to interpret Qur'anic verses considering modern scientific understanding. They often acknowledge that evolution as a biological process does not necessarily negate divine intervention or oversight. It is worth mentioning that more conservative scholars and clerics may disagree with the concept of theistic evolution, insisting on a literal interpretation of the Qur'anic verses regarding creation. They would argue that God created each species, including humans, in their present form as described in the Qur'an.

Since the laws that govern the universe are well known, does that negate the need for a Creator?

From a theistic perspective, the laws governing the universe do not necessarily negate the need for a Creator; instead, they can be seen as evidence of a divine organizing principle. For example, one of the longstanding arguments for the existence of God in theistic traditions is the argument from design, also known as the teleological argument. This argument posits that the complexity, order, and beauty observed in the universe suggest purpose or design, which in turn implies a Designer. From this standpoint, the universe's laws can be seen as evidence of this design. Likewise, a fundamental question arises as to why these laws exist in the first place and why they take the form that they do. The theistic viewpoint often posits that the laws of the universe are not self-originating but instead require a Lawgiver, who instilled these laws for the governance of creation. In classical theism, God is often described as necessary, whereas the universe and its laws are contingent. This means that while God's existence is independent and self-sufficient, the universe relies on something else. In this view, even if the laws of the universe are well understood, they are still contingent upon a Creator for their initial inception and continued existence.

Science is an empirical endeavor that seeks to describe how things work, not why they exist. While science can explain the laws of the universe, it does not necessarily provide answers to metaphysical or existential questions about the ultimate origin or purpose of these laws. Islamic theistic perspectives often see science and religion as complementary, with science explaining the "How?" and religion addressing the "Why?" In many religious traditions, the concept of a Creator is tied to creating and maintaining physical, moral, and spiritual laws. In this view, understanding the physical laws of the universe needs to address questions about meaning, purpose, morality, or the nature of consciousness, which many theists believe are also grounded in a divine Creator. In summary, from an Islamic standpoint, the existence of laws that govern the universe is not seen as negating the need for a Creator but rather as affirming the presence of a divine order. Despite being well explained by science, these laws still raise fundamental questions about their creation, existence, and the contingent nature of the universe, which theistic viewpoints contend are best answered by invoking a Creator.

An atheist may assume that laws are sufficient to create the universe and cause it to appear. Some atheists have relied on the law of gravity as sufficient for the emergence of the universe. Regardless of the collapse of this claim by just thinking about the source of the law of gravity, or who codified it, or who gave it the property of interference and showing the effect, regardless of these self-evident intuitions, the law of gravity does not cause the billiard ball to roll. Law alone is unable to cause anything without the appearance of that thing. The law of gravity cannot produce a billiard ball; it just causes it to move. In fact, the law of gravity is not independent, but it is a description of a natural occurrence. Moreover, the law of gravity will not move the billiard ball without a force pressing on the billiard stick and moving it. Only at this moment will the billiard ball move and the effect of the law of gravity appear.

Nonetheless, an atheist assumes that the law of gravity is sufficient to create a billiard ball, billiard stick, and roll the ball. Which one is closer to good reason and logic regarding the cause of the appearance of the universe: the Creator or the law?

Similarly, the internal combustion laws of a car engine cannot create a car engine. If the laws of internal combustion are added to the car engine, it will not work, either. There must be petrol, which gives energy, and there must be a spark for combustion, and before that, there must be an engine, and only then will the laws of internal combustion appear and the engine work. It is not reasonable to assume that the laws of internal combustion are sufficient to create the engine, the spark of combustion, petrol, the driver, and the road. In fact, the idea that a law is sufficient to explain the emergence of the universe is an idea that is completely alien to reason. Additionally, if one assumes the idea, it will lead to the sequence of actors explained in the answer to the previous question. If a claim is made to another law, it will lead to the sequence of actors that entails the non-emergence of any law or any beings.

Why can't a coincidence be the source of the universe?

Adopting the idea of coincidence is ignorant of the fundamentals of possibilities, given that coincidence has two indispensable conditions: time and place. Coincidence stipulates a time when it makes its effect and stipulates the existence of a material place where it produces its influence. Then, how can one say that coincidence played a role in creating the universe, even though the universe came out of no time and no place? How can the effect of coincidence appear without the appearance of the coincidence itself? How can coincidence provide an effect before its own existence or the existence of time and place, which are the two essential conditions for coincidence? No, coincidence can't be the source of the universe.

Why can't the universe be eternal, with no beginning?

According to the second law of thermodynamics, it is impossible that the universe is eternal. Here is an example to simplify this law: If a cup of hot water is in the room, heat is transferred from the hot water to the room until the room's temperature equals the temperature of the cup. This is the second law of thermodynamics, where energy flows from high levels to low levels over time. This law takes place in everything in the universe at every moment since the emergence of the universe until the temperature of everything in the universe becomes equal, and when this happens, what is known as the thermal death of the universe will occur. If the universe was eternal, it would have been suspended by now—thermally dead. However, the universe is now in a state that is less than maximum entropy and has not yet reached thermal death. Thus, it is not eternal; rather, it has a fixed beginning during which time and space had appeared. It has been proven that the universe began at a minimum of entropy, which means that its occurrence was without a precedent example; it was created out of nothing. This is a scientific law on one side, whereas atheism is completely on the other side.

There has also been a discovery that the universe is expanding, and the Big Bang Theory, which refutes the idea that the universe is eternal.

If everything is created from something, what was God created from?

The question implies that God did not exist before, but God is eternal, meaning He has always existed. The question of "What was God created from?" is illogical and absurd because He is the Creator of everything. It is impossible to describe or explain what He is made of or from since God is the Creator of everything. No being can ever describe the nature of God's existence or attempt to do so. The Qur'an answers this same question, *"Say, 'He is God the One, God the eternal. He begot no one, nor was He begotten. No one is comparable to Him"* [Qur'an 112:4].

Muslims do not conceptualize God as an image, physical or mental, but they know God through His many beautiful names and attributes mentioned in the Qur'an and Prophetic teachings. The Qur'an says, *"Call on God, or on the Lord of Mercy– whatever names you call Him, the best names belong to Him"* [Qur'an 17:110]. He is Allah—the First, the Last, the Compassionate, the Merciful, the Sovereign, the Holy, the Giver of Peace, the Protector, the Creator, the Sustainer, the Maker, the Shaper, the Forgiving, the All-Provider, the All-Knowing, the All-Seeing, the All-Hearing, the Judge, the All-Aware, the Watchful, the Truth, the Loving, the Generous, the Powerful, the Hidden, the All-Exalted, the All-Strong, the Witness, the Trustee, the Resurrector, the Sublime, the Wise, and many more.

What is God made of? Nothing makes Him, but He makes everything. The Creator does not require anything; instead, He is independent of everything. We often have a problem because we try to place God in our realm physically. Remember, God has no frames, no references, no bodies. If someone asks, "How do I conceptualize Him?" The answer is to conceptualize and understand Him through His creation. Everything in existence is His sign pointing to Him.

The laws of the created beings do not apply to the Creator; this is a self-evident fact. Otherwise, one could also say, "Who cooked the cook? Who painted the painter?" It is self-evident that the Creator is the one who brought time and place into existence. So, it is inconceivable to say that the laws He created out of nothing should apply to Him. It is true that every created being should have a creator; however, in the case of the Creator, Allah says in the Qur'an, *"There is nothing like unto Him"* [Qur'an 42:11].

How can we, with our small size, be a center in a gigantic universe?

Within the Islamic tradition, the question of human centrality in the face of a vast universe is often addressed through theological, philosophical, and ethical dimensions. The Qur'an, the Hadith, and subsequent Islamic scholarship assert that human beings hold a unique and dignified position within the cosmic order, primarily based on their spiritual essence and moral responsibilities. In Islam, human beings are described as the "vicegerents" (*khalifah*) of God on Earth. This is explicitly mentioned in the Qur'an, where God declares His intention to place a vicegerent on Earth. Allah says in the Qur'an, *"And [mention, O Muhammad], when your Lord said to the angels, 'I will create a vicegerent on earth...'"* [Qur'an 2:30]. The term *"Khalifah"* implies both honor and responsibility. As God's representatives, humans are endowed with faculties like intellect, will, and moral discernment, and they are charged with the ethical stewardship of the Earth and its creatures. This signifies a unique role and purpose for human beings, granting them a form of centrality in the grand scheme of creation.

Moreover, Islam encourages the study of the natural world to understand God's attributes better. Verses in the Qur'an often refer to the heavens, the Earth, and other elements of nature as "signs" (*ayaat*) of God's majesty and wisdom. While the universe is expansive and beyond human scale, the ability to contemplate it and recognize it as a sign of God's greatness is considered a uniquely human attribute. This capability for reflection and understanding further accentuates the central role that human beings occupy in an Islamic worldview. It is also important to note that the Islamic perspective on human centrality is not merely anthropocentric but theocentric; it is rooted in a relationship with the Divine. According to Islamic teaching, the ultimate purpose of human life is to worship God and live a life following His guidance. This special relationship with God lends a unique spiritual and moral dimension to human existence, making it central in a way that transcends mere physical or spatial considerations.

Therefore, from an Islamic standpoint, human centrality in the cosmos is not one of size or scale but of divine purpose and moral responsibility. As God's vicegerents, human beings possess intrinsic dignity and a unique moral and intellectual growth capacity, which confers a special status and purpose within the broader cosmic order. Religion is the trust that man bears, which is the greatest test one must go through. One may easily perceive this divine assignment and suffer the tingling of moral conscience, acknowledging that there is something within that tells us what to do and what not to do. Humans perceive, realize, understand, and know the reality of their existence and the universe around them, grasping the meaning of their existence well. They are the ones liable for duties, responsibilities, assignments, and reckoning. They are beings aware of the splendor of careful formulation, the laws of perfection, and the ability to carry out assignments or reject them. They possess the full capacity for choice and can be believers or disbelievers. Humans occupy a central position in this universe. Allah says in the Qur'an, *"Indeed, we offered the Trust to the heavens, the earth, and the mountains, yet they refused to bear it and were afraid of it. But man assumed it; he is indeed wrongful and ignorant"* [Qur'an 33:72].

Since there are so many planets, based on the theory of possibilities, would it not be correct to assume that one of these planets would be suitable for life?

What is the relation between the existence of many planets and discrediting perfection and creation as proof? It is not a matter of raw materials. Being in a forest full of every vegetable, fruit, and animal does not mean that there must suddenly appear a dish of delicious, cooked food. The issue is not about the raw materials. The mere existence of a group of planets is not a sufficient argument to have among them a planet that is so perfectly created like the Earth. It is a case of perfection, creation, and making. Allah says in the Qur'an, *"...such is the design of Allah, who has perfected everything"* [Qur'an 27:88]. The presence of many other planets does not at all justify that there is life on Earth, nor does it justify the existence of the genetic code, consisting of four billion letters that impressively control all functions, organs, and hormones. Life is information, not matter. If an atheist and another person were to ascend to a planet and discover a complex device that works with impressive precision, even if they cannot yet understand its function, can the maker of this device be denied just because of the huge size of the planet they are on? Mental intuition prompts them both, when they see this device, to admit the existence of the capable Creator. The one who denies this logical intuition, who denies the existence of the Creator, is the one who is required to present the evidence, not the one who affirms His existence. The atheist in this dazzling universe is the one who is required to provide the evidence, not the believer.

The agnostic Carl Sagan once wrote a novel called "Contact," in which he recounts how scientists are looking for extraterrestrial intelligence. In this fictional novel, scientists discovered a long series of prime numbers coming from outer space. This initial sequence implies a specific mathematical value, a value that indicates a kind of precision, which was enough mental evidence to conclude that this message was coming from another civilization trying to communicate with humanity. What is ironic is that Carl Sagan is a famous agnostic himself, yet his mind accepts the fact that the complexity and organization of a small message are proof of creation and perfection. A mere series of prime numbers would prove the presence of a giant civilization. So, how can one attribute the perfection of the four billion letters inside each cell of our body, where even the absence of a single letter could lead to catastrophe, to the illogical notions of atheism? It is not reasonable to resort to quirks (oddities) to prevent the interpretation of the phenomenon in its framework as an indication of the existence of the Creator. Allah says in the Qur'an, *"Say, 'look at what is in the heavens and earth.' But the signs and warnings are of no avail to those who do not believe."* [Qur'an 10:101].

If God does not need us, why did He create us?

A rich and reputable doctor may treat people without needing anything from them but treat them for their own benefit. Here, we do not describe his actions as absurd. Moreover, a swimmer may rescue a child out of mercy, then leave him and go without waiting for the child's parents to thank him. Here, this action is not classified as a need or absurdity; rather, this is a generous act, a noble purpose, and one of good character. So, need and absurdity are not necessarily correlated.

Allah is quoted to have said in a Hadith *Qudsi*: "O My servants, were the first of you and the last of you, the human of you and the *jinn* (spirit) of you to be as pious as the most pious heart of one of you, it would not increase in My dominion anything. O My servants were the first of you and the last of you, the human of you and the jinn of you to be as wicked as the most wicked heart of one of you, it would not decrease from My dominion anything. It is but your deeds that I count for you and then recompense you for them" [Sahih Muslim]. So, whoever finds good, let him praise Allah, and whoever finds other than that, let him blame none but himself.

Allah is free from the needs of the world. Our endeavors, efforts, and work are only for ourselves and our benefit. Allah says in the Qur'an, *"Whoever strives, he only strives for his own good. Indeed, Allah is in no need of the worlds"* [Qur'an 29:6]. We know that Allah has wisdom in all His creation, even if one is ignorant of it. Knowledge of divine wisdom does not require understanding all dimensions of wisdom, but it is sufficient to understand some of them. It is sufficient to know that all are charged with worshiping Allah and know that there is divine wisdom. Otherwise, one is like those who disbelieve in all that they do not understand: *"But they rejected that which they did not comprehend, and its warning has not yet been fulfilled against them"* [Qur'an 10:39]. Allah is Wise, and He created us for a wise purpose. He alone is the one truly worthy of worship. Allah says in the Qur'an, *"O mankind, worship your Lord, who created you and those before you, so that you may become righteous"* [Qur'an 2:21]. He is the One who guides, the One who legislates, decrees, commands, and prohibits. Allah says in the Qur'an, *"His is the creation and the command"* [Qur'an 7:54]. It is not just the creation that belongs to Allah but the command, as well. All must obey His commands. Worship is the right of Allah due upon the slaves.

He, the Almighty, created humanity, gave life, provided sustenance, offered guidance, and sent His messengers to humankind to test who among them excels in deeds. Allah says in the Qur'an, *"He is the One Who created death and life to test you as to which of you is best in deeds, and He is the All-Mighty, the Most Forgiving"* [Qur'an 67:2]. Our worldly life and that of the Hereafter will not be set aright except with worship, nor will our morals be reformed except with worship, for worship prevents immorality and evildoing, and with it, the worldly life will be reformed. Allah says in the Qur'an, *"Recite [O Prophet] what is revealed to you of the Book and establish prayer, for indeed prayer restrains one from immoral acts and wickedness"* [Qur'an 29:45]. Paradise can only be attained through worship and the mercy of Allah, as it is salvation in the Hereafter and bliss in the worldly life. Worship is for humanity and for their own benefit, and it is obligatory upon them towards Allah Almighty because He is their Creator, and its benefit returns to humanity only, and negligence affects them only. Paradise is expensive, so whoever desires Paradise should work for it.

Why does God punish people?

No one can disagree that punishment is necessary in the pursuit of justice. Punishment has long been woven into the fabric of every justice system throughout history. God has created humankind with the ability to choose how to live and, in turn, be accountable. Those who sincerely strive to obey God will earn mercy and enter paradise. But those who are careless about their purpose in life and deny God have ultimately made their own choice and will be held accountable. No one can blame God. God did not create people to punish them—instead, He intends to shower them with His mercy. The fact that God knows the choices made does not diminish the voluntary nature of one's actions or exempt one from responsibility. Islam is a practical religion that encourages a balance between hope in God's mercy and fear of His punishment—both of which are required to lead a positive and humble life in this short journey of earthly life. God is the Most Merciful, but also, He is the Most Just. Without a Day of Judgment, it would have contradicted the perfect justice of God, and life would be unfair. Imagine those who caused corruption, bloodshed, and human suffering in this worldly life and died before they were brought to justice. Islam makes a promise to those criminals that they will not escape God's justice on the Day of Judgment.

Why can't the universe create itself?

The proposition that the universe created itself has an intrinsic logical contradiction: It would need the universe to exist before it existed, which is an ontological impossibility. This claim violates the law of non-contradiction, a fundamental premise of classical logic that asserts that something cannot be both "A" and "not-A" simultaneously and in the same way. The idea that the universe may create itself means that it would have to simultaneously be both a being (to perform its creation) and a non-being (to be the recipient of the creative act). This is an unresolvable problem. If one claims that the universe formed itself, one is violating the basic rules of rational thought, compromising the validity of reasonable discourse. The concept of a "necessary being" is frequently addressed in philosophical discourse, particularly in discussions involving the cosmological argument. An essential being exists due to the necessity of its nature; it does not exist because of anything else. God is frequently stated in classical theism as this necessary being—self-existent, eternal, and not dependent on anything else. To argue that the universe is self-created would imply that it has the attributes of a necessary being, contradicting scientific evidence and theoretical models such as the Big Bang Theory, which posits a temporal beginning to the universe. If the cosmos had a start, it could not be self-existent or necessary; rather, it would depend on something outside of itself. Furthermore, the universe's properties, like its laws and constants, show a degree of fine-tuning that suggests design or purpose. A self-created cosmos would have to have laws that govern its traits and behavior, resulting in another logical paradox. In conclusion, the hypothesis that the universe formed itself poses significant logical and ontological obstacles that look insurmountable. Not only does the concept contradict empirical data and well-established scientific theories, but it also violates basic logic principles. As a result, the concept is widely seen as implausible from both a theistic and a rational standpoint.

CHAPTER 19

The Most Common Atheists' Objections About Religion

"And We certainly sent into every nation a messenger,
[saying], "Worship Allah and avoid tyrant. And among
them were those whom Allah guided, and among them
were those upon whom error was [deservedly] decreed. So,
proceed through the earth and observe how was the end of
the deniers." ~ *(*Qur'an 16:36*)*Top of Form

There are many religions and many gods in the cultures of the Earth, but there is only one atheism; therefore, it is true.

Responding to atheists' claim of the plurality of religions versus the singularity of atheism, the argument that "there are many religions and many gods, but there is one atheism; therefore, it is true" is an exciting but flawed attempt to suggest that the sheer diversity of religious belief systems undermines their credibility, whereas atheism's purported singularity provides it with more validity.

However, this claim needs to be more logically rigorous and epistemologically robust upon closer investigation for numerous fundamental reasons. To begin, the argument commits a false dilemma fallacy by providing an oversimplified binary between the diversity of religions and the oneness of atheism. The variety of religious perspectives does not invalidate their worth or credibility. Multiple religious frameworks can provide legitimate insights into existential concerns, even if they do so in different ways and through distinct traditions. The diversity of religions also reflects the complexities of existential problems, necessitating different perspectives to appreciate them fully.

Second, if singularity is considered a hallmark of truth or validity, it must be applied consistently across all disciplines, including atheism. Despite its appearance, atheism is divided into several subcategories, including agnostic atheism, gnostic atheism, secular humanism, existentialist atheism, etc. These groupings disagree on essential issues in epistemology, ethics, and philosophy of mind.

Third, the argument is based on an ambiguous definition of "truth." Truth is frequently holistic in religious contexts, attempting to provide a complete worldview encompassing human life's moral, ontological, metaphysical, and experiential dimensions. Atheism, primarily a rejection of believing in gods, does not inevitably present an alternative "truth" or worldview encompassing these various elements.

The fourth point of complaint is that the argument fails to address crucial epistemological difficulties. Multiple paradigms, such as scientific empiricism, philosophical rationalism, and religious revelation, provide diverse strategies for pursuing knowledge and truth. The argument simplifies this epistemic diversity by claiming that diversity in religion diminishes its credibility, but unity in atheism promotes it. This rash assumption ignores the limitations and scope of other epistemological perspectives.

Finally, the argument provides no positive proof for atheism. The criticism of religious diversity is a negative argument against religious belief but not a positive argument for atheism. To demonstrate atheism as "true," supporters must show empirical or rational evidence that substantively supports the atheistic worldview rather than simply criticizing the alternatives.

In conclusion, the claim that the singularity of atheism makes it true while the variety of religious beliefs undermines its validity is founded on several logical and epistemological problems. A thorough debate on the matter necessitates significantly more depth and analysis of different factors, such as the nature of truth, the complexities of epistemological frameworks, and the necessity for positive evidence to sustain any worldview, atheistic or otherwise.

All religions recognize and worship the one supreme entity, the Creator and Sustainer of the universe, whom Islam calls Allah. Islam differs from all other world religions in that other religions have worshiped various gods alongside Allah, such as Jesus in Christianity, Vishnu and Shiva in Hinduism, Buddha in Buddhism, and so on. Associating partners with the one true God is the main issue here.

All faiths acknowledge one supreme entity, yet they worship different gods alongside Him. Even the idols of pagan Greece or pagan Makkah were not worshiped as deities because the people acknowledged that the Creator is the one supreme entity, still they made them intermediaries to Him. Allah says in the Qur'an, *"If you ask them who created the heavens and earth and subjected the sun and moon, they will undoubtedly say Allah; How are they deluded?"* [Qur'an 29:61]. Anyone who thinks that idol worshipers believed that idols created the Earth or that they sent down rain, grew vegetation, or created creatures is mistaken. For example, most Hindus believe in the one supreme God despite the various partners they associate with Him. In all religions on the planet, Allah is One. Allah says in the Qur'an, *"...and our God and your God are One"* [Qur'an 29:46]. Idols, animals, and human gods are all wrongly taken as intermediaries to Allah; however, associating partners with Him is considered a *Shirk* – an antithesis of *Tawheed*. In the Qur'an, Allah says, *"As for those who take others as guardians besides Him, [saying], We only worship them so that they may bring us closer to Allah"* [Qur'an 39:3].

What about the criticism of religions as sources of violence?

The assertion that religions are intrinsic sources of violence has been a recurring theme in public discourse, particularly in the writings of figures associated with the New Atheist movement, such as Richard Dawkins, Sam Harris, and Christopher Hitchens. While it is indisputable that numerous acts of violence have been carried out under the banner of various religious faiths, attributing the impetus for such violence solely or predominantly to religion risks oversimplification of a complex interplay of factors that give rise to human conflict.

There is a need to deconstruct this criticism by offering a multifaceted understanding of the issue. Firstly, it is vital to situate the argument within a historical context. The claim that religion is the primary cause of violence is empirically unsound when one considers the tapestry of human history. For most religious people across the world, religion is a source of peace, tranquility, and human fraternity. Numerous conflicts and wars have been waged for entirely secular reasons, such as territorial conquest, political power, and resource allocation. For instance, the Mongol invasions or Roman conquests were motivated more by territorial gains than religious fervor. Even when religious rhetoric has been invoked, it is often a veneer that masks underlying motives, making religion one of multiple factors rather than the root cause of conflict.

Understanding religion's role in violence necessitates considering the complex social, cultural, and political ecosystems within which religions operate. For example, the Northern Ireland troubles, often labeled as a religious conflict between Catholics and Protestants, had roots in national identity and political sovereignty issues. In such instances, religion is not an isolated factor but is entangled with other social and political variables.

It is crucial to differentiate between the theological tenets of a religion and the actions of individuals or groups who identify with that religion. Critics often resort to textual literalism, quoting religious scriptures out of context without considering the diverse interpretive traditions that have developed within religious communities. Misinterpretation of sacred texts is not confined to religious traditions; any text, whether religious or secular, is susceptible to misuse for justifying violent ends. Religious traditions are not static but are subject to interpretation and reform. For example, the Christian Reformation, Islamic traditions of Ijtihad (independent reasoning), and the Jewish practice of Talmudic study all represent the internal mechanisms for self-criticism and ethical amelioration within religious communities. Such processes enable religious traditions to adapt and evolve, mitigating the tendencies that could lead to violent extremism.

One must also scrutinize the selective focus on religious violence while ignoring secular ideologies, resulting in tremendous suffering. From the devastating impacts of World Wars to the genocidal policies of totalitarian secular regimes, secular philosophies and ideologies have been equally, if not more, effective in propagating violence.

Lastly, it's worth noting that religious teachings have been a cornerstone for moral and ethical frameworks that inspire acts of kindness, charity, and social justice. Humanitarian figures like Mother Teresa (d. 1997), Martin Luther King Jr. (d. 1968), and Abdul Sattar Edhi (d. 2016) illustrate how religious beliefs can catalyze profoundly beneficial impacts on human society.

In summary, while it is essential to rigorously scrutinize and critique instances where religious ideologies have been used or misused to legitimize or incite violence, the wholesale denunciation of religion as inherently violent is intellectually untenable and empirically unfounded. Such a perspective fails to account for the myriad of other factors contributing to human conflict. It overlooks the significant positive impacts that religious belief can exert on individual and communal life. Understanding the nuanced relationship between religion and violence necessitates a scholarly engagement with historical context, social complexities, and ethical frameworks rather than blanket criticisms that only polarize and oversimplify a multifaceted issue.

CHAPTER 20

Why Does God Allow Evil and Suffering in the World?

*"Do people think that they will be left alone because they say: 'We believe,' and will not be tested? And We indeed tested those who were before them. So, Allah will certainly know those who are true, and will certainly know those who are liars." ~ (*Qur'an 29:2-3*)*

The Difficult Question of Evil and Suffering in Islamic Theology

The difficult question surrounding the existence of evil and suffering, especially when juxtaposed with the belief in a benevolent and omnipotent Deity, has been a perennial challenge for theologians and philosophers across various religious traditions. Among these traditions, Islamic theology and philosophy have grappled with this issue and produced many profound insights and reflections. Central to this discourse is the Qur'an, the paramount religious text for Muslims. This sacred scripture lays the foundational parameters for discerning the nature and reason for evil and suffering in the world. Through its passages, the Qur'an articulates that human worldly life is a test of trials and tribulations. It is a crucible in which human souls undergo refinement and evolution. A pivotal verse encapsulates this worldview: *"He who created death and life to test you [as to] which of you is best in deed..."* [Qur'an 67:2]. From this perspective, challenges, adversities, and tribulations are not anomalies but integral components of this divine examination.

Furthermore, the Qur'an underscores the free will granted to human beings. While this agency is indeed a divine gift, it also bears the potential for decisions that may culminate in the emergence of evil and suffering in the worldly realm. The Qur'an repeatedly revisits this theme, iterating humans' responsibility for their actions and the subsequent ramifications of their choices. The Qur'anic narrative also highlights the transient nature of our earthly existence. In contrast to the enduring realm of the afterlife, our current life is fleeting, an amalgam of happiness and grief.

The brief worldly existence is a minuscule fraction in the grand picture of eternity. Muslims believe in the life Hereafter. There may be some inconveniences in this life, which will be compensated for in the life hereafter. The Prophet Muhammad (PBUH) is quoted to have said in an authentic Hadith, "Amazing is the situation of the believer. If a thorn pokes the believer and he praises God, it gets stored up as a reward in a life hereafter" [Sahih al-Bukhari]. In another Hadith, the Prophet Muhammad (PBUH) said, "No fatigue, nor disease, nor sorrow, no sadness, nor hurt, no distress befalls a believer, even if it were the prick he receives from a thorn, but Allah expiates some of his sins" [Sahih al-Bukhari]. Therefore, it does not matter what happens to the believer; the outcome is always good.

Using the metaphor of this life as a pixel and eternity as a picture, from God's point of view, He looks at the entire big picture—not only this life but the whole eternity. He sees the final good that manifests itself, the outcome of everything that has transpired in this life. However, we see that which is close—what is near to us. That is what we are preoccupied with. We only see the evil and suffering of this world. We do not see that in the outcome. People who have served God or been wronged in this world are rewarded generously by being admitted into Paradise. So that the final outcome is such that, the way that God sees it, ultimately good and justice prevails. Moreover, with all of its evil and suffering, this world still leads to an ultimate good.

Islamic intellectual history is replete with scholars who have delved deeply into this matter. For instance, the esteemed philosopher Ibn Sina (d. 1037 CE), who amalgamated Aristotelian and Neoplatonic ideas, posited that evil is not a standalone entity. Instead, it represents a lack or absence of good (Goodman, 2020). This standpoint offers a resolution to the seeming paradox of the coexistence of evil in a world crafted by an absolute and perfect Being. Al-Ghazali, another luminary in Islamic thought, explored the nuanced nature of evil in his seminal works. For him, evil is relative and context dependent (Griffel, 2019). What may seem detrimental in one scenario could be a harbinger of a broader beneficial outcome in another. On decreeing fighting for self-defense, Allah says in the Qur'an, "*Fighting has been enjoined upon you while it is hateful to you. But perhaps you hate a thing, and it is good for you; and perhaps you love a thing, and it is bad for you. And Allah Knows, while you know not*" [Qur'an 2:216].

He also emphasized the limitations of human cognition, implying that the vast expanse of divine wisdom often transcends human comprehension. In the annals of Islamic rationalist tradition, Ibn Rushd postulated that evil manifests in harmony with divine sagacity (Taylor, 2018). He emphasized that the natural world, subject to inherent laws, produces positive and negative outcomes. Furthermore, he accentuated the pivotal role of human agency, attributing many worldly afflictions to human decisions. This view is corroborated in the Qur'an. Allah says in the Qur'an, "*Corruption has appeared throughout the land and sea by [reason of] what the hands of people have earned so He may let them taste part of [the consequence of] what they have done that perhaps they will return [to righteousness]*" [Qur'an 30:41].

Islamic Perspectives on Evil and Suffering: A Comprehensive Exploration

Distinct from the rationalist trajectory, Ibn Taymiyyah opined that life's challenges are divinely ordained evaluations (Hoover, 2018). He argued that these trials discern the genuinely devout and act as avenues for spiritual enhancement. In another area, Islamic mystical traditions offer a distinctive vantage point. Celebrated Sufi thinkers like Rumi perceive suffering as a pathway leading to spiritual enlightenment (Chittick, 1983). Such adversities, they argue, are instruments that purify the soul, bringing it into closer communion with the Divine. Advancing into metaphysical terrains, Mulla Sadra envisages existence as a graded continuum (Kamal, 2006). In his schema, evil manifests the absence or lack of good. He also emphasizes the overarching principle of divine justice, urging a shift from purely human-centric evaluations.

Contemporary Muslim intellectuals have revisited this age-old dilemma, weaving traditional insights with modern philosophical paradigms. These thinkers often underscore the existential ramifications of suffering, viewing tribulations not as random occurrences but as catalysts for introspection, personal development, and spiritual elevation. Thus, probing deeper into Islamic theological perspectives, it becomes evident that trials, tribulations, and adversities are often perceived not as mere punishments or tests but as opportunities for spiritual refinement and elevation.

From this viewpoint, challenges and hardships are not obstacles hindering human progress; they are transformative experiences that can propel individuals toward greater moral and spiritual heights (Nasr S. H., 2010). This transformative potential of suffering underscores its integral role in the human journey toward self-realization and closeness to the Divine. Furthermore, by integrating modern philosophical paradigms, these thinkers can present a more comprehensive understanding of suffering. Drawing upon existentialist thought, for instance, they highlight human existence's inherent uncertainty and unpredictability, suggesting that suffering can serve as a medium through which individuals confront the profound questions of life, purpose, and meaning. In doing so, individuals are often compelled to seek solace and guidance in their faith, fostering a deeper and more intimate relationship with God.

In conclusion, the rich mosaic of Islamic thought, from the foundational Qur'anic teachings to the musings of classical scholars, mystics, and modern philosophers, presents a holistic and multi-faceted approach to understanding the enigma of evil and suffering. By emphasizing the transformative and elevating potential of trials and tribulations, these thinkers present a perspective that resonates deeply with the existential concerns of the modern individual, reaffirming the timeless relevance of Islamic teachings in addressing the perennial questions of human existence. Furthermore, by situating human experiences within the boundless realm of divine wisdom, Islamic thought offers pathways for comprehension, solace, and spiritual advancement amidst the inherent tribulations of life.

CHAPTER 21

The Islamic View of the Origin of the Universe

"Have those who disbelieved not considered that the heavens and the earth were a joined entity, and We separated them and made from water every living thing? Then will they not believe?" ~ (Qur'an 21:30)

Islamic Perspectives on the Origin and Fate of the Universe: A Quranic Exploration

The Qur'an doesn't have a chapter on the genesis as in the Bible to explain the origin of the universe, but it has various passages scattered throughout the book that deal with the creation of the universe and human beings. We learn from the Qur'an that the creation of the universe and its content was not an instant event but rather a process with many stages, not the least important is the Hereafter. The Qur'an states that the universe was created in six days, but these days are not earthly days; they are passages of time. The Arabs used to refer to the universe as "the heavens and the earth," but the Qur'an describes the heavens and the Earth as a single entity that God split into the heavens (galaxies) and the earth [Qur'an 21:30]. The Qur'an further implies that the universe evolved from a gaseous state that is described as "smoke" [Qur'an 41:11]. The Qur'an represents the universe as one that is expanding [Qur'an 81:15-16] and one that has a beginning and an "appointed term" for existence—not eternal [Qur'an 46:3]. The Qur'an presents the Hereafter as a new universe that will spring out after the end and destruction of the current universe [Qur'an 14:48].

Science has come to agree with what the Qur'an described in the 7th century on the creation and fate of the universe. Today, most astrophysicists concur with the idea that the universe began with the Big Bang; at the earliest stage, the universe was filled with radiation and elementary particles such as quarks, then hydrogen and helium were formed from elementary particles in the inferno of the Big Bang. They believe the gaseous clouds condensed and gave birth to stars that eventually took shape to form galaxies. Following the massive explosion of the Big Bang, the universe began an expansion that is still ongoing today. The growth of the universe will come to a halt at some point, and they speculate that the universe will rebound to the end of singularity, which they referred to as the Big Crunch, after which a new universe will spring out of the singularity. In fact, modern scientists appear to be repeating verbatim pertinent Qur'anic passages when it comes to events at the end of the universe.

Modern science maintains that the universe originated from the Big Bang and evolved into its present state over earthly time. Allah says in the Qur'an, *"On the day when We shall roll up heaven as a scroll for writings; As We originated the first creation, so We shall bring it back again—A promise binding on Us; so, We shall do it"* [Qur'an 21:104]. Modern science also asserts that the universe, at some point, will start contracting where the galaxies will begin to recede, and the galaxies that are receding from one another will start approaching each other, always gathering speed. Allah says in the Qur'an, *"So verily, I call to witness the stars that recede"* [Qur'an 81:15-16]. During the final collapse of the universe, astronomers believe that under the combined influence of hydrogen fusion on the solar surface and the high-temperature helium fusion in its interior, the exterior of the sun will inflate and cool. Allah says in the Qur'an, *"When the Sun shall be darkened"* [Qur'an 81:1]. The sun will become a giant red star. Allah says in the Qur'an, *"Upon the day when heaven shall be as molten copper"* [Qur'an 70:8]. When the sun enlarges, it will swallow other planets. Allah says in the Qur'an, *"And the Sun and Moon are united"* [Qur'an 75:9]. Scientists also believe that as the sun gradually becomes red and inflated, its overwhelming heat will melt Arctic and Antarctic ice, resulting in coastal flooding worldwide. Allah says in the Qur'an, *"And the ocean filled will swell"* [Qur'an 52:6]. The soaring ocean temperature will lift clouds of steam into the air, and the unforgiving extreme heat of the sun will make the ocean boil. Allah says in the Qur'an, *"When the sea shall be set boiling"* [Qur'an 81:6]. The observer will no longer be able to discern individual galaxies, for these would now have begun to merge as intergalactic space close-ups. Allah says in the Qur'an, *"When the sky stripped bare"* [Qur'an 81:11].

Modern scientists predict that as the end of the current universe approaches, the galaxies and, subsequently, the stars will collapse and merge into each other until an explosive inferno ensues, resulting in a singularity identical to where our universe originally began (i.e., all matter in the universe will be compressed into a single point of space and time). Allah says in the Qur'an, *"The day the heaven shall be rent asunder with the clouds…"* [Qur'an 25:25]. Allah also says, *"When the sky cleft asunder when the stars are scattered"* [Qur'an 82:1-2]. Allah also says, *"When the stars fall, losing their luster"* [Qur'an 81:2]. Furthermore, Allah states, *"And (on that day) the earth is moved, and its mountains, and they are crushed to powder at one stroke"* [Qur'an 69:14]. Additionally, Allah says, *"When the sky is split open, and it becomes red like ointment"* [Qur'an 55:37]. Allah also says, *"It will be no more than a single blast…"* [Qur'an 36:53]. Modern science speculates whether the universe will rise again after the collapse and what would be the nature and properties of the new universe. Allah says in the Qur'an, *"On the day when We shall roll up heaven as a scroll for writings; As We originated the first creation, so We shall bring it back again—A promise binding on Us; so, We shall do it"* [Qur'an 21:104]. Allah also says, *"On the day when the earth is changed into a different earth and heavens into new heavens, mankind shall stand before God, the One, who conquers all"* [Qur'an 14:48].

Finally, while the above passages juxtapose modern scientific understanding with Qur'anic verses related to the beginning and end of the universe, showcasing potential parallels between the two, it's important to approach such comparisons with both reverence and intellectual rigor, acknowledging that both religious texts and scientific theories possess their own unique domains and epistemologies.

CHAPTER 22

Islamic View of Human Nature and Human Life

"We have certainly created man in the best of stature. Then We return him to the lowest of the low, Except for those who believe and do righteous deeds, for they will have a reward uninterrupted." ~ (Qur'an 95:4-6)

While the Qur'an doesn't explicitly discuss biological evolution from lower species as presented by the theories of "Darwinian evolution" and "natural selection," nor does it give any clue as to when the creation of the first human happened, it does emphasize the step-by-step transformation in the creation of humankind. Man's physical form is a product of the Earth, evolving gradually. The Qur'an describes the infusion of the spiritual soul as the culmination of this evolutionary process, marking the transition to a living Adam. Qur'anic passages, such as *"(The One Almighty God) Who perfected everything which He created and began the creation of man from clay. Then, He made his posterity out of the extract of a liquid disdained. Then He proportioned him and breathed into him from His [created] soul and made for you hearing and vision and hearts; little are you grateful."* [Qur'an 32:7-9] encapsulate this entire evolutionary process.

The signs of Allah are evident in His creations, as each reflects Allah's exquisite names and attributes. These manifestations serve as a bridge connecting human understanding to the Divine. Among Allah's attributes, there are four that specifically explain His Divine role in the realm of creation: *"Ar-Rabb"* (The Lord, The Sustainer), *"Al-Khaaliq"* (The Creator), *"Al-Baari"* (The Evolver), and *"Al-Musawwir"* (The Designer) [Qur'an 96:1-2; 59:24]. *Ar-Rabb* encapsulates the nurturing aspect of Allah, guiding His creation progressively from one stage to the next until it reaches its goal of perfection. *Al-Khaaliq* is the Divine act of fashioning something into existence meticulously so that it assumes its intended form without being based on a prior model. *Al-Baari* signifies the Divine wisdom behind differentiating creations, setting each one apart in its own unique manner, alluding to the process of creation as evolutionary. Lastly, *Al-Musawwir* signifies designing and sculpting a thing and giving definite form and/or color to make things exactly suitable for a certain end or object, distinguishing it with variety and multitude.

If we consider God the Evolver, He is also the Creator of novel life forms from those He originally fashioned. Moreover, He is the Designer who gives forms and colors so that His creations function suitably in environments to achieve certain ends or objects. By changing genetic configuration, He creates new species capable of adapting to the changes in the environment over the various ages of the Earth, but such modifications exist and are the result of God's will. Thus, the meanings of these attributes confirm the belief that evolution and creation are not necessarily contradictory but mutually complementary. These evolutionary adjustments must exist as a manifestation of God's Divine intent. Consequently, these attributes underscore that evolution and creation may not inherently be conflicting but could relatively harmoniously be intertwined. Creation is the Divine act, while evolution could be the human interpretation of that Divine act of creation.

The Qur'an tells us that life began from water for all living things, and the creation of the "prototype" human species (Adam) began from clay; however, his "progenies" were created from an emitted drop of semen. Through the study of embryology, we know that the birth of humans involves the evolution of cells (yoked sperm and ova) through all later stages of fetal growth to human progeny—a step-by-step process in finite Earthbound time. Many Qur'anic verses on human creation unequivocally state that the creation of humankind, both the prototype and the progeny, was not an ex-nihilo instant event but a step-by-step transformation and that man's physical material form is, in fact, a product of the Earth. Unlike his spiritual soul, his body is not a foreigner or alien on this planet. For instance, consider the following verse: *"And Allah has caused you to grow from the Earth a [progressive] growth."* [Qur'an 71:17]. Also: *"... He has produced you from the Earth and settled you in it, so ask forgiveness of Him and then repent to Him. Indeed, my Lord is near and responsive."* [Qur'an 11:61]. Additionally, *"From the Earth We created you, and into it We will return you, and from it We will extract you another time."* [Qur'an 20:55]. Finally, Allah says, *"What is [the matter] with you that you do not attribute to Allah [due] grandeur, while He has created you in stages?"* [Qur'an 71:13-14].

The Qur'an frequently references water, soil, and clay concerning the creation of man and the origin of life, and these references are perfectly harmonious with the modern view. For example, *"O People, if you should be in doubt about the Resurrection, then [consider that] indeed, We created you from dust, then from a sperm-drop, then from a clinging clot, and then from a lump of flesh, formed and unformed - that We may show you. And We settle in the wombs whom We will for a specified term, then We bring you out as a child, and then [We develop you] that you may reach your [time of] maturity. And among you is he who is taken in [early] death, and among you is he who is returned to the most decrepit [old] age so that he knows, after [once having] knowledge, nothing. And you see the Earth barren, but when We send down upon it rain, it quivers and swells and grows [something] of every beautiful kind."* [Qur'an 22:5]; and *"It is He who created you from clay and then decreed a term and a specified time [known] to Him; then [still] you are in dispute."* [Qur'an 6:2]. In other passages, Allah says, *"Then inquire of them, [O Muhammad], Are they a stronger [or more difficult] creation or those [others] We have created? Indeed, We created men from sticky clay."* [Qur'an 37:11].

Furthermore, Allah states, *"He created man from clay like [that of] pottery."* [Qur'an 55:14]; and *"And We did certainly create man out of clay from an altered black mud."* [Qur'an 15:26]. Moreover, in the Qur'an, Allah states, *"And it is He who has created from water a human being and made him [a relative by] lineage and marriage. And ever is your Lord competent [concerning creation]."* [Qur'an 25:54]. Allah adds, *"Have those who disbelieved not considered that the heavens and the Earth were a joined entity, and We separated them and made from water every living thing? Then will they not believe?"* [Qur'an 21:30]. Finally, *"Allah has created every [living] creature from water. And of them are those that move on their bellies, and of them are those that walk on two legs, and of them are those that walk on four. Allah creates what*

He wills. Indeed, Allah is over all things competent." [Qur'an 24:45].

In the light of Qur'anic narrations, it is not entirely inconceivable to believe that man biologically evolved, but regarding the gradual creation of man from the Earth's material, the Qur'an describes the gradual creation of man's physical body—not from a lower species. When God's creative design was completed, He breathed His (created) soul into man, Adam. From the same soul breathed into Adam, God created Eve—the two became the first pair of human prototypes. Allah says in the Qur'an, *"O Mankind! fear your Lord, who created you from one soul and created from it its mate and dispersed from both of them many men and women..."* [Qur'an 4:1]. The Qur'an enunciates that humans are descendants of this primordial human pair, Adam and Eve. Allah says in the Qur'an, *"O Mankind! We have created you from a male and a female and made you into nations and tribes so that you might come to know each other. The noblest of you in God's sight is the one who fears God most (pious, righteous). God is All Knowing and All Aware"* [Qur'an 49:13]. The Qur'an also affirms that God can bring us into being anew in an unknown form [Qur'an 56:61]. The Qur'anic locution, *"When I have fashioned him (in due proportion)..."* as God refers to the creation of man [Qur'an 38:72; 15:29], encapsulates the entire evolutionary process of the development of humans and life on Earth. From the Qur'anic rendition of human development, if humans truly underwent biological evolution, there were intermediate stages of form and not intermediate stages of living creatures, referred to as microevolution. In other words, the evolving form of man was not living until God breathed His (created) soul into the body, and then it became the living Adam. The spiritual soul was breathed into the chosen primordial pair, Adam and Eve. The Qur'an refers to the prefigured primate as "Bashar," the term used in the Qur'an to refer to man when his physical qualities are highlighted [Qur'an 15:28-29; 38:71-72]. In this context, the significance of the infusion in man of his spiritual soul must be understood as the crowning of man as God's vicegerent on Earth, which was finalized by the Divine commandment for all angels to prostrate before Adam (the first human prototype), thus submitting to his superiority as the Lord's deputy on Earth [Qur'an 2:34; 18:50]. When translating Homo sapiens in the context of evolutionists, it is portrayed as a prefigured primate lacking the attributes of self-consciousness and spirituality. It would have remained nothing more than an intelligent brute. Consider the following verses from the Qur'an, specifically how the reference to a man suddenly shifts from the third person to the second person following the infusion of a spiritual soul. Allah says in the Qur'an, *"(The One Almighty God) Who gave everything its perfect form. He originated the creation of man from clay, and then He made his progeny from an extract of a humble fluid. Then He molded him; He breathed His Spirit into him. He gave you hearing, sight, and hearts. How seldom you are grateful"* [Qur'an 32:7-9)].

Islam also views human life as God-oriented and must revolve around Him, which means that man should build a life based on the concept of God. Man should surrender to God through sheer free will because this God-consciousness is the actual ascension of man, and in it lies the secret of all his success. The God-oriented life begins with the discovery of God. When individuals, whether men or women, discover God, it means they have found the truth that permeates their whole being. This feeling of having discovered the truth becomes such a thrilling experience that fills one with everlasting conviction that removes all frustrations from life. Through suffering from health, wealth, loss of loved ones, jobs, or material losses, one never loses the feeling that God is present, providing solace to the pain and suffering. He is the only one worthy of worship, and it is Him from whom help is sought. Muslims resonate this verse many times every day, *"It is You we worship, and You we ask for help"* [Qur'an 1:5]. When disasters befall believers, they would respond, *"Who, when disaster strikes them, say, 'Indeed we belong to Allah, and indeed to Him we will return'"* [Qur'an 2:156].

The Qur'an generally employs the term *"ayah"* to designate anything that gives news of or points towards the existence of God. It is equally correct to translate *"ayah"* as a "sign" or "evidence," and these terms are helpful for those who want to pursue a specifically rationalistic approach to the question of God's existence. According to the Qur'anic view, everything in the universe is a sign pointing toward the existence of God. Allah says in the Qur'an, *"We shall show them Our signs in the horizons and in themselves until Truth becomes manifest to them. Is it not enough that your Lord is witness over all things?"* [Qur'an 41:53]. Man can realize the truth of God's existence by pondering upon God's creations. The universe is an expression of God's signs for people of intellect to consider, leading to His glorification. God is not visible, but His existence can be realized by observing His signs in His creation. Among the observable signs is the vastness of space of the universe, the solar system with the sun at the center and the planets orbiting, the moon and the stars, the galaxies, the heights of the mountains, the waves of the sea, and the flow of the river, the greenery of plants and trees, the minerals under the Earth, the formation of clouds, rain, and snow, the seasons, and climatic changes. Man's existence and all things and phenomena around him prove God's existence. In the breeze of air, a Divine touch can be experienced. In the chirping of the birds, God's praise can be heard.

Allah says in the Qur'an, *"The seven heavens and the Earth and whatever is in them exalt Him. And there is not a thing except that it exalts [Allah] by His praise, but you do not understand their [way of] exalting. Indeed, He is Ever Forbearing and All-Forgiving"* [Qur'an 17:44]. In another verse, *"He is Allah, the Creator, the Inventor, the Fashioner; to Him belong the best names. Whatever is in the heavens and Earth is exalting Him. And He is the Exalted in Might, the Wise"* [Qur'an 59:24]. Allah also says, *"Do you not see that Allah is exalted by whomever is within the heavens and the Earth and [by] the birds with wings spread [in flight]? Each [of them] has known his [means of] prayer and exalting [Him], and Allah is Knowing of what they do"* [Qur'an 24:41]. Finally, Allah says, *"Do you not see that to Allah prostrates whoever is in the heavens and whoever is on the Earth and the sun, the moon, the stars, the mountains, the trees, the moving creatures, and many of the people? But upon many the punishment has been justified. And he whom Allah humiliates - for him there is no bestower of honor. Indeed, Allah does what He wills"* [Qur'an 22:18].

One's life changes toward a God-centric life after acknowledging God's existence, which is characterized by ongoing consciousness and remembrance of the Divine. This recognition instills an intense sense of God's presence, with every experience as a reminder of Him. The heart and mind are perpetually filled with thoughts of God, making every morning and evening feel like one resides near the Divine. Much like rain nourishing crops, this individual is continuously immersed in the remembrance of God, establishing Him as the spiritual epicenter of life. A heart devoted to God is graced with spiritual revelations at every turn. This belief becomes a wellspring of spiritual and moral growth, saturating one's being with Divine love and eliminating the desire for anything else. God's boundless mercy is perceived as an expansive ocean to delve into, where the soul never encounters constraints. Through spiritual enlightenment, one attains such unparalleled richness that worldly desires fade. For the individual who truly understands God, the universe transforms into a Divine testament. Each tree leaf emerges as a sacred scripture page, and witnessing the sun feels like God has kindled a celestial torch, illuminating His teachings. The universe evolves into a grand cosmic academy, with the individual as its devoted scholar. Humans long for a supreme, limitless entity that anchors their existence. Upon discovering the Creator, one finds unparalleled contentment, akin to a child nestled in a mother's embrace. To know God is to find the true center of love.

The discovery of God saves one from regarding something other than God as a god and mistakenly and unrealistically thinking it to be the answer to the urge inherent within. The discovery of God is also to fulfill their honest desire to find God, and failing to discover God means failing to find that which is man's greatest need. One who fails to find God is compelled by his natural urge to give the place of God to something other than God. This place is sometimes accorded to a particular human being, sometimes to a particular animal, sometimes to a phenomenon of nature, sometimes to a specific material power, sometimes to a particular supposed concept, and sometimes just to the self or desires. Allah says in the Qur'an, *"Have you seen the one who takes as his god his own desire? Then would you be responsible for him?"* [Qur'an 25:43]. Even if one fails to discover God or if one denies God, it is not in his or her power to stifle the urge in his nature to find God. That is why those men and women who have not found God inevitably come to hold something other than God as God—even atheists and agnostics do that. By nature, it is possible for man not to accept the One true God as God, but it is not possible for anyone to save himself from granting the status of divinity to something other than God when he or she failed to find Him.

Making God one's object of worship and devoting oneself to God elevates a person's status. Conversely, worshiping anything other than God diminishes oneself from the level of humanity. *"There is no deity worthy of worship except the One true God"* [Qur'an 3:18]. Allegiance to the One true God is the fundamental path for both humanity and the cosmos, and rejecting the One true God and attributing the universe's origin to concepts like self-origination, necessity, or randomness is a profound misconception and a grave injustice. There are many manifestations of God's supreme knowledge, unmatched wisdom, firm will, and ultimate power that can be seen in the universe. Therefore, the notion of self-origination, necessity, or chance lacks tangible existence and thus cannot encapsulate knowledge, wisdom, will, and power. It is expected to refer to a system with unobservable laws as "nature," but nature is not itself the source of the laws. Nature represents the laws, not the Composer or Lawgiver, a design, not the Designer; it receives but does not act; it reflects order but is not the orchestrator of the order. Essentially, nature comprises laws set forth by God's Divine intent—laws that our intellect can comprehend but lack tangible substance or force. The primordial covenant results in the innate impulse within people to seek out the higher power that they can sense, as they have done in some form or another throughout all recorded history, to the point where some scientists today argue that belief in God or a higher power is hardwired into our DNA (Hammer, 2004).

CHAPTER 23

General Islamic Worldview

"[Those] Who believe in the unseen, establish prayer, and spend out of what We have provided for them, and who believe in what has been revealed to you, [O Muhammad], and what was revealed before you, and of the Hereafter they are certain [in faith]. Those are upon [right] guidance from their Lord, and it is those who are the successful?"
~ *(Qur'an 2:3-5)*

The Islamic worldview represents an expansive and intricate framework that profoundly shapes the beliefs, values, and perspectives of nearly two billion Muslims across the globe. This worldview comes from the teachings of the *Qur'an*—the holy book of Muslims, and *Hadith* Prophet Muhammad's sayings, actions, and what he approved or disapproved. Islamic worldview embraces many elements of life, including spirituality, ethics, social interactions, and governance. The concept of monotheism, called "*tawheed*," is central to this worldview, emphasizing God's Oneness and surrender of all creation to His sovereign will.

Spirituality is essential in the Islamic worldview. Muslims believe that prayer, fasting, supplication, remembrance of God, and other acts of worship can help them create a solid and close connection with Allah. The Five Pillars of Islam—testimony of faith (*shahada*), prayer (*salat*), almsgiving (*zakat*), Ramadan fasting (*sawm*), and pilgrimage to Mecca (*hajj*)—serve as foundational rituals that guide a Muslim's spiritual journey. These rituals encourage a devotional life and emphasize the value of self-discipline, humility, and compassion.

Ethics and morals are central to the Islamic worldview. Muslims are encouraged to cultivate values such as honesty, kindness, generosity, and justice in their dealings with others. The concepts of "*akhlaaq*" (exemplary moral conduct) and "*adaab*" (refined etiquette) emphasize treating people with dignity and empathy. Islamic ethics extends to economic and social issues, encouraging equal income distribution and caring for the less fortunate through acts of charity and welfare.

The Islamic worldview recognizes a harmonious blend of individuality and emphasizes community responsibility and social harmony. Muslims are urged to participate in communal prayers, assemble for religious celebrations, and help one another in need. The *ummah*, or global Muslim community, crosses national and cultural boundaries, encouraging Muslims to unite. Furthermore, the principle of *"amr bil ma'ruf wa nahi anil munkar"* is a bedrock principle in the Islamic worldview that commands enjoining good and prohibiting evil, asking Muslims to oppose oppression and injustice in all forms, and promote righteousness in individual and society at large.

The Islamic worldview, therefore, has implications for law and governance. The term *"Shari'ah,"* which means "path" or "way," refers to a comprehensive set of rules and norms taken from Islamic sources (the *Qur'an, Sunnah*, and rational tools) to guide individuals, families, and society at large. While interpretations differ, *Shari'ah* seeks to create an equitable and harmonious community by addressing issues ranging from family law to business transactions. It also emphasizes leaders' accountability and the importance of governance aligning with ethical and Islamic moral standards.

The Islamic worldview emphasizes knowledge and intellectual pursuits. Muslims are encouraged to pursue knowledge and meditate on Allah's signs in nature and the scriptures. This pursuit of knowledge is exemplified by Prophet Muhammad's famous saying, "Seeking knowledge is obligatory upon every Muslim" (*Sunan Ibn Majah*). Science, technology, philosophy, and various fields of study are viewed as avenues to understand the intricacies of Allah's creation and to fulfill one's role as Earth steward.

Time is likewise regarded as an essential part of the Islamic worldview. The Islamic calendar is based on lunar cycles and has religious significance, with significant events such as Ramadan and Hajj taking place in specified months. The concept of *"barakah"* emphasizes the sanctity and blessing of time. Muslims are encouraged to make good use of their time by participating in acts of prayer, personal growth, and positively contributing to society. Furthermore, the Islamic worldview encourages a balanced way of life.

The notion of *"mizan"* (balance) encourages moderation in all aspects of life, whether in questions of faith, personal conduct, or dealings with others. Extremism and excesses are discouraged, and Muslims are encouraged to avoid activities that could endanger themselves or others. A deep feeling of accountability and belief in the Day of Judgment is also part of the Islamic worldview. The concept of *"muhasabah"* (personal accountability) on the Day of Judgment is crucial, such that Allah will judge all people based on their actions, intentions, and faith during their worldly life. This belief in the Hereafter and the notion of *"Akhirah"* (Afterlife) inspires believers to live a life that represents their faith and make decisions consistent with Islamic teachings.

Finally, the Islamic worldview is a rich tapestry of beliefs and values that shape the lives of Muslims worldwide. It includes spiritual devotion, ethical behavior, community togetherness, and governance ideas. The concept of monotheism and submission to Allah's Divine will is central to this worldview. Muslims strive to live lives consistent with their understanding of Islam's teachings and ideals by embracing spirituality, promoting ethics, building strong communities, and advocating for social justice and just governance.

In summary, the Islamic worldview encompasses a holistic approach to life, consisting of spirituality, ethics and morals, justice, knowledge, time, balance, accountability, and compassion. It provides a framework for Muslims to navigate various aspects of life, striving for personal growth, community welfare, and a harmonious relationship with Allah, His creation, and the environment. Through their beliefs and actions, Muslims seek to embody the teachings of Islam and contribute positively to the world around them.

The following are concise and contextualized overviews of the seven philosophical and theological elements underpinning a worldview: ontology, epistemology, anthropology, teleology, morality/ethics, law/

governance, and aesthetics.

Islamic ontology is concerned with the nature of existence and reality, and central to Islamic ontology is again the concept of "*tawheed*," which asserts the Oneness and Uniqueness of Allah as the ultimate source of all existence. Muslims believe that Allah is the Creator of everything, and all aspects of the universe are dependent on His will. The concept of contingency asserts that everything in the universe is contingent upon Allah's existence. The material world is seen as a manifestation of Allah's attributes and a reflection of His Divine will. This perspective leads to a holistic view of reality, where the material and spiritual realms are intertwined, and everything points towards the presence of the Divine.

Islamic epistemology deals with how knowledge is acquired, understood, and applied. The Qur'an emphasizes the importance of knowledge and encourages believers to reflect upon the signs of creation. The Islamic tradition distinguishes between two main sources of knowledge: revelation (*wahy*), which includes the Qur'an and the Hadith, and reason (*'aql*), which involves rational thinking and reflection. The harmony between revelation and reason is seen as essential in understanding the world and living a balanced and fulfilling life. Muslims are encouraged to reflect upon the signs of creation (*ayaat*) and use reason to understand the world around them. The balance between revelation and reason ensures that knowledge is acquired through both spiritual insight and intellectual inquiry, fostering a holistic understanding of reality.

Islamic anthropology delves into the nature of human beings as understood in Islam. Muslims believe that humans are a unique creation of Allah, endowed with free will and the capacity to choose between right and wrong. Human beings are considered Allah's vicegerents (*khalifah*) on Earth, responsible for stewardship and caretaking of the planet and its resources. Islamic anthropology also centers on the concept of *fitrah*, the natural disposition with which humans are created. The *fitrah* encompasses an inherent inclination towards recognizing the existence of Allah and adhering to moral values. Human being is honored. His life is sanctified, and he is the carrier of God's trust (consciousness and free will). By having free will, humans are accountable for their choices.

All creations have been made subservient to a human being, in return, a human being serve God alone.

Islamic teleology is concerned with the purpose and ultimate goals of human life. The Islamic worldview asserts that the purpose of human existence is to worship and submit to Allah, as it is clearly stressed in the Qur'an, *"I have not created jinn and mankind except to worship Me"* [Quran 51:56]. Muslims believe that their actions in this world will be judged in the Hereafter, and their ultimate goal is to attain Allah's pleasure and Eternal Paradise. The pursuit of righteousness, good deeds, and adherence to ethical and moral values are seen as pathways to attaining Allah's pleasure and Eternal Paradise. This teleological perspective influences Muslims' choices, motivations, and priorities, guiding them towards a life that aligns with their understanding of Divine purpose.

Islamic moral and ethical values are rooted in the teachings of the Qur'an and the Hadith. The Five Pillars of Islam serve as a foundation for ethical behavior, encompassing acts of worship and acts of compassion towards others. The concept of *ihsan* encourages believers to act with excellence and sincerity in all aspects of life, whether in prayer or in their interactions with people. Concepts like *'adl* (justice), *rahma* (mercy), and *shukr* (gratitude) underscore the importance of treating others with kindness and fairness. Muslims are encouraged to practice virtues such as humility, patience, gratitude, and forgiveness in their interactions with others.

Islamic law, known as *Shari'ah*, encompasses a comprehensive system of guidance for various aspects of life, including personal conduct, family matters, commerce, and governance. While interpretations of *Shari'ah* can vary, it generally seeks to promote justice, equity, and the well-being of individuals and society at large. The relationship between religious and political authority varies across different historical and cultural contexts, but the underlying aim has always been to create a just and ethical society. Concepts like *shura* (consultation), *'adl* (justice), and *maslaha* (public good) are central to Islamic political thought.

Islamic aesthetics are characterized by their unique visual language, often defined by geometric patterns, arabesques, and intricate calligraphy.

The prohibition of depicting living beings stems from the belief that only Allah can create life. Islamic art aims to reflect the harmony and order of the cosmos, invoking a sense of contemplation and connection with the Divine. From mosques to manuscripts, Islamic aesthetics serve as a visual representation of the spiritual and philosophical dimensions of the Islamic worldview. The goal of Islamic aesthetics is often to reflect the beauty and order of the cosmos and to inspire a sense of contemplation and connection with the Divine.

In conclusion, the Islamic worldview encompasses a wide array of philosophical and practical dimensions, ranging from understanding existence to shaping ethical and moral behavior and governance. It's a comprehensive framework that guides Muslims' understanding of reality, their relationship with Allah, and their interactions with the world around them. Different aspects of the Islamic worldview interconnect to provide a holistic approach to living a meaningful and purposeful life in accordance with Islamic teachings. Rooted in monotheism and the teachings of the Qur'an, this worldview offers a comprehensive framework that guides Muslims in navigating the complexities of life, fostering a deep connection with the Divine, and contributing positively to their communities and the world at large.

CHAPTER 24

Why Religion and Why Islam?

"Indeed, the religion in the sight of Allah is Islam [Submission to His Will]." ~ (Qur'an 3:19)

True success for human beings means fulfilling the purpose of their creation or their existence, thus attaining eternal happiness in this life and in the Hereafter. Eternal happiness is achieved only through *peaceful self-submission to the will of the Creator* (this is the literal meaning of *Islam*). In other words, *Islam* = peaceful, self-submission to the will of the Creator. *Islam* is the religion that was given to Adam, Noah, Abraham, Moses, and Jesus (PBUT) and, in its final form, to Muhammad (PBUH) as a complete, perfected, and universal way of life for all mankind. A Muslim is one who chooses to submit or surrender willingly to the will of the Creator and adopts a way of life, based completely on the Creator's guidance, obeying every order. Ultimately, the Muslim seeks to gain peace with the Creator, within oneself, with fellow humans, and with the environment, to gain the reward of salvation and paradise in the Hereafter by the mercy of the Creator.

God created us and all that we see in the material world and all that we don't see in the unseen world for a purpose. While human beings (body and spirit) vary in essence from the sky, Earth, mountains, birds, and trees, they share a unified goal: to possess unwavering submission to the Divine will, even without the privilege of direct vision, and to venerate Him as though we stand before Him. Creatures, from animals to birds to all creatures on Earth, inherently understand and fulfill their Divinely ordained roles, as God has woven this understanding into their very essence. Allah says in the Qur'an, *"The seven heavens and the earth and whatever is in them exalt Him. And there is not a thing except that it exalts [Allah] by His praise, but you do not understand their [way of] exalting. Indeed, He is ever Forbearing and Forgiving"* [Qur'an 17:44]. In another passage, *"Do you not see that to Allah prostrates whoever is in the heavens and whoever is on the earth and the sun, the moon, the stars, the mountains, the trees, the moving creatures, and many of the people? But upon many, the punishment has been justified. And he whom Allah humiliates - for him there is no bestower of honor. Indeed, Allah does what He wills"* [Qur'an 22:18]. But it is the human being, whom God has exalted above much of His creation and granted dominion over a vast expanse of the known and unknown, to their will, that has been endowed with the most profound gift: consciousness and the freedom of choice.

However, these two gifts come with their own set of consequences. First, God instilled in mankind the innate belief to recognize that He is the sole Creator, yet unlike the rest of creation, the disposition to believe in and worship God alone sleeps within each soul and must be awakened, exercising the mind and the heart. Second, God may or may not choose to hold the bee or the flower accountable for its actions, but He will surely call on mankind and hold each one responsible for the choices made. This morality, coupled with mortality, are the two defining qualities of the human being. The idea that we are liable in life and after death for our beliefs and actions brings up two important questions. First, why has God obliged mankind to seek faith instead of programming it like the rest of creation? Second, how will God resurrect (putting the soul onto the reassembled body) of every being who has existed since the beginning of time?

The initial answer is that, by leading humans to recognize the existence of a Creator, God tests gratitude toward Him for transitioning from nonexistence to the experience of life and from complete unawareness to the state of rational beings. The second is that God, who created everything from nothing, can recreate it all over again with complete precision whenever He chooses and with no weariness. In fact, He promises this in the Qur'an and intends to do exactly this with His entire human creation. Allah says in the Qur'an, *"The Day when We will fold the heaven like the folding of a [written] sheet for the records. As We began the first creation, We will repeat it. [That is] a promise binding upon Us. Indeed, We will do it"* [Qur'an 21:104]. In another passage: *"And the disbeliever says, "When I have died, am I going to be brought forth alive? Does man not remember that We created him before, while he was nothing?"* [Qur'an 19:66-67].

Many religions teach the essence of all that has been said so far. Moreover, the human sense of moral conduct and value system across time and the world is remarkably common. Yet, how can we know that these ideas are true? Why are the concepts of right and wrong so widely and persistently shared? The response is twofold: God set free-willed people upon the planet to journey back to pure belief in Him alone and to strive for all that is good for themselves and the rest of creation along the way. He did not strand them in the lonely vastness of a planet adrift in space without the sustenance their bodies require or the guidance their souls need. God provides everything in the world for mankind, including water, food, fuel, and shelter, reflecting how He created different genders and connected people through family ties. Regarding the desires of human spirits, God sent two forms of guidance to humanity to awaken souls to the remembrance of Him and to facilitate the emotional and social aspects of human existence. He sent down from among mankind elevated beings as prophets and messengers. Nearly every community in the history of humanity has had them. He also revealed heavenly books through some of His messengers that all people could access. These scriptures are inscribed in remembrance of God in His own words, meant to explain who the Creator is, what He expects of humankind, and what to hope for in Him in the days of the world and the everlasting life after. Allah says in the Qur'an, *"And for every nation is a messenger. So, when their messenger comes, it will be judged between them in justice, and they will not be wronged"* [Qur'an 10:47].

The revelations that these prophets and messengers propagated enjoin belief in the same God, practice of the same human virtues, and admonition of the same ultimate destiny. However, God evolved their traditions and systems of human self-governance regarding the rights and obligations of the individual, the community, and human interaction as humankind itself developed personally, socially, and globally. It is God's way that whatever He does should come to perfection; thus, from the beginning, He willed that the human leadership of His prophets and messengers and the revealed guidance of His Books would reach a culmination at precisely the right moment in history, with Muhammad (PBUH) as His last prophet and messenger and the Qur'an as His last revelation to mankind until the end of time. The work that was re-introduced by Prophet Muhammad (PBUH) as written in the Qur'an represents the fruition of that anciently sacred tradition. The last revealed testimony in its original Arabic language is named the *Qur'an*, meaning the Recitation, the Reading, or the Proclamation, because God intended for believing men and women to read and recite it repeatedly and proclaim what is into others as a grace and as a reminder to them. It makes clear to them who they are, where they come from, where they are headed, what they are to do, what will happen if they do not listen, what will be theirs if they do, and Who it is that brought them to life and why.

Any translation of the Book is not the Qur'an itself, and this is an important distinction to keep in mind. The Qur'an only exists as God Himself revealed it, and in the specific Arabic language, He revealed it to the final messenger through His archangel Gabriel (*Jibreel*): letter-by-letter, word-by-word, verse-by-verse, segment-by-segment, and chapter-by-chapter. Prophet Muhammad (PBUH) then conveyed it verbatim to all those around him as he received it and saw to it that his companions memorized it accurately and transcribed it meticulously in writing. Fourteen hundred years later, it still holds the same language and order as when God's last messenger transmitted it to the world, bringing it to life and others to life with it, and memorized by millions around the world.

God's blessings and peace be upon Muhammad, God's last messenger, and upon all his brothers, whom God sent as prophets and messengers before him. These include Jesus, Moses, Abraham, Noah, and many others, some of whom are mentioned in the Qur'an and others who are not; peace and blessings be upon them. Allah says in the Qur'an, *"And We have already sent messengers before you. Among them are those [whose stories] We have related to you, and among them are those [whose stories] We have not related to you. And it was not for any messenger to bring a sign [or verse] except by the permission of Allah. So, when the command of Allah comes, it will be concluded in truth, and the falsifiers will thereupon lose [all]"* [Qur'an 40:78]. All the prophets and messengers have been presented to mankind as role models. The Qur'an makes no distinction between them or between their creeds. They are a single fellowship charged with bringing to the world a solitary faith: the belief in one God without associating any partner and living a righteous life. Allah says in the Qur'an, *"And We certainly sent into every nation a messenger, [saying], 'Worship Allah and shun false gods'"* [Qur'an 16:36]. Islam does not take its name from any one of the prophets and messengers, nor from their people or lands; rather, from its central, fundamental truth comes its title: Islam, the religion of willing human submission or surrender to the will of One God.

CHAPTER 25

Moral And Ethical Foundation of Islam

"Righteousness is not that you turn your faces toward the East or the West, but [true] righteousness is [in] one who believes in Allah, the Last Day, the angels, the Book, and the prophets and gives wealth, in spite of love for it, to relatives, orphans, the needy, the traveler, those who ask [for help], and for freeing slaves; [and who] establishes prayer and gives charity; [those who] fulfill their promise when they promise; and [those who] are patient in poverty and hardship and during battle. Those are the ones who have been true, and it is those who are the righteous." ~ (Qur'an 2:177)

Islam suggests a harmonious relationship between religious and scientific pursuits, acknowledging human limitations in comprehending the Divine plan. It rejects the notion of antagonism between the external (scientific) and internal (religious) realms, emphasizing that humans are an integral part of a Divinely orchestrated universe. A balanced lifestyle based on hopes and fears reinforces this perspective's ingrained sense of spiritual security. While Islam shares with other faiths the belief in a Supreme Being, it distinguishes itself by offering a theological framework and a practical guide for living. In Islam, spirituality is not a separate realm requiring renunciation of worldly matters. Instead, Islam encourages a balanced life that integrates the spiritual and material aspects founded on natural laws decreed by God.

Central to Islamic thought is the concept of *Tawheed*—the Oneness of God—around which all human activities, devotional or practical, must revolve. Islam offers a broad understanding of "worship," extending it beyond ritualistic acts like prayers and fasting to include all aspects of human life. This concept reframes life as a continuous moral responsibility, whereby every action, even the most trivial, is an act of worship. Unlike other religions that propose various pathways to spiritual perfection, either through renunciation or cycles of rebirth,

Islam asserts that perfection is attainable in this earthly life. It advocates for maximizing human potential without violating the Divinely ordained laws, offering a wide margin for individual differentiation. Islam deviates from religious doctrines like the Christian notion of original sin or the Hindu cycle of transmigration, instead asserting that humans are born pure and potentially perfect. This idea empowers individuals with the vision that spiritual and moral perfection can be achieved through continuous submission to God's laws.

Finally, Islam neither glorifies earthly life, as seen in contemporary secular liberalism nor denigrates it, as found in some interpretations of Christianity. Instead, it presents a balanced viewpoint, acknowledging earthly life as a step towards a higher form of existence. This position is epitomized in the Qur'anic verse that encourages prayers for well-being in this world and the Hereafter, *"But among them is he who says, 'Our Lord, give us in this world [that which is] good and in the Hereafter [that which is] good and protect us from the punishment of the Fire"* [Qur'an 2:201]. The Qur'an serves as an all-encompassing guide that addresses various dimensions of life, including moral, social, and spiritual dimensions. While the Qur'an addresses a multitude of topics and issues, its moral and ethical teachings can be considered central to the faith and practice of Islam.

Below are some of the foundational principles and moral teachings conveyed in the Qur'an:

- The concept of *Tawheed*, or the Oneness of God, is central to Islamic belief and serves as a foundation for ethical and moral behavior [Qur'an 112:1].

- Being truthful and honest are highly valued traits considered essential for a righteous life [Qur'an 9:119].

- The Qur'an commands believers to uphold justice at all costs, even if it is against themselves or their kin [Qur'an 4:135].

- The Qur'an encourages believers to show kindness and compassion to others [Qur'an 2:195; 76:8-9], and teaches that the only thing that differentiates people in the eyes of God is their level of piety [Qur'an 49:13]—not color, race, ethnicity, wealth, education, social status, power, fame, etc.

* While the Qur'an permits warfare under certain conditions, such as self-defense, it imposes strict ethical guidelines [Qur'an 16:126].

* The Qur'an places a strong emphasis on the acquisition of knowledge [Qur'an 96:1-5].

* The Qur'an gives considerable attention to family life, advises believers to treat their family members with respect and kindness, and puts parents' status right after the Almighty Himself [Qur'an 17:23].

* The Qur'an speaks frequently of personal accountability, underscoring the belief that individuals are responsible for their actions [Qur'an 41:46].

* Islam encourages ethical financial practices and warns against exploitative behaviors like usury [Qur'an 2:275].

* Being truthful and honest are paramount virtues in Islamic moral ethics. Speaking the truth is not just encouraged but commanded [Qur'an 33:70].

* The Qur'an often encourages Muslims to help others, particularly those who are in need; this extends to giving charity and assisting the oppressed [Qur'an 2:261]. Giving charity and assisting the oppressed transcends religious affiliation.

* Arrogance is strongly discouraged in the Qur'an—instead, humility is promoted as a virtue [Qur'an 31:18].

* In the Qur'an, patience is not just a virtue but a skill to cultivate— whether in the face of adversity or in dealing with others, patience is highly valued [Qur'an 2:153].

* The Qur'an considers human life to be sacred and cautioned against taking a life unjustly. Slaying a soul for no just cause is equated

to slaying the whole of humanity and saving a soul is equated to saving the whole humanity [Qur'an 5:32].

•   Being grateful, both to Allah and to people, is a recurring theme in the Qur'an [Qur'an 14:7].

•   The Qur'an encourages the honoring of contracts and keeping one's promises as a sign of a believer's integrity [Qur'an 5:1].

•   The Qur'an advises treating neighbors kindly and strongly emphasizes the importance of maintaining kinship ties. The severing of such ties is seen as a serious moral failing. Family is regarded as a cornerstone of a stable and healthy society, and individuals are encouraged to extend kindness, support, and understanding toward their family members [Qur'an 47:22]. Another verse states the importance of family ties as part of a broader ethical framework, *"Worship Allah and associate nothing with Him, and to parents do good, and to relatives, orphans, the needy, the near neighbor, the neighbor farther away, the companion at your side, the traveler, and those whom your right hands possess. Indeed, Allah does not like those who are self-deluding and boastful"* [Qur'an 4:36].

•   The Qur'an also places considerable emphasis on the protection and moral and ethical education of one's offspring. Parents are encouraged to safeguard their children's welfare, provide them with sound upbringing and education, and guide them in matters of morality, ethics, and faith. This is considered not only a social responsibility but also a spiritual one [Qur'an 66:6].

•   Additionally, the Qur'an offers narratives of prophets and righteous people who are models of parental concern and guidance, such as the story of Luqman advising his son, *"And [mention, O Muhammad], when Luqman said to his son while he was instructing him, 'O my son, do not associate [anything] with Allah. Indeed, association [with Him] is great injustice'"* [Qur'an 31:13].

These Qur'anic teachings form part of the moral and ethical fabric that Islamic tradition aims to weave into both individual character and communal life. The values of family cohesion and protection of progeny serve multiple functions: they contribute to individual well-being, fortify social stability, and are means for the transmission of ethical and religious values to future generations. Hence, they are given significant attention in the moral and ethical framework of the Qur'an. Kindness to others and to animals is emphasized [Qur'an 90:17]. The Qur'an considers all humans as equal in the eyes of God [Qur'an 49:13]. Family cohesion and maintaining good relations are commanded [Qur'an 13:25]. Individual responsibility for one's actions is highlighted [Qur'an 99:7-8]. The prohibition of usury and usurious practices are laid out [Qur'an 2:275] for just economic and commercial transactions. Honesty and fairness in trade and commerce, and in all business and financial transactions is commanded [Qur'an 83:1-3]. Giving to the poor and needy is not just encouraged but is also obligatory through zakat (almsgiving)—which is the third pillar of Islam [Qur'an 9:60]. Physical purity is often associated with spiritual purity [Qur'an 5:6]. This compilation offers a glimpse into the rich ethical framework that the Qur'an provides for the moral and social conduct of individuals and communities, aiming to foster personal development, social harmony, and spiritual growth. For a more detailed study of moral and ethical teachings of the Qur'an, see the work of M. A. Draz, The Moral World of the Qur'an (Draz, 2008) and the work of Ismail Raji Al-Faruqi, Al-Tawhid (Al-Faruqi I. R., 2000).

The ethical and moral framework within Islamic tradition is not solely derived from the Qur'an, despite its primary position as the ultimate source of guidance for Muslims. The Hadith literature, which encompasses the sayings, actions, and approvals of the Prophet Muhammad (PBUH), significantly complements and elaborates upon the ethical and moral directives found in the Qur'an. The Hadiths are a practical manifestation of the Qur'an's teachings, providing a tangible application of its principles through the Prophet's life.

For instance, where the Qur'an provides commandments to uphold justice, the Hadiths detail what justice looks like in various situations, ranging from commerce to interpersonal relationships. They explain the general good qualities that the Qur'an talks about, like kindness, honesty, and compassion. They also show how the Prophet lived these excellent qualities, making him a role model for all Muslims.

Additionally, the Hadith literature talks about situations and issues that might not be directly addressed in the Qur'an. This makes it possible for a flexible interpretation of right and wrong behavior that can be changed to fit different situations. This collection of works is not only crucial for understanding how Islamic morals and ethics work in real life, but it is also necessary for Islamic law (*fiqh*), which uses the Hadith to make decisions about how Muslims should behave morally and ethically.

So, the Hadith does not work independently; it is connected to the Qur'an in a way that cannot be separated. It is a secondary but essential source that gives Islam's moral and ethical teachings more depth and dimension.

For a more detailed study of moral and ethical teachings of the Prophetic teachings, visit www.sunnah.com—the online resource of major Hadith collections.

CHAPTER 26

The Prophet of Islam and What He Taught

"There has certainly been for you in the Messenger of Allah an excellent pattern for anyone whose hope is in Allah and the Last Day and [who] remembers Allah often." ~ (Qur'an 33:21)

Muhammad (PBUH) was born in Makkah in the Arabian Peninsula, a town known as a hub of trade and pilgrimage; it was visited by people from Yemen in the south and the Levant in the north. Arabs are descendants of Prophet Abraham (PBUH) through his firstborn child, Ishmael (PBUH), Ismail in Arabic. Prophet Abraham (PBUH) made a supplication for the Arab guardianship of the sacred house of Ka'abah, and for a prophet to be sent to guide them and the world. Arabs had solid characteristics of bravery, generosity, altruism, trustworthiness, and sharp memory to receive, preserve, and propagate God's last message.

Arabia was an isolated piece of land, but at the same time, it was situated between two rival powers of its time - the Byzantines in the west and the Sassanids in the east. Due to the geographic location of the Arabian Peninsula and being isolated from the rest of the world, Arabs were not influenced or assimilated by either culture or civilization—a perfect condition for maintaining the last message in its pristine form.

The political culture of Arabia consisted of tribal laws where clans formed alliances to defend each other, their territories, resources, and land. Tribal rulings and customs were the only laws and were enforced with no mercy and in accordance with the whims and caprices of the rulers. Verbalized history, poetry, and verbal literature of tribal storytelling helped tribes preserve their identity. Most Arabs were unlettered, and for that reason, verbal tradition was common. Poets from different tribes would attempt to outshine one another at public poetry forums. Poetry was something that could trigger conflicts and violence, but it also had the ability to be the cause of peace.

For this reason, the highly sophisticated eloquence of the Qur'an, with its rich meaning in its verses, beauty in its expressions, and greatness in its style, posed a big challenge to the Arab pagans. They knew that Prophet Muhammad (PBUH) was unlettered and was not a poet, yet they could not explain why he had suddenly become eloquent in literature. The Qur'an itself poses a challenge to anyone who thinks that it did not come from the Almighty God to produce something similar, and because Makkan pagans could not fulfill the challenge, they resorted to discrediting the prophet (PBUH)—a pattern that has since been repeated throughout history.

In pre-Islamic Arabia, the concept of human rights was non-existent. The strong would crush the weak, and tyrants were celebrated. It was an extremely patriarchal society where women had no rights, and newborn baby girls were buried alive. Idolatry was the dominant faith, and people worshiped all kinds of idols. There were a few Arabs who called themselves *"Hanifs,"* who worshiped one God and could be traced back to Prophet Abraham (PBUH). While, in general, Arabs of that time had some good qualities, they were also characterized by extremely unpleasant morals and values that had become norms within their society—particularly related to women, orphans, slaves, the poor, and the vulnerable, and in relation to their religion. The Qur'an refers to this pre-Islam period as *jahiliyyah*, or "the age of ignorance." But *jahiliyyah* is a state of mind that breeds injustice, corruption, violence, and terror. Therefore, the events of the seventh century Arabia that the Prophet Muhammad (PBUH) had to grapple with have much to teach us about the events of our time, in any geographical context.

Prophet Muhammad (PBUH) challenged three core matters that upset the status quo in Makkah. First, the irrational idea that material things are worthy of worship; instead, he invited people to worship the One true God who created and sustains the universe and everything in it. Second, the social hierarchy that maintained the superiority of certain tribes and families at the expense of others, and instead, he proclaimed that no human being is superior to another because of race, gender, or any physical quality; he rejected all forms of racism, and he argued that the only superiority among people is that of moral excellence or piety. Third, he demolished the socio-economic system of injustice, corruption, and harmful practices of society. Instead, he built a society based on social justice, charity, dignity, respect for others, and a strong spiritual and moral foundation.

The Prophet (PBUH) propagated his message in Makkah for thirteen years, but as Islam began to impact society, he and his followers were perceived by the Makkan elites as a direct threat to their social, economic, and political privileges that came with their control of the Ka'abah. The Ka'aba is a cubic structure situated at the heart of Islam's holiest mosque in Makkah. The Ka'aba, the first house of worship ever built on Earth dedicated to One God, has endured as the sanctum of Islam. It symbolizes unity for all Muslims by providing a directional focal point for their daily prayers, regardless of their location in the world. Our father, Adam, first built the Ka'aba when he descended to Earth. Later, it went into disuse after the floods of Prophet Noah. It was Prophet Abraham and his first son, Ishmael, who were asked by Allah to rebuild it on the same site. Today, Muslim men and women of diverse races, nations, languages, colors, cultures, and statuses unite in their daily prayers facing the Ka'aba, making for one human community worshiping one God. However, at the time, the Prophet Muhammad (PBUH) was met with strong opposition, hostility, anger, intense hatred, and slander, as well as violence, torture, and boycott.

In the early years of Islam's formation, the elites of Makkah adopted varying approaches to dealing with the nascent Muslim community, contingent upon the social standing of those involved. Physical violence and torture were standard suppression methods for the less privileged Muslims, who lacked the protective sponsorship of powerful clans. These vulnerable individuals bore the brunt of the elite's campaign to snuff out the fledgling Islamic movement. Conversely, for those Muslims hailing from noble backgrounds or influential clans, the Makkan leadership employed a subtler approach. These individuals were subjected to ridicule, scorn, and social ostracization, like today's "cancel culture". The elites sought to delegitimize their views and undermine their credibility, engaging them in a battle for intellectual and social capital rather than physical coercion.

Yet, when it became evident that neither physical nor psychological duress would sway the Prophet Muhammad (PBUH) and his followers from their path, the Makkan leadership resorted to an alternative tactic. Acknowledging the stubbornness of the Prophet's convictions and the expanding base of his following, the Makkan elites extended an olive branch, albeit one steeped in their vested interests. They approached the Prophet Muhammad (PBUH) with a proposition: in exchange for ceasing his religious preaching, they offered him a catalog of temptations, including significant wealth, political power, and even a marriage into one of the city's leading families.

This was a pivotal moment, symbolic of the Makkan leadership's realization that neither coercion nor disdain would impede the momentum of the Islamic movement. Desperate to maintain their sociopolitical hierarchy, they aimed to lure the Prophet (PBUH) with worldly allurements. However, the Prophet (PBUH) unequivocally rejected these offers, reinforcing the spiritual core of his mission and his unwavering commitment to the monotheistic message he was propagating.

In light of these failures, the Makkan elites escalated their campaign against the Muslims, applying maximum pressure on all fronts to stifle the Islamic message and those who adhered to it. Increased tensions, persecution, and several sociopolitical plots intended to isolate and weaken the Muslim community characterized the era that followed the Prophet's rejection of their alluring offers.

Throughout the Makkan period, the Prophet (PBUH) forbade Muslims to respond unkindly or use any form of violence as retaliation. Instead, he nurtured them away from hatred, violence, and extremism. The Prophet (PBUH) established *Dar Al-Arqam* as a center of learning to educate and develop his followers both intellectually and spiritually and to keep them away from the conflict zones.

The Prophet (PBUH) knew he was sent as a mercy to all humanity, and he asked Muslims to be patient and persistent in their suffering to overcome short-term challenges so that the last message of God could reach all people. When the pressure became unbearable, and some Muslims complained to the Prophet (PBUH), he reminded them of previous believers who suffered more but did not turn away from the faith and reassured them that the Lord would accomplish His purpose.

After thirteen years of persistent suffering, the Prophet (PBUH) and his followers received an invitation to migrate to Madinah. The Arabs of Madinah pledged to take the Prophet (PBUH) as their leader and to defend him and his message. The migration or *Hijrah* took place in 622 CE when close to 200 Muslim families from Makkah migrated to Madinah with the Prophet (PBUH). This marked a shift for Muslims from persecution to nation-building.

Moving away from tribalism, the Prophet (PBUH) established the first civil society in Madinah. A civil treaty was signed by all community members of Madinah that laid out the framework for a political constitution that had never been seen before in Arabia, and for that matter, in the world, until the publishing of the Magna Carta in 1215 CE. The document is referred to as the "Constitution of Madinah," and it defined the reality of a city nation-state with a common citizenship, consisting of Makkan Muslim migrants, Madinan Muslim hosts, Madinan Jews, and Madinan polytheists. These groups made a unified community (*Ummah*), having equal rights and responsibilities, being a unique phenomenon at the time.

The treaty provided a federal structure with a centralized authority on matters of public finance, security, and national defense, while at the same time, the distinct tribes and clans in various districts enjoyed autonomy in certain matters of social, cultural, and spiritual character. The Prophet (PBUH), as the leader and arbiter of the community, based his actions on the common law and negotiated in this legally binding civil treaty.

Madinah became a paradigm of a multi-ethnic, multicultural, pluralistic society, with a rule of law and religious and cultural tolerance, and where each member of the community was guaranteed protection and religious freedom—a forerunner of a contemporary nation-state.

In Madinah, the Prophet (PBUH) introduced many other political, social, and economic reforms. Madinah, as a city-state, was modeled on

Islamic values of human rights, women's rights, the rights of minorities, and peaceful co-existence. It was governed by a civil constitution and a system of consultation (*shura*), with full respect, tolerance, and acceptance of other religions and cultures. This level of pluralism (religious and cultural) and tolerance would be the hallmark of Muslim governance—something that was scarce in Europe at that time.

Madinan society moved away from tribalism, and into a centralized political system abiding by the rule of law, diplomacy, and international relations, as well as a national army for maintaining peace and security. The diplomacy of the Prophet (PBUH) was exceptional, especially his effort to reach out to the Christian communities. He negotiated and signed treaties of peace and friendship with the Christians of Najran, the Monks of Sinai, the Christians of Persia, the Christians of the world, the Assyrian Christians, and the Armenian Christians of Jerusalem (Morrow, 2013).

The Prophet (PBUH) established the public treasury or *Baytul al-Maal* and introduced reforms on commercial ownership, contracts, social security, distribution of wealth through institutions of charity, and endowments. He also redefined economic activities and factors of production free from usury and moral hazards. In the social sphere, reforms were introduced on rules related to marriage, inheritance laws, and child support. There was also a lot of emphasis on education and learning.

For the thirteen years of struggle in Makkah to eradicate idolatry and corruption, the Muslims were violently persecuted, tortured, and embargoed. On more than one occasion, Muslims had asked for permission to fight back, but the Prophet (PBUH) replied that the Almighty God had not given him permission to fight back. The Prophet (PBUH) knew that aggression breeds further aggression, and the holy city would have turned into a nightmare of violence and a bloodbath. He was trying to teach them forgiveness, tolerance, mercy, and perseverance.

However, even after the migration (hijrah), the Makkan elites did not leave the Prophet (PBUH), and Muslim migrants lived in peace in Madinah. They waged many consecutive aggressive battles against the

Prophet (PBUH) for about six years until they signed the peace treaty of Hudaybiyyah before the peaceful opening of Makkah. In Madinah, the Almighty God granted permission to those who had been attacked, wronged, or driven out of their homes to fight back on condition that they do not commit aggression and always opt for peace. All the battles fought during the Prophet's lifetime adhered to those Divine commands, and he set the standard and rules of engagement for those who followed him. They were defensive battles, not aggressive battles, which is contrary to frequent European misrepresentation and distortion of these battles.

During these defensive battles, the Prophet (PBUH) established moral rules of engagement that were previously unknown in any civilization, whether in the East or West, in ancient or contemporary times. For instance, he commanded that fighting should be directed only at those who initiated hostilities. There was to be no fighting against or killing of women, children, the elderly, or people engaged in worship from any faith. The conditions also outlined that there would be no collateral damage, no destruction of places of worship, no killing of animals or cutting of trees, no mutilating and disrespecting dead bodies, and no torture or harm of prisoners of war.

The opening of Makkah was the greatest conquest in the history of mankind, through which the Almighty God honored His religion, His Prophet (PBUH), and believers in general. The opening of Makkah was preceded by the peace treaty of Hudaybiyyah that was signed between the Prophet (PBUH) and Makkan elites two years earlier, such that there would be no aggression and fighting from both sides for ten years. The treaty proved to be the turning point in Islamic history by giving the Prophet (PBUH) the needed breathing space to propagate the message of Islam freely. Due to the Makkan elites' tough negotiations, the terms of the agreement were perceived unfavorable to the Muslims by his companions, yet the Prophet (PBUH) opted for peace and was farsighted enough to see it as a great victory, as the Qur'an describes it.

The Makkan elites broke the treaty two years after its enforcement, and the Prophet (PBUH) responded by marching to Makkah with a large army, which entered the city peacefully, without any resistance or bloodshed. It was here that the Prophet (PBUH) exhibited great acts of graciousness, benevolence, magnanimity, and peace as he entered the gates of Makkah, his head down with humility, and proclaimed a general amnesty to all the people of Makkah. He also gave a special privilege to his archenemy, Abu Sufiyan, the Makkan leader, by declaring that whosoever took refuge in Abu Sufiyan's house was safe, whosoever confined himself to his house was safe, and whoever entered the Ka'abah was safe.

The Prophet Muhammad's prophethood took place in the "daylight of history," where almost everything about him is known: the place he was born, the places where he lived, where he died, and where he was buried. His lineage and his descendants are fully known. The names of his friends, companions, and adversaries are also known. What he liked, what he ate, how he dressed, and even how he grew his hair and beard is known. There are details of what he looked like, without images, and what his mannerisms were like, as well. The chronicles of his practice, his sayings, and his approvals have been extensively documented (Hadith collections), separate from the revelation he received (the Qur'an). These chronicles are supported and authenticated by documented unbroken chains of communication handed down and leading up to a source among the Prophet's (PBUH) companions and contemporaries. Hundreds of Prophet Muhammad's (PBUH) biographies have been written, both in classical and contemporary periods. Many of these biographies have been translated and are available in different languages. More recently, there are Western scholars who are more sympathetic to the figure of Prophet Muhammad (PBUH), who have also written biographies that are more objective than the traditional Western distorted view of the Prophet (PBUH), such as Karen Armstrong (2021), Craig Considine (2020), Lesley Hazleton (2014), and Juan Cole (2018), among others. There is no justification for one to remain uninformed about the esteemed Prophet of Islam (PBUH) and leave themselves vulnerable to the distortions presented by critics, Islamophobic individuals, and far-right elements that have influenced discussions about Islam in the West.

A prophet is a unique person—a human being—yet he speaks for the Almighty God. The difficult task has always been that of dealing with the human being as a prophet. It is easy to go to one extreme of making him a Divine (as the Christians did to Jesus) or making him an ordinary person, as we see in the contemporary Western discourse about the Prophet Muhammad (PBUH). One must contrast the delicate balance offered by Islam. Muhammad (PBUH) is presented as a servant, messenger, and "perfect example" of a human being, but he is not a Divine or ordinary person. He speaks for God, but he is not God. He is the object of our gratitude, ardent love, devotion, and unswerving allegiance, but he is not the object of our worship. The testimony of faith, "There is no god, but God; Muhammad (PBUH) is the servant and messenger of God," prevents Muslims from making him Divine. Muslims are also asked in the Qur'an to invoke God's blessings and peace on Muhammad (PBUH). It is not possible for those who invoke God's blessings and peace to the Prophet (PBUH) to denigrate him to the level of just an ordinary person. Muslims, thus, find in the Prophet Muhammad (PBUH) the perfect example to follow and a mighty servant of God and messenger to love and respect.

The Prophet Muhammad (PBUH) left behind a rich human legacy, and to love him and follow him is tantamount to loving and obeying God Himself as per the Qur'anic injunctions [Qur'an 4:80]. It is also to set upon a lifelong journey of aligning oneself to the Divine will. He was an orphan and a father, a husband and a widower, a shepherd and a trader, a commander and a spiritualist, a ruler of his people and among the poorest of them, a father who suffered the heartbreak of burying his children, and a grandfather who relished the delightful time with his grandchildren. He embodied and exemplified truthfulness, justice, forgiveness, compassion, tolerance, restraint, perseverance, thankfulness, gratitude, cleanliness, modesty, and many more characteristics of beauty.

The Prophet Muhammad (PBUH), commenting on the purpose of his mission, said, "I was sent to perfect moral and ethical behavior." Allah says in the Qur'an, "*There has certainly been for you in the Messenger of Allah an excellent model (of moral and ethical behavior) for anyone whose hope is in Allah and the Last Day and (who) remembers Allah often*" [Qur'an 33:21]. Indeed, he was the embodiment of the Qur'anic teachings in his day-to-day life and dealings with others. The Prophet

(PBUH) left behind a corpus of his teachings on moral and ethical behaviors. These are some of his teachings:

The Prophet (PBUH) emphasized the worship of God without associating any partners with Him. He stressed the importance of good manners, ethical behavior, and a compassionate disposition. He advocated for justice, fairness, and equality among all members of society, regardless of their status, race, or gender. The Prophet (PBUH) laid significant emphasis on acquiring knowledge. He gave special importance to family bonds, particularly the relations between parents and children. He advocated for the fair and respectful treatment of women. Following the Qur'an, he prohibited usurious practices, emphasized the importance of charity, and provided guidelines on fair economics and trade. The Prophet (PBUH) was a champion of kind treatment of animals and respect for the environment. Following the Qur'an, he taught environmental protection through the reduction of waste and conservation of natural resources. The Prophet (PBUH) taught the importance of forgiveness and advised his followers to treat others with kindness and compassion. He also encouraged people to be aware of their actions and to judge themselves before being judged by God. As part of his teachings, the Prophet (PBUH) gave instructions about cleanliness and basic hygiene. He emphasized the importance of honesty and integrity in all dealings. He also taught that humility is a virtue and arrogance is a vice. He defined the rights and responsibilities of neighbors. He emphasized the importance of showing respect to elders and kindness to young people. The Prophet (PBUH) promoted peaceful coexistence with people of other faiths, peaceful resolution of conflicts, and discouraged unnecessary violence. Following the Qur'an, he instituted a mechanism of obligatory and voluntary charity for social welfare. He emphasized the significance of personal freedom within the boundaries of ethical conduct. He warned against the dissemination of falsehood and encouraged intellectual honesty and honesty in financial transactions. The Prophet (PBUH) encouraged being generous and showing hospitality to guests. He warned against the squandering of time and encouraged individuals to strive for self-sufficiency and dignity through work. Following the Qur'an, the Prophet (PBUH) commanded the honoring of treaties, agreements, and promises.

He also emphasized the concept of collective responsibility of the community. The Prophet (PBUH) placed a high value on education and the sacredness of human life.

It was narrated from 'Aisha, the wife of the Prophet (PBUH) that when she was asked about the character of the Prophet Muhammad (PBUH), she replied by saying, "His character was the Qur'an." What she meant was that the Prophet Muhammad (PBUH) exemplified the teachings of the Qur'an in his actions, behaviors, and interactions. He was a living embodiment of the Qur'an, practicing what was revealed and serving as a model for his followers. This Hadith stresses the importance of aligning one's actions with the teachings of the Qur'an and exemplifies the high moral and ethical standards of the Prophet Muhammad (PBUH).

CHAPTER 27

What the Qur'an Says About the Purpose of Life

"And I did not create the jinn and mankind except to worship Me." ~ (Qur'an 51:56)

In Islamic theology, the purpose of life is perceived through a rich tapestry that encompasses various dimensions including the worship of Allah, moral and ethical upliftment, and a commitment to community service. Central to this theological perspective is the mandate to worship Allah, a directive emphatically stipulated in the Qur'an [Qur'an 51:56], which states that the primary reason for the creation of *jinn* (spirit) and mankind is to worship Allah. This essential act of worship extends far beyond the realm of ritualistic practices, extending to a deep-seated acknowledgment and reverence of the Divine. The five foundational pillars—the testimony that there is no god, except Allah; Muhammad is the last messenger and servant of Allah, the five daily prayers (*salat*), fasting during the month of Ramadan (*sawm*), the giving of alms (*zakat*), and the pilgrimage to Mecca (*hajj*) are a mere entry point into a much deeper, more extensive commitment to God that permeates every facet of human existence.

Within this framework, the pursuit of knowledge about Allah is an integral aspect of worship. Knowing Allah is not merely an intellectual exercise, it is a transformative endeavor that deepens one's faith, enhances moral and ethical conduct, and strengthens the spiritual connection with the Divine. Knowledge of Allah's attributes, actions, and signs in the universe instills awe and reverence, motivating the believer to engage more diligently in acts of worship. Thus, the quest to know Allah is both an act of devotion and a means to enrich and deepen one's relationship with the Divine.

The pursuit of moral excellence, known as "*Ihsan*," also emerges as a significant purpose of life in Islamic teaching, promoting the cultivation of virtues such as honesty, integrity, patience, and kindness. This moral and ethical landscape navigates beyond personal development to embrace a broader societal context where individuals are urged to foster justice, equality, and fairness, laying the foundations for a harmonious and just society. It encourages an active service to others, translating the principles of compassion and mercy that are central to Islamic teachings, into tangible actions that uplift communities and foster environments of mutual respect and empathy.

Moreover, Islam advocates for a robust intellectual engagement with the world, encouraging the acquisition of knowledge and intellectual growth as vital aspects of human life. This perspective was established with the first revelation to the Prophet Muhammad (PBUH) being "*Iqra!*" (Read! or Recite!). Allah says in the Qur'an, "*Recite in the name of your Lord who created. Created man from a clinging substance. Recite, and your Lord is the most Generous. Who taught by the pen. Taught man that which he knew not*" [Qur'an 96:1-5], a powerful endorsement of learning, seeking knowledge, and exploration. Consequently, Islamic tradition venerates scientific discovery and the scholarly exploration of the natural world as a medium through which individuals can appreciate the intricacies of Allah's creation, developing a deeper understanding and appreciation of the Divine through the study of His signs in the natural world.

When it comes to knowledge and learning, Islamic civilization established itself as a rational, knowledge-based, human-focused, ethical-based, and religious- and cultural-tolerant civilization. Fortunately, it did not experience intellectual tension between faith and reason, religion and science, religion, and philosophy, as the case of other traditions. In Islam, respect for truth is common to religion, science, and philosophy. The distinction between them lies in the kind of knowledge they seek and the methods they use to obtain it. The Qur'an not only provided the essential teachings for human salvation, but it also inspired early Muslims to acquire knowledge and learning, gave them the spirit of rational investigation, discovery, and embrace of science and innovation. Furthermore, the Islamic worldview articulates life on Earth as a transient stage, a preparation ground for life Hereafter through intellectual, moral, and spiritual development. This notion also instills a sense of accountability in individuals, urging them to lead lives of righteousness guided by the ethical and moral precepts of Islam, all aimed at seeking Allah's pleasure and preparing for eventual accountability in the Afterlife. It nurtures a consciousness of the transient nature of earthly life, guiding individuals to prioritize actions and choices that align with the Divine principles and favorably position them in the life Hereafter. At the time when Medieval Europe was in the "Dark Ages," Muslims gathered knowledge of the world, translated it into Arabic, studied it, synthesized it, built new ideas on it, and shared it freely with the rest of humanity. They found great institutions of learning and research. They also produced many new scientific ideas and innovations that formed the foundation of modern science and the modern world and became the basis for the European Renaissance (Saliba, 2011).

From a strategic verse, *"And I did not create the jinn (spirit) and mankind except to worship Me"* [Qur'an 51:56], Islamic teachings outline a multi-dimensional life's purpose by harmonizing spiritual, ethical, intellectual, and social dimensions into a unified and a cohesive framework. It provides individuals with a navigational compass grounded in the central principle of Tawheed—the unequivocal Oneness of God— guiding them to lead lives that harmoniously balance these various dimensions in a manner that fosters spiritual depth, moral integrity, intellectual rigor, and societal harmony. It paints life as a rich and diverse landscape, a nurturing ground for individuals to cultivate a deep connection with the Divine, achieve personal growth, and contribute positively to the community, all while keeping an eye on the ultimate success in the Hereafter. This rich, nuanced, and integrated approach to life's purpose offers a fulfilling and meaningful pathway, guiding individuals to navigate the complexities of human existence with wisdom and grace, aligned with a deep spiritual resonance and a commitment to the upliftment of the self and the community.

In the Qur'an, the story of the creation of Adam, the first human, is of paramount importance as it sets the foundation for many of the theological and philosophical underpinnings of Islam. It highlights the essential purpose of human life according to Islamic teachings. Let us delve into the pertinent aspects of this narrative, as delineated in various passages throughout the Qur'an. At the outset, it is noted that Adam was created by Allah from clay, a symbol of humility, as it is a substance found ubiquitously and which possesses malleable properties. This creation event signifies the beginning of humanity and, by extension, the commencement of the human capacity for knowledge, will, and agency.

Following the creation, Adam was endowed with knowledge by Allah, a process that emphasized the noble stature of humans, standing as God's vicegerents (*khalifa*) on Earth. It is narrated that Allah taught Adam the names of all things, illustrating the profound capacity for understanding and learning that humans are gifted with. After the process of endowing knowledge, Adam was commanded to dwell in the Garden with his spouse, Eve. The primary objective of their life, and by extrapolation, the life of all humans, was to worship Allah through a life of righteousness, conscious obedience, and the seeking of knowledge to better appreciate the signs of God in the cosmos. This purpose is further underlined through various narratives in the Qur'an, where the emphasis is placed on the obligation of humans to recognize the Oneness of God (*Tawheed*) and to lead a life rooted in ethical principles that uphold justice, compassion, and truth. Worship in this context is not limited to ritualistic practices but encompasses all actions undertaken with a consciousness of God's presence and guidance.

Central to the Islamic worldview is the notion of life as a test (trials and tribulations), with Adam's story being the primordial example. The transgression of God's order by Adam and Eve in consuming the forbidden tree stands as an allegory for human fallibility and the propensity to err. Yet, it is through seeking forgiveness and mending one's ways with God (since He is the Only One who accepts repentance) that human beings can fulfill their purpose on Earth. The earthly life is thus perceived as a transient phase, a preparation for the Afterlife, where individuals would be held accountable for their actions. It instills a sense of moral responsibility, urging individuals to cultivate virtues such as patience, honesty, and humility, grounded in the Divine guidance that is encapsulated in the Qur'an and the traditions of the Prophet Muhammad (PBUH). The story of Adam in the Qur'an articulates the rich tapestry of life's purpose in Islam, marked by a deep-seated call to knowledge, worship, moral uprightness, and societal activism. It navigates the dialectics of freedom and responsibility, error and repentance, worldly engagement and spiritual transcendence, forging a pathway that aims at the realization of human potential in its fullest measure, and guided by the beacon of Divine light. It encourages individuals to traverse the Earthly sojourn with a heart and mind grounded in God's remembrance, working tirelessly towards achieving a state of balance and harmony in oneself and the world at large.

The teaching of Adam by Allah holds profound theological and philosophical significance in the Islamic tradition. When Allah taught Adam the names of all things, as mentioned in [Qur'an 2:30-33], it was a clear affirmation of the intellectual potential and the nobility of human beings. This was a demonstration of the distinctive cognitive abilities endowed to humans, setting them apart even from angels, who are well-regarded in Islamic theology. Angels do not carry the capacity to disobey God, and they spend all moments of their lives obeying and praising God. The process of teaching Adam thus exalts the status of humans, portraying them as beings capable of learning, understanding, rationalizing, and utilizing knowledge in multifaceted ways. The direct endowment of knowledge by Allah to Adam implies that humans are the crown of creation, entrusted with a special role and responsibility on Earth. This act amplifies the nobility of humans, placing them in a position of leadership and stewardship on Earth to govern the Earth based on the principles of justice, wisdom, and mercy as derived from the Divine knowledge imparted to them.

The act of teaching Adam personally by Allah also illustrates Allah's mercy, benevolence, and nurturing aspect, wherein He prepares Adam (and, by extension, humanity) to carry out their Earthly responsibilities proficiently. This nurturing relationship lays the foundations for a life guided by the conscious realization of God's presence and seeking knowledge through His guidance, fostering a path of righteousness and closeness to the Divine. By teaching Adam, Allah essentially established the precedent for the process of revelation, a Divine mechanism through which knowledge, guidance, and wisdom would be transmitted to humanity through the series of prophets that followed, culminating in the revelation of the Qur'an to Prophet Muhammad (PBUH). This establishes a continuously guided pathway, affirming the necessity of seeking knowledge and wisdom through Divine revelations and guidance.

Even though Adam was taught a vast amount of knowledge, Islamic tradition encourages the continuous pursuit of knowledge, endorsing a humble disposition acknowledging that what one knows is just a tiny fraction of the vast ocean of knowledge that Allah possesses, as Allah states in the Qur'an, "*Should He not know what He created? And He is the Subtle, the Aware*" [Qur'an 67:14]. This promotes a culture of humility, introspection, and continuous learning, seeking to understand the Divine signs in the cosmos. The fact that it was Allah who taught Adam, magnifies the honor and responsibility bestowed upon humans. It paints a picture of humans as beings of immense potential and capability, encouraging a diligent pursuit of knowledge, grounded in Divine guidance. It sets the stage for a deep, nurturing relationship between the Creator and the created, underscoring the central role of knowledge in fulfilling the purpose of life as delineated in Islamic theology and fostering a landscape rich with exploration, understanding, and a continuous journey towards attaining wisdom and closeness to the Divine. It firmly establishes the foundations of a tradition steeped in the reverence for knowledge, grounded in the Divine pedagogy imparted by Allah to Adam, framing a path of righteousness navigated through wisdom, understanding, and a deep-seated consciousness of Allah's guidance.

The Prophet Muhammad (PBUH) is reported to have said, "Seeking knowledge is an obligation upon every Muslim" (Sunan Ibn Majah). This stresses the importance of seeking knowledge in Islam—religious or worldly. Furthermore, the Qur'an often encourages believers to reflect, ponder, and seek knowledge, highlighting the signs in the universe as indicators of the Creator's magnificence. Nevertheless, no matter how much knowledge a human being attains, it remains essential to maintain a humble disposition. This humility arises from recognizing the limitations of human knowledge and Allah's infinite knowledge and wisdom.

The narrative of Adam and Eve eating from the forbidden tree, as detailed in various passages in the Qur'an including [Qur'an 7:19-22] and [Qur'an 2:35-36], holds deep philosophical connotations, offering insights into the nature of human beings, moral choices, and their consequences. The ability to choose to obey or disobey Allah epitomizes the presence of free will in humans. It sets the stage for a world where moral and ethical dilemmas exist, and individuals are accorded the agency to navigate through these dilemmas by making choices, thereby delineating a pathway of moral development and growth. The notion of disobedience introduces the concept of moral accountability, where actions are met with consequences. This provides a robust framework for a morally conscious society where individuals are cognizant of the repercussions of their actions. The act of consuming the forbidden fruit mirrors the intrinsic human tendency to err and transgress boundaries. It depicts a fundamental aspect of human nature: curiosity and propensity to overstep limits set for them, illustrating the Islamic perspective on the innate imperfections and vulnerabilities of humans.

From the Islamic standpoint, making mistakes and learning from them is a vital aspect of human growth and development. It portrays the journey of self-improvement and refinement through experiences and lessons learned from past errors. The involvement of Satan in encouraging disobedience highlights the external influences that can lead individuals astray. It warns against the perils of succumbing to negative influences and encourages individuals to be vigilant of the potential deceptive allure that diverges them from the path of righteousness. Simultaneously, it presents an opportunity for resistance, emphasizing the role of Divine guidance in aiding individuals to resist and overcome evil, fostering a morally upright character through conscious efforts and Divine assistance. Following their disobedience, Adam and Eve experienced shame and remorse, showcasing the inherent moral compass in humans (fitrah or natural disposition) that guides them to differentiate between right and wrong, and nurturing a space of moral introspection and personal accountability. Their realization of the mistake provides a pathway to repentance, illustrating the Islamic philosophy of *"Tawbah"* (repentance) that encourages individuals to turn back to Allah in moments of transgression, thereby mending the spiritual and moral fabric through sincere repentance. Allah is most compassionate, merciful, loving, and forgiving. One should not have a feeling that one's mistakes are too great and too many for Allah to forgive, because that would go against the very idea and belief of the Merciful God. Allah says in the Qur'an, *"Say, 'O My servants who have transgressed against themselves, do not despair of the mercy of Allah. Indeed, Allah forgives all sins. Indeed, it is He who is the Forgiving, the Merciful"* [Qur'an 39:53]. In another passage, *"And who—other than those who have utterly lost their way—could ever abandon the hope of their Sustainer's mercy?"* [Qur'an 15:56], which means that losing hope in Allah's mercy and forgiveness is tantamount to disbelief.

Thus, the narrative of eating from the forbidden tree and the subsequent fall of Adam is steeped in Islamic insights into the complex matrix of free will, moral accountability, human tendency towards error, and perpetual struggle against external evil influences. It explores the profound dynamics of moral consciousness, the continuous journey of self-improvement through learning from one's mistakes, and the unwavering hope in the mercy and forgiveness of Allah. It lays the groundwork for understanding the psychological underpinnings of human existence in the Islamic worldview, marked by a delicate balance between Divine guidance and human agency, urging individuals towards a path of moral rectitude through conscious choice and a committed relationship with the Divine grounded in repentance and forgiveness. It offers a rich canvas illustrating the intricacies of the human moral landscape, inviting reflective contemplation on the deeper meanings of existence, free will, and moral choice in the light of Islamic theology.

The concept of growing through mistakes, facilitated by the exercise of free will, is a fundamental aspect of understanding human development from an Islamic perspective. This intricate relationship between making mistakes and subsequent growth can be elaborated through various dimensions including moral, intellectual, and spiritual growth. Making mistakes and facing the consequences tend to shape and refine an individual's conscience. It cultivates a deeper understanding of the demarcation between right and wrong, thus fostering a morally responsible individual. Learning from mistakes often engenders empathy and compassion. Individuals who have erred are generally more understanding and forgiving of others' mistakes, promoting a society grounded in empathy and mutual respect. The pathway of making and learning from mistakes encourages critical thinking. Individuals learn to analyze situations better, anticipating potential pitfalls and making more informed decisions as a result of their past experiences. If we take lessons from history, traditionally, many innovations and discoveries have been the results of trial and error. Making mistakes often leads to unforeseen discoveries, encouraging a culture of exploration and intellectual curiosity. Thus, navigating through mistakes allows individuals to gain a deeper understanding of themselves, their inclinations, and their weaknesses, nurturing a journey of self-improvement and greater self-awareness, aligned with the principles of moral and spiritual upliftment.

In Islamic jurisprudence, sins are commonly classified into two categories: major and minor. Major sins have been explicitly mentioned in the Qur'an or Hadith as deserving of severe punishment in this world or the Hereafter. These include, but are not limited to, murder, theft, adultery, and bearing false witness. Minor sins are less severe and for which specific punishments are not outlined in the Islamic texts, such as idle talk, backbiting, waste, miserliness, etc. Avoiding major sins is paramount for a Muslim aiming to be at the mercy of Allah. Major sins attract severe penalties in the temporal sphere and compromise one's standing in the eternal life to come. As Allah says in the Qur'an, "*If you avoid the major sins which you are forbidden, We will remove from you your lesser sins and admit you to a noble entrance [into Paradise]*." [Qur'an, 4:31]. This verse explains that abstaining from major sins can lead to the expiation of minor sins, elevating the individual's spiritual status.

The act of continuously seeking repentance (*Tawbah*) is encouraged in Islam for all sins—major or minor—as humans are fallible beings prone to err. The Prophet Muhammad (PBUH) stated, "By Him in Whose Hand is my life, if you were not to commit sin, Allah would sweep you out of existence, and He would replace you with a people who would commit sin and then seek forgiveness from Allah, and He would have pardoned them" (Sahih Muslim). This Hadith stresses the importance of avoiding sin and the constant act of seeking forgiveness as a form of spiritual self-renewal.

Repentance in Islam is more than just a feeling of remorse; it is a process that involves several key steps:

1)   Acknowledgment of the sin: The first step is acknowledging the sin committed without justification or rationalization.

2)   Sincere Remorse: Feeling genuine remorse or guilt for sinning, as repentance without remorse is considered invalid.

3)   Immediate Cessation: Discontinuing the sinful act immediately is crucial for sincere repentance. (4) Making Amends: If the sin involves infringement upon the rights of others, then restitution or seeking forgiveness from the aggrieved party is essential.

4)   Firm Resolve: Making a firm intention not to sin again.

5)   Seeking Forgiveness: After fulfilling the above steps, one should offer a prayer of repentance, asking Allah for forgiveness.

6)   Good Deeds: Good deeds are highly recommended as expiation for sins. By understanding the hierarchical nature of sins and the necessity of continuous repentance, one understands the ethical and spiritual landscape within which Muslims strive to cultivate piety and righteousness.

In conclusion, the interplay between making mistakes and the subsequent moral, intellectual, and spiritual growth forms a crucible for human development in the Islamic worldview. It is through the exercise of free will, which sometimes results in errors, that individuals embark on a continuous journey of learning, self-improvement, and closer connection with the Divine. This perspective encourages a hopeful outlook on human potential, emphasizing the opportunities for growth and betterment that lie in each mistake, developing a dynamic and enriching pathway of human development, and fulfilling the purpose of human life.

CHAPTER 28

The Qur'an (Chapter 55): Surah *Ar-Rahman* (The Merciful)

"So, which of the favors of your Lord would you deny?"
~ *(Qur'an 55:13)*

As you near the end of this book, you are encouraged to delve deeper into the concept of "faith," promoting rigorous scholarly exploration and an unwavering quest for truth within the rich domain of Islamic thought. A good starting point will be to pick a copy of the Qur'an translation and have a first-hand reading of the English meanings of God's word. The translation of the meanings of chapter 55 of the Qur'an, known as Surah Ar-Rahman (The Merciful) is highly recommended, and is presented below; also following an accompanied thematic commentary.

Ar-Rahman (The Merciful)

In the Name of Allah, the Most Beneficent, the Most Merciful. [1] The All-Merciful Allah [2] has taught the Qur'an. [3] He has created man. [4] He has taught him (how) to express himself. [5] The sun and the moon are (bound) by a (fixed) calculation. [6] And the vine and the tree both prostrate (to Allah). [7] He raised the sky high, and has placed the scale, [8] so that you should not be wrongful in weighing. [9] Observe the correct weight with fairness, and do not make weighing deficient. [10] As for the Earth, He has placed it for creatures, [11] in which there are fruits and date palms having sheaths, [12] and the grain having chaff, and fragrant flowers. [13] So, which of the favors of your Lord will you deny? [14] He has created man from dry clay, ringing like pottery, [15] and created *jann* (father of the *jinn*) from a smokeless flame of fire. [16] So, which of the favors of your Lord will you deny? [17] He is the Lord of both points of sunrise and both points of sunset. [18] So, which of the favors of your Lord will you deny? [19] He let forth the two seas to meet together, [20] while there is a barrier between them; they do not encroach (upon one another). [21] So, which of the favors of your Lord will you deny? [22] From both of them come forth the pearl and the coral. ²³ So, which of the favors of your Lord will you deny? ²⁴ And His are the sailing ships raised up in the sea like mountains. ²⁵ So, which of the favors of your Lord will you deny? ²⁶ Everyone who is on it (the Earth) has to perish. ²⁷ And your Lord's Countenance will remain, full of majesty, full of honour. ²⁸ So, which of the favors of your Lord will you deny? ²⁹ All those in the heavens and the Earth beseech Him (for their needs). Every day He is in a state of action. ³⁰ So, which of the favors of your Lord will you deny? ³¹ Soon We are going to spare Ourselves for you (to reckon your deeds), O two heavy species (of *jinn* and mankind)! ³² So, which of the favors of your Lord will you deny? ³³ O company of *jinn* and mankind, if you can penetrate beyond the realms of the heavens and the Earth, then penetrate. You cannot penetrate without power. ³⁴ So, which of the favors of your Lord will you deny? ³⁵ A flame of fire and a smoke will be loosed against you, and you will not (be able) to defend. ³⁶ So, which of the bounties of your Lord will you deny? ³⁷ So, (it will be a terrible event) when the sky will be split apart and will become rosy, like (red) hides. ³⁸ So, which of the favors of your Lord will you deny? ³⁹ On that day, neither a man will be questioned about his sin, nor a Jinn. ⁴⁰ So, which of the favors of your Lord will you deny? ⁴¹ The guilty ones will be recognized (by angels) through their marks and will be seized by foreheads and feet. ⁴² So, which of the favors of your Lord will you deny? ⁴³ This is Jahannam (Hell) that the guilty people deny. ⁴⁴ They will circle around between it and between hot, boiling water. ⁴⁵ So, which of the favors of your Lord will you deny? ⁴⁶ And for the one who is fearful of having to stand before his Lord, there are two gardens, ⁴⁷ So, which of the favors of your Lord will you deny? ⁴⁸ both having branches. ⁴⁹ So, which of the favors of your Lord will you deny? ⁵⁰ In both there are two flowing springs. ⁵¹ So, which of the favors of your Lord will you deny? ⁵² In both there are two kinds of every fruit. ⁵³ So, which of the favors of your Lord will you deny? ⁵⁴ (The people of these gardens will be) reclining on floorings whose (even) linings will be of thick silk, and the fruits plucked from the two gardens will be at hand. ⁵⁵ So, which of the favors of your Lord will you deny? ⁵⁶ In them there will be maidens restraining (their) glances, whom neither a man might have touched before them, nor a *Jinn*. ⁵⁷ So, which of the favors of your Lord will you deny? ⁵⁸ They will look like rubies and corals. ⁵⁹ So, which of the favors of your Lord will you deny? [60] Is there any reward for goodness other than goodness? [61] So, which of the favors of your Lord will you deny? [62] And besides these two, there are two other gardens (for the second category of the Godfearing), [63] So, which of the favors of your Lord will you deny? [64] both (gardens are) dark green! [65] So, which of the favors of your Lord will you deny? In both there are two springs gushing forth profusely. [67] So, which of the favors of your Lord will you deny? 68 In both there are fruits and date-palms and pomegranates. [69] So, which of the favors of your Lord will you deny? [70] In them there will be women, good and gorgeous, [71] So, which of the favors of your Lord will you deny? [72] the houris, kept guarded in pavilions, [73] So, which of the favors of your Lord will you deny? [74] whom neither a man might have touched before them, nor a Jinn. [75] So, which of the favors of your Lord will you deny? [76] (The people of these gardens will be) reclining on green cushions and marvellously beautiful mattresses. [77] So, which of the favors of your Lord will you deny? [78] Glorious is the name of your Lord, the Lord of Majesty, the Lord of Honour.

CHAPTER 29

Thematic Commentary on Surah
Ar-Rahman (The Merciful)

"So, whoever Allah wants to guide - He expands his breast to [contain] Islam; and whoever He wants to misguide - He makes his breast tight and constricted as though he were climbing into the sky. Thus, Allah places defilement upon those who do not believe." ~ (Qur'an 6:125)

The opening verse of this surah, "[*God,*] *The Merciful taught you the Qur'an*" [Qur'an 55:1–2], which gives the chapter its name, refers to one of the most exalted names of God. This name, "*Ar-Rahman*," is frequently mentioned in the Qur'an, emphasizing God's boundless compassion for all His creations. Among the many blessings bestowed upon humanity by God is the guidance provided through the Qur'an. This Divine scripture encompasses all previous revelations given to earlier prophets, offering timeless teachings, principles, and ideas that enable humans to lead fulfilling lives. The Qur'an's wisdom and guidance are the foremost gifts from God to the seal of the prophets, Muhammad (PBUH), as stated in [Qur'an 4:113].

Moreover, Allah extends the blessings of the Qur'an to all who study and teach it. Prophet Muhammad (PBUH) emphasized the significance of learning and imparting its teachings, proclaiming, "The best among you is he who learns the Qur'an and teaches it" [Sahih Bukhari]. This noble act of disseminating Qur'anic knowledge continues the tradition of God's Prophet and contributes significantly to the enlightenment and education of individuals and communities. Language, a unique attribute of humanity, enables the articulation of ideas and facilitates communication among diverse languages, accents, and dialects. The language of the Qur'an displays linguistic beauty that is manifested through its unparalleled syntactical elegance, profound layers of meaning, and a mesmerizing rhythm that resonates with a deep sense of divine orchestration.

The chapter delves further, asserting that the cosmos operates within a meticulously predetermined and precise system. Stars, planets, and galaxies do not drift aimlessly but follow precise orbits and speeds. Likewise, terrestrial vegetation adheres to a deliberate and well-integrated system for its life cycle. This surah portrays a universe as intricately regulated as a finely tuned mechanism, with the heavenly bodies and Earthly flora all attesting to God's Divine order. Although human activities may disrupt elements of this natural order, the overall balance remains under the supreme Creator's control. Men bear the responsibility of protecting the environment and establishing justice in all facets of life. The chapter urges, *"And establish weight in justice and do not make deficient the balance."* [Qur'an 55:9]. God's blessings are abundant, including providing sustenance through crops, plants and trees, minerals, water, etc. essential for human and animal survival. The Earth is adorned with exquisite flora for human enjoyment and pleasure.

The chapter features a recurring exhortation, posed as a question to remind both humans and *jinn* (spirits) about God's blessings: *"So, which of the bounties of your Lord will you deny?"* Beyond this, the chapter can be divided into four main sections, each addressing distinct themes. The first section emphasizes creation and its intricate design. The second section discusses death, resurrection, and the consequences of wrongdoing. The third section highlights faithful believers, while the fourth section portrays individuals with heightened devotion to God. From the Qur'anic perspective, human creation began with Adam, molded from Earth and clay, and continues through stages within the mother's womb, culminating in a fully developed human being. God's divine-will dictate that human-will occupy and rule the Earth for a designated period before facing accountability in the Afterlife.

This chapter reaffirms that all living beings on Earth will ultimately die, yet the majesty and glory of God will endure forever. No one is exempt from the final judgment. The righteous will experience eternal peace and happiness, while the disbelievers and wrongdoers will face appropriate consequences. The chapter suggests that the accountability process unfolds in multiple stages before the final judgment. The repeated exhortation, *"So, which of the bounties of your Lord will you deny?*" emphasizes specific aspects of the chapter and draws attention to scenes on the Day of Judgment. It conveys a sense of admonishment towards those who are ungrateful and deny God's kindness and grace. The chapter concludes with a breathtaking description of the paradisiacal gardens reserved for the most righteous, portraying them as places of opulence, tranquility, and everlasting peace, rich with greenery, flowers, and flowing rivers.

CHAPTER 30

Conclusion

"Say, 'Indeed, my Lord has guided me to a straight path - a correct religion - the way of Abraham, inclining toward truth. And he was not among those who associated others with Allah.'" ~ *(Qur'an 6:161)*

In these pages, a profound exploration of faith, theology, philosophy, and science through the lens of Islamic teachings culminates in a comprehensive understanding of Islamic perspectives on belief, disbelief, doubts, and truth-seeking. The discourse highlights the simplicity of belief in the one true God, the creator of the universe and the source of moral and ethical values, in contrast to the complexity of unbelief rooted in conjecture and supposition. It also delves into the historical origins of disbelief in the Western world, revealing a mosaic of intellectual endeavors that have evolved over centuries.

The central question of whether God truly exists is addressed through a rigorous examination of Islamic theology and philosophy, unveiling nuanced narratives and arguments. The focus is on Islamic epistemology and ontology, which navigates the realms of certainty and doubt. The dialogue between science and the Qur'an initiates a discussion between empirical evidence and religious texts, fostering a multidimensional understanding that bridges the gap between the visible and the invisible, the tangible and the intangible. This exploration also sheds light on the Islamic concept of God, arguments supporting God's unity as the sole entity deserving of worship, and the rational foundations underpinning belief in God and in the Afterlife. These insights are presented through a lens combining reason, faith, and empirical and metaphysical evidence.

Furthermore, the search probes into Islam's moral and ethical foundations, elucidating the guiding principles that shape human behavior and interactions based on Islamic teachings. The life and teachings of the Prophet of Islam (*PBUH*) are portrayed as beacons illuminating the intricate tapestry of religion and its significance in individual and societal contexts. At this juncture, the text emphasizes that this exploration is not the end but an invitation to further delve into the journey of faith and the pursuit of truth, fostering understanding and nurturing dialogues rooted in empathy and compassion.

In conclusion, this book is a starting point for those open-minded, truth-seeking individuals searching for the Divine reality. It aims to equip readers with the tools and insights to grasp theism, atheism, agnosticism, and truth-seeking within the framework of the Islamic intellectual tradition. It encourages readers to embark on a thoughtful journey to faith in the One true God, understanding diverse perspectives and using the knowledge within to navigate the complexities of faith, reason, science, and disbelief.

About the Author

HAFIDH SAIF AL-RAWAHY'S educational and professional journey reflects a dedicated shift from a foundational expertise in computer science and information management to a deep engagement with Islamic studies and interfaith dialogue. He currently imparts Islamic teachings at a local college and contributes as a volunteer at the Islamic Information Center of the Sultan Qaboos Grand Mosque in Muscat, Sultanate of Oman, where he works to promote understanding and dialogue on issues of faith and religion. The convergence of his technical background and theological study has provided him with a unique interdisciplinary approach to advancing effective interfaith communication.

Bibliography

Adams, F. C., & Laughlin, G. (1997). A dying universe: the long-term fate and evolution of astrophysical objects. *Reviews of Modern Physics, 69*(2), 337.

Adams, F. C., & Laughlin, G. (1997). A Dying Universe: The Long-Term Fate and Evolution of Astrophysical Objects. *Reviews of Modern Physics, 69*(2), 337.

Ahmed, I. (2013). *The Process of Creation: A Qur'anic Perspective.* Lahore: Markazi Anjuman Khuddam-ul-Qur'an.

Al-Bar, M. A., & Chamsi-Pasha, H. (2015). The Source of Common Principles of Morality and Ethics in Islam. *Contemporary Bioethics: Islamic Perspective*, 19-48.

Al-Faruqi, I. R. (1973). The Essence of Religious Experience in Islam. *Numen, 20*(3), 186-201.

Al-Faruqi, I. R. (2000). *Al Tawhid.* Virginia: International Istitute of Islamic Thought.

Al-Ghazali, M. (1972). *al-Munqidh min al-Dalal.* Cairo: Dar al-Kutub al-Haditha.

Ali, S. S. (2015). The Qur'anic Morality: An Introduction to Moral-System of Qur'an. *Islam and Muslim Societies: A Social Science Journal, 8*(1), 94-108.

Ali, S. S. (2015). The Qur'anic Morality: An Introduction to the Moral-System of the Qur'an. *Islam and Muslim Societies: A Social Science Journal, 8*(1), 94-108.

Atkins, P. (2010). *The Laws of Thermodynamics: A Very Short Introduction.* Oxford: Oxford University Press.

Barnes, L. A. (2012). The Fine-Tuning of the Universe for Intelligent Life. *Publication of Astronomical Society of Australia, 29*(4), 529-564.

Barrett, J. L. (2004). *Why Would Anyone Believe in God?* Lanham: AltaMira Press.

Barrett, J. L. (2011). *Cognitive Science, Religion, and Theology.* West Conshohocken: Templeton Press.

Behe, M. J. (1996). *Darwin's Black Box.* Toronto: Simon & Schuster.

Bladel, K. v. (2007). Heavenly Cords and Prophetic Authority in the Qur'an and its Late Antique Context. *Bullentin of the School of Oriental and African Studies, 70*(2), 223-246.

Bloom, P. (2005, December). Is God An Accident? *Atlantic Monthly.*

Bucaille, M. (2001). *The Bible, The Qur'an, and Science.* Delhi: Islamic Book Service.

Callen, H. B. (1985). *Thermodynamics and an Introduction to Thermostatistics.* New Jersey: Wiley.

Chalmers, D. J. (2010). *The Character of Consciousness.* Oxford: Oxford University Press.

Chan, M. H. (2017). *The Fine-Tuned Universe and the Existence of God.* Theses and Dissertation, Hong Kong Baptist University, Hong Kong.

Chittick, W. C. (1983). *The Sufi Path of Love: The Spiritual Teachings of Rumi".* New York: SUNY Press.

Chong, E. K. (2005). *Theistic Arguments: The Craig Program.* Retrieved from https://www.engr.colostate.edu/~echong/apologetics/4%20 Theistic%20Arguments.pdf

Collins, R. (2012). The Teleological Argument. In W. L. Craig, & J.

P. Moreland, *The Blackwell Companion to Natural Theology* (pp. 202-281). Oxford: Blackwell.

Connor, J. A. (2006). *Pascal's wager: the man who played dice with God.* San Fransisco: HarperSanFransisco.

Darwin, C. (1859). *On the Origin of Species* . London: John Murray.

Dawkins, R. (1976). *The Selfish Gene.* Oxford: Oxford University press.

Dawkins, R. (2006). *The God Delusion.* New York: Bantam Books.

Dawkins, R. (2008). *River Out of Eden: A Darwinian View of Life.* London: Orion Publishing Group.

Dembski, W. A. (1998). *The Design Inference: Eliminating Chance Through Small Probabilities.* New York: Cambridge University Press.

Denova, R. (2002). *God: Definition.* Retrieved from World History Encyclopedia: https://www.worldhistory.org/God/

Draz, M. A. (2008). *The Moral World of the Qur'an.* London: I. B. Tauris.

Dupret, B., & Gutron, C. (2016). Islamic Positivism and Scientific Truth: Qur'an and Archeology in a Creationist Documentary Film. *Human Studies, 39*(4), 621-643.

Durant, W. (1993). *The Age of Faith: The History of Civilization.* New York: MJF Books.

El-Naggar, Z. N. (2003). *The Geological Concept of Mountains in the Qur'an.* Cairo: Al-Falah Foundation.

Evans, C. S., & Bagget, D. (2014). *Moral Arguments for Existence of God.* Retrieved from Stanford Encyclopedia of Philosophy: https://plato.stanford.edu/moral-arguments-god/

Flew, A. (2007). *There is a God: How the World's Most Notorious Atheist Changed His Mind.* New York: HarperOne.

Friederich, S. (2017). *Fine-Tuning*. Retrieved July 2023, from Stanford Encyclopedia of Philosophy: https://plato.stanford.edu/entries/fine-tuning/

Gamow, G. (1948). The Evolution of Universe. *Nature*, 680-682.

Gary, J. (2002). *Straw Dogs*. London: Granta Books.

Gay, P. (1969). *The Enlightenment: The Science of Freedom*. New York: W.W. Norton & Company.

Glass, J. I., Assad-Garcia, N., Alperovich, N., Yooseph, S., Lewis, M. R., & Maruf, M. (2005). *Essential Genes of a Minimal Bacterium*. Rockville, Maryland: J. Craig Venture.

Goodman, L. E. (2020). *Ibn Sina*. Retrieved from Stanford Encyclopedia of Philosophy: https://plato.stanford.edu

Griffel, F. (2019). *Al-Ghazali*. Retrieved from Stanford Encyclopedia of Philosophy: https://plato.stanford.edu

Guessoum, N. (2011). *Islam's Quantum Question*. New York: I. B. Tauris.

Haack, S. (2003). *Defending Science - Within Reason: Between Scientism and Cynism*. New York: Prometheus Books.

Hadith. (2011). *Sahih Collections*. Retrieved from Online Hadith: www.sunnah.com

Haleem, M. A. (2005). *The Qur'an (A New Translation)*. Oxford: Oxford University Press.

Hammer, D. H. (2004). *The God Gene: How is Hardwired into Our Genes*. New York: Doubleday.

Hawi, S. S. (1975). Ibn Tufayl: On the Existence of God and His Attributes. *Journal of the American Oriental Society, 95*(1), 58-67.

Hawi, S. S. (1975). Ibn Tufayl: On the Existence of God and His Attributes. *Journal of the American Oriental Society, 95*(1), 54-67.

Hawking, S. (1998). *A Brief History of Time.* New York: Bantam Books.

Hoover, J. (2018). *Ibn Taymiyya.* Retrieved from Stanford Enclyclopedia of Philosophy: https://plato.stanford.edu

Hussaini, S. H. (2016). Islamic Philosophy Between Theism and Deism. *Revista Portuguesa de Filosofia, 72*(1), 65-83.

Ikpendu, E. L., & Ahmed, D. (2020). An Overview of the Cosmological Bing Bang Theory of the Universe. *African Scholar Journal of Agriculture and Agricultural Tech, 18*(1), 105-124.

Imamoglugil, H. K. (2020). The Relationship Between Reason and Revelation from the Perspective of an Extraordinary Salafi Abu al-Wafa Ibn Aqil. *Entelekya Logico-Metaphysical Review, 4*(2), 119-128.

Johnson, A. (2021). *The Moral Arguments for God's Existence.* Retrieved from Moral Apologetics: https://www.moralapologetics.com/wordpress/malecture

Johnson, A. (2021). *The Moral Arguments for God's Existence.* Retrieved from Moral Apologetics: https://www.moralapologetics.com/wordpress/malecture

Kaku, M. (1995). *Hyperspace: A Scientific Odyssey Through Parallel Universes, Time Warps, and the 10th Dimension.* Oxford: Oxford University Press.

Kamal, M. (2006). *Mulla Sadra's Transcendent Philosophy.* Farnham: Ashgate Publishing Ltd.

Keith, J. (2003). Philosophy of the Muslim World: Authors and Principal Themes. *14.* CRVP.

Kelemen, D. (2004/5). Are Children "Intuitive Theists"? Reasoning About Purpose and Design in Nature. *Psychology Science, 15*(5), 295-301.

Kikanovic, K. (2021). Moral Argument for God. *Master's Thesis.* Istanbul: Ibn Haldun University.

Kimble, K., O'Connor, T., & Kvanvig, J. (2011). The Argument From Consciousness Revisited. *Oxford Studies in Philosophy of Religion*(3), 110-141.

Languages, O. (2023). *Oxfor English Dictionary.* Oxford: Oxford University press.

Latifa, R., Hidayat, K., & Sodiq, A. (2019). Commentary on Place Spirituality: An Islamic Perspective. *Archive for the Psychology of Religion, 41*(1), 38-42.

LeDrew, S. (2016). *The Evolution of Atheism.* Oxford: Oxford University Press.

Lennox, J. C. (2019). *Can Science Explain Every Thing?* Charlotte: The Good Book Company.

Lings, M. (1965). *Ancient Beliefs and Modern Superstitions.* London: Perennial Books.

Lugo, L., Cooperman, A., Bell, J., O'Connell, E., & Stencel, S. (2013). *Morality.* Pew Research Center, The Worl's Muslims: Religion, Politics, and Society. Pew Research Center.

Manson, N. A. (2009). The Fine-Tuning Argument. *Philosophy Compass, 4*(1), 271-286.

Mark, K. (2020). *The End of Everything: (Astrophysically Speaking).* London: Penguin Books.

McGinnis, J., & Reisman, D. C. (2007). *Classical Arabic Philosophy:*

An Anthology Sources. Indianapolis: Hackett Publishing Co. Inc.

McGrath, A. E. (2010). *The Open Secret: A New Vision for Natural Theology*. Oxford: Wiley-Blackwell.

Meisami, S. (2013). *Makers of the Muslim World: Mulla Sadra*. London: Oneworld Publications.

Mihirig, A. A. (2022). The Existence of Arguments in Classical Islamic Thought: Reply to Hannah Erlwein. *International Journal of Philosophy and Traditions (SOPHIA)*(61), 429-444.

Moore, K. L. (1986, June). A Scientist's Interpretation of References to Embryology in the Qur'an. *The Journal of IMA, 18*, 15-17.

Morris, T. (1999). *Philosophy for Dummies*. New Jersey: Wiley Publishing.

Morrison, R. G. (2019). Cosmology and Cosmic Order in Islamic Astronomy. *Early Science and Medicine, 24*(4), 340-366.

Morrow, J. A. (2013). *The Covenants of the Prophet Muhammad with the Christians of the World*. New York: Angelico Press/Sophia Perrenis.

Mufti, K. I. (2014). *Fine-Tuning of the Universe (Part 1 of 8): Physical Laws*. Retrieved from The Religion of Islam: https://www.islamreligion.com/articles/10518/viewall/fine-tuning-of-universe/

Naik, D. Z. (2007). *Qur'an and Modern Science: Compatible or Incompatible?* . Riyadh: Darussalam.

Nasr, S. H. (2010). *Islam in the Modern World*. New York: HarperOne.

Nasr, S. H., Dagli, C. K., Dakake, M. M., Lumbard, J. E., & Rustom, M. (2015). *The Study Qur'an*. New York: HarperCollins.

Nowacki, M. R. (2007). *The Kalam Cosmological Argument for God*. New York: Prometheus Books.

Oppenheimer, M. (2007, November 4). The Turning of an Atheist. *The New York Times Magazine.*

Parrott, J. (2022, April 19). *The Case for Allah's Existence in the Qur'an and Sunnah.* Retrieved from Yaqeen Institute: www.yaqeeninstitute.com

Paul, H. (1998). John Calvin, the Sensus Divinitatis, and noetic effects of sin. *International Journal of Philosophy, 43*(2), 8-10.

Pecorino, P. A. (2015). *Philosophy of Religion and the Problem of God.* (Q. C. College, Producer) Retrieved July 2023, from An Introduction to Philosophy: https://www.qcc.cuny.edu/socialsciences/ppecorino/intro_text/Chapter%203%20Religion/Cosmological.htm

Peebles, P. J., Schramm, D. N., Turner, E. L., & Kron, R. G. (1991). The Evolution of the Universe. *Scientific American, 265*(5), pp. 53-62.

Penrose, R. (1979). *Singularities and Time-Asymmetry.* Cambridge: Cambridge University Press.

Penrose, R. (2007). *The Road to Reality: A Complete Guide to the Laws of the Universe.* London: Vintage Books.

Peterson, D. C. (2009). *The Physics of the Healing, Book I & II.* Provo, Utah: Brigham Young University Press.

Petrovich, O. (2021). Piaget's Construction of the Child's Reality. *Educational Psychology: An International Journal of Experimental Educational Psychology.*

Philips, B. A. (1997). *The Pupose of Creation.* Retrieved July 2023, from http://www.islam-korea.com/english/pdf/The%20Purpose%20of%20Creation-334316.pdf

Popkin, R. (1999). *The Columbian History of Western Philosophy.* New York: Columbia University Press.

Qur'an. (2007). *Qur'an Project.* Retrieved from Sahih International

English Translation: www.tanzil.net

Reichenbach, B. R. (2004). *The Cosmological Argument.* Illinois: Northwestern University.

Rizvi, S., & Terrier, M. (2021). The Challenge of Evil in Islamic Thought: A Brief Survey. *Orlens, 49*(3-4), 173-180.

Sagan, C. (1997). *Contact.* New York: Simon & Schuster.

Saleh, A. W. (2019). *Prophecy and Revelation in Islam.* Retrieved from British Library: https://www.bl.uk/sacred-texts/articles/prophecy-and-revelation-in-islam

Saliba, G. (2011). *Islamic Science and the Making of the European Renaissance.* Massachusetts: The MIT Press.

Shanks, N., & Green, K. (2011). Intelligent Design from a Theological Perspective. *Synthese, 178*(2), 307-330.

Shapin, S. (2018). *The Scientific Revolution.* Chicago: University of Chicago Press.

Stefon, M. (2009). *Encyclopedia Britannica, 8th Edition.* Chicago: Encyclopedia Britannica Inc.

Tal'at, H. (2020). *Islam and Atheism Face to Face.* Rabwa: Islamic Guidance & Community Awareness Association.

Taylor, R. C. (2018). *Ibn Rushd.* Retrieved from Stanford Encyclopedia of Philosophy: https://plato.stanford.edu

Voltaire. (1773). *Epistle to the author of the book, The Three Impostors.* (L. Moland, Ed.) Paris: Garnier.

WAMY. (2014). *What is Islam?* Retrieved from World Associaltion of Muslim Youth: https://wamy.org/what-is-islam/

Ward, K. (2001). *God, Chance & Necessity.* Oxford: One World.

Williams, G. (2012). *Teleological Argument*. Retrieved July 2023, from Philosophical Investigations: https://peped.org/philosophicalinvestigations/handout-teleological-argument/

Yaran, C. S. (2003). *Islamic Thought on the Existence of God: Contributions and Contrasts with Contemporary Western Philosophy of Religion*. Retrieved July 2023, from Council for Research in Values and Philosophy: https://www.crvp.org/publications/Series-IIA/IIA-16-Contents.pdf

www.ingramcontent.com/pod-product-compliance
Lightning Source LLC
Chambersburg PA
CBHW052033260626
47163CB00006B/203